THE FOURTH LEVEL
DRAGON'S DEN
BOOK TWELVE

I0622388

NICHOLAS HUNTLEY

First Edition, February 2020

nichhuntley.ca

WHITEWOLF PUBLISHING

Paperback ISBN 978-1-988765-34-1

Digital ISBN 978-1-988765-35-8

The text of this book is set in Times New Roman.

"Yet either way, it was physical strength that fought, that ran fleet of foot, that cried aloud… For I had begun to believe that it was the muscles – powerful, statically so well organized and so silent – that were the truth source of clarity of my consciousness. The occasional pain in the muscles of a blow that missed the shield gave rise instantly to a still tougher consciousness that suppressed the pain, and imminent shortage of breath gave rise to a frenzy that conquered it."

– Yukio Mishima

Act 1, Scene 1

The dense deciduous trees of the monsoon forest were lit by the lunar light that kept the starry night sky a bright, dark blue. The moon shined in all its entirety and in the absence of urban life, the stars were bountiful and sparkling from all across the universe. Across the large horizon, the diverse variety of trees, including the teak trees that stood up straight with a large bush of lively green leaves at the top, a shade of green that was the greenest of greens, sprouted out and defined the mountainous landscape. Between the land, a river snaked through the smooth green mountains, brown and narrow, essential to the small village below. Either side of the river was nothing but green by the flora – not even the beach could be seen until one reached this small bank where little homes and its people rested.

The village consisted of only so many structures constructed out of wood with grass rooftops. At the bank of the river, wide wooden steps led down to a small pier where boats were moored. The river continued through the countryside where the forest continued to cover limestone ridges and peaks. Further along, a small pack of elephants could be seen roaming the shallow waters to cross the other side.

The landscape continued for miles in every direction and only in the midst of it, lost in nature, were the ruins of a large temple. Even against the bluish-green stone of the temple walls and structure, the green of the monsoon forest consumed at the shrine to reclaim what was lost from man. The central piece of the Buddhist stupa was crowned with a hemispherical dome, and beneath it were many layers where at the corner were squared mounds with peaked rooftops. At the front of the temple were a set of stairs that led to the large looming doors. At the base of these stairs was a courtyard where at the front of the front were a set of two lion-like creatures with feathered mains and vicious teeth, at the flanks of the pathway. The breadth of the temple became more visible as time and night passed on, the skies turning to an orange-red. At the top of the gates of the wall that surrounded the temple was a scaled-reptilian-like or serpentine-like creature with little arms that carried long claws. The creature was cast in gold and had two lone whiskers from the top of its mouth, next to its nostrils and huge horns. The head of the creature was like that of a crocodile, open and from its mouth one could see in the background, the rising sun shining down.

Within the dense jungle, Charlemagne de la Cabernet lunged forward with a slash across a loose set of vines before him from his machete so that he could proceed. He led the way for those behind him: Miklos, Lukas, Dr. Vidkunsen, and a few locals who were hired to assist with the expedition. Charlemagne was dressed for the climate, which was halfway between tropical and temperate. He wore khaki shorts, hiking boots, and a long-sleeved beige dress shirt with a brown slouch hat with the strings tied underneath his chin. His eyes were tired. His skin as fair as it has always been. His face clean-shaven apart from his steel-white moustache. At his feet, he had white socks pulled up just a few inches above his ankles. Charlemagne had a large rucksack that contained his own spade at the side and rifle at the other side.

Both Miklos and Lukas were out of uniform, but armed with semiautomatic rifles. Each of them were well-equipped with whatever supplies the Global Defense Project permitted them to carry. Dr. Vidkunsen appeared similar to how she had appeared over a year ago during the Arctic voyage. The clothes she wore were similar to what she wore in Egypt and she was equipped with the necessary first aid equipment. The locals were dressed in their traditional garb, sandals at their feet, and shovels at their backs to assist with any excavating that would need to take place.

Charlemagne continued to lead them forward, through the forest as they listened to the local ambience of the many animals throughout the land, but the most poignant of all came from the littlest – cicadas rhythmically chirping in the background and birds that sang their morning tune. In addition to the fauna, there was a humidity that sank into the skin. Charlemagne's forehead was moist by the natural sauna that was this land, causing him to wipe the top of his face with a handkerchief as they came to stop before a set of stones.

A small set of ruins were in front of them. Charlemagne looked at them and then took out a journal from his backpack without removing it from his shoulder. He flipped through the book, looking up and down. He then stepped forward and looked around them, up to the yellowish sky and then back down to the leftovers of the past. There was little left from what had been some sort of ancient structure. All that remains were remnants of a foundation. The ruins consisted of beige stone bricks that stuck out of the ground.

Charlemagne looked around, made an evaluation and then took out a compass.

"We're nearby," Charlemagne stated. "Very nearby."

"How much more?" Miklos questioned.

"A kilometer at best," Charlemagne remarked, looking around, "but thanks to these tall damn trees, it's been lost on us just how far we had to go."

Charlemagne continued to lead the team through the jungle. He took them uphill and then downhill, towards a stream, and then uphill again until they passed through a small tunnel at the side of a limestone cliff wall. At the other side, Charlemagne looked forward and saw what he had been looking for, the stupa that was hidden and being digested by the monsoon forest. The team had approached the Buddhist temple from the left flank and was about half a kilometer from them – a little more to reach the front gates. Charlemagne continued to lead the team downhill, back into the midst of the forest, and then all a way around until they reached a clearing with tall grass.

By now, the sun was storming down a blaze of heat against them and was high over the horizon. The skies were now a clear blue, still without a cloud among them. The eyes of the dragon sculpture over the gate of the temple were fierce and looked down to the expedition group. Charlemagne's old, light blue eyes looked back at them. The sculpture was immense and grabbed around the beams of the gate to look down at strangers with intimidation and fear. In length, it was approximately six meters and in width less than a meter, but its height was two meters. Around its right front claw was a spherical translucent clear stone. The sun caused the stone to be bright to them.

Charlemagne looked at this stone with intent. He pointed it out to Miklos as he nudged him.

"We're here," Charlemagne stated. "Surely, this is the place where the second orb has come to rest after all these years."

Charlemagne took out his journal and flipped through the pages. He retrieved a pencil from his backpack and crossed through some notes. The two locals that had travelled with them looked frightened as they looked at the terrifying creatures, so much so that they instantly fled the team. Charlemagne looked to them as they left, did not say anything, and instead put his book away to continue forward. The team stepped into the courtyard, looked around what had once been a bountiful garden to only see vines and shrubs overgrown. Charlemagne looked at the lion-like creature, or *chinthe* as they were known locally. The leogryph was made out of a smooth stone and had sinister eyes that looked out at them.

The team continued and Charlemagne made his way towards the many steps to reach the top. There were more than a hundred steps approximately ten meters wide in order to reach the top. The team proceeded upwards and at the top, Charlemagne looked around to see the vastness of the forest with all its mountains. Miklos and Lukas set off to open the wooden doors that barricaded the inside. The doors were easily opened, unlocked and provided them access. The team then continued inside where they were forced to produce spotlights to guide them.

The entry corridor had a fair length to it, and at the end, they came to a balcony that looked forward to a large stone statue of Buddha in a standard cross-legged pose with his right hand up and eyes closed. In his left hand, at his palm, was a stone lily. The statue was immense, between fifty to a hundred meters in height. Beneath them, below, the ground floor had tunnels at each flank of the statue. There were also tunnels at their level at each flank which went deeper into the temple.

Charlemagne led them deeper inside, through the simple, but wide and tall corridors that wrapped around and then came together at the rear to a set of stairs that went down even more. The team reached the sublevel and then went around, all the way back to the feet of the statue. At the lateral sides of the temple on this floor were exits outside through smaller wooden doors than the one at the front. Before the statue, underneath the balcony, there was a set of stairs that went deeper below. Charlemagne led the team even further down, then around, and then down a narrow staircase to reach a set of narrow corridors.

The team navigated through, entering small rooms that connected to each other, and then other parts of narrow corridors until at last they reached a different room. The room had another statue of a Southeast Asian local in a gown, but this one on its side with a simple fountain before it. The thin fountain was filled with water that dripped down from the ceiling above, but as much as water dripped, none spilled over. It was less than an inch deep and a drop only fell down every other minute. The statue lied on its side with an arm covering its head, and next to its head was a sealed passageway with a smooth stone wall blocking the path. The team stopped in this room as Charlemagne examined the door.

Charlemagne brought his hands over the stone wall and rubbed around. He then turned around to Miklos and nodded. Miklos and Lukas stepped forward, removing their backpacks, and taking out a set of small plastic explosives to plant at the corners of the wall. The team then stepped away from the blast zone so that they could detonate a controlled explosion. The stone wall blew forward and bits of rock littered the room. The team re-entered and stepped into the corridor behind the wall, entering the tomb on the other side. Charlemagne rushed in with haste to see what awaited him.

The tomb was small and austere. There were no possessions or treasures, but instead a simple urn atop of a pedestal. The pedestal had a simple inscription in a Brahmic script. Charlemagne looked around the desolate space with his spotlight. He clenched a fist around the handle of his spotlight and held a frown. He then turned around and looked at his team. They appeared to be anxious as well as disappointed. The tomb and surrounding structure then began to shake.

The team froze for a moment before Charlemagne looked at them.

"Everyone out," Charlemagne ordered.

The team vacated the tomb and proceeded to go through the narrow corridors they had come from before reaching the narrow staircase. The seismic activity appeared to have stopped with minor damage to the structure with bits of rock fallen around. The team then scrambled into cover as the first round of gunfire came their direction.

Charlemagne produced his rifle from his backpack and began to return fire down the left corridor where hostiles were firing towards them. Miklos and Lukas fired with their own rifles at these unknown characters. A series of ropes were thrown down from the balcony above. At either side of the corridor, smoke began to envelop and provide cover for the hostiles. Dr. Vidkunsen produced a pistol she had been given to defend herself. Charlemagne looked around with a nervous expression.

"Attila, do you still have any explosives?" Charlemagne questioned.

Miklos threw Charlemagne some of the plastic explosives. He took them and attached the detonator capsules into them before rushing over to the corner of the archway into the left hall. Miklos and Lukas took care of the hostiles attempting to rappel down. Charlemagne placed explosives at either side of the archway and then returned into cover. He then threw a piece onto the top of the arch, sticking onto the stone, and then detonated it.

The archway collapsed and gave them cover against one side of the advancing forces, allowing them to shift their attention to the right hallway. Charlemagne continued to return fire to the right-side. An enemy soldier landed next to him, dead, and Charlemagne examined the uniform briefly to see the type of weapon – it was black like their uniforms and a type of assault rifle. Charlemagne took it into his hands and then looked at the eyes of the fallen soldier. The skin was yellowish-brown and eyes slanted. They were East Asian with no insignia on their shoulders. Charlemagne took some magazines from the soldier and proceeded to return fire with this weapon that carried more impact. With the archway behind blown and forces attempting to fall from above taken care of, Miklos and Lukas also armed themselves with one of the assault rifles that had fallen around them, and pushed back as the smoke began to dissipate.

A propelled rocket hit the neck of the Buddha statue above. Charlemagne looked and shouted out to the team to get out of the way as it fell over and crashed between them. The impact left a cloud of dust, but did not separate them. Charlemagne simply went around and rejoined the others as they prepared to rush the corridor by taking cover against the parallel wall. Another propelled rocket flew from above, which told them that they weren't clear from hostiles above.

Charlemagne looked up in anticipation of another rappel attack, but none came. He then looked over to one of the bodies that had fallen over and saw some grenades he could take. Charlemagne went over and picked up a canister, taking the pin off, and throwing it towards the opposite corner from where the team was to provide them with some smoke.

"Go!" Charlemagne shouted, rushing into the smoke to come through.

Charlemagne led the charge and threw another smoke grenade further towards the corner of the corridor. The team followed from behind and joined him. Charlemagne checked his corner and then opened fire ahead to where there were more hostiles. The hostiles scrambled without any cover to hide behind, allowing them to rush forward some more and come to the foyer of the lateral exit. The doors had been opened from where the hostiles had entered. Miklos and Lukas each took a side of the door while Charlemagne stuck behind a large piece of rubble in the middle of the room to watch the left and right. Dr. Vidkunsen stayed behind Lukas. Charlemagne reloaded his rifle and continued to fire at either side.

Once his rifle was spent, Charlemagne began to mold some of the leftover plastic explosives to throw towards the archways at either side. He was able to create six small pieces with the remainder of the detonator caps and threw them at key points of the archway before detonating them. The arches toppled and blocked the path for them to be surrounded. Once the archways were cleared, Charlemagne went to rejoin Miklos to give him a chance to reload. Charlemagne reloaded his own rifle before switching with him.

The courtyard below was simple in comparison to the one at the front and didn't have any statues or fountains, or even plants. It consisted solely of stone brick floor and an archway at the end where the wall opened up to the monsoon forest. On the left and right there were transport helicopters parked with various hostiles taking cover around. Charlemagne attempted to pick off as many as he could before getting into cover to trade with Miklos again. The courtyard was packed and Charlemagne was on his last magazine.

"We don't have enough resources to take care of an army of this size," Charlemagne remarked.

"We'll push on as much as we can," Miklos insisted.

"We can't push at all," Charlemagne argued. "There's too many of them."

"In that case, it was nice fighting with you, Charles," Miklos replied.

Charlemagne finished reloading his rifle and waited for Miklos to be spent. Once his rifle ran out of bullets, Miklos traded spaces with him again. Charlemagne opened fire with the last bullets he had, and when that was done, Miklos and he moved once more as Miklos produced a pistol he had to continue firing back. Charlemagne breathed steadily as he unloaded the magazine from his rifle and tossed the two pieces aside. He produced his own revolver and raised it up in preparation to exchange places with Miklos again. Charlemagne closed his eyes and his lips moved as though he was speaking, praying.

Miklos and he changed places again and Charlemagne shot out with his revolver, which was barely effective. He shot out against the hostiles with a firm rage, shooting his six shots before the revolver clicked. Miklos attempted to get him to move so they could trade places again, but Charlemagne didn't move. He instead looked up as his ears twitched and he saw a familiar sight in the skies – it was the vertical-takeoff and landing, or V-TOL, aircraft belonging to the GDP. Miklos saw what Charlemagne saw as the V-TOL landed between the helicopters.

The hostiles ceased their fire as did Charlemagne's team. The rear of the aircraft opened and a small team of six elite forces stepped out, armored in a beige tactical uniform and spreading out with their weapons pointed. Behind them, a woman in a black blazer and skirt, set with brown leggings and a white blouse. Her hair was black, skin fair, and she wore a pair of shades over her eyes.

"It's Ms. Black," Charlemagne said with slight disgust. "What is she doing here?"

One of the G.D.P. soldiers stood up and shouted out to the soldiers in an East Asian language. Director Black looked up the steps to where Charlemagne and his team were. A helicopter could be heard from nearby and landed beyond the walls. Director Black stepped towards the steps into the temple, tapping her foot with her hands at her waist. Charlemagne came out from around the corner and stepped forward like a child awaiting to see his mother after he's done something he shouldn't have. The G.D.P. soldiers spread out in packs of three and provided cover against the hostiles who were forced to lower their arms.

Director Black looked at Charlemagne and said, "Well, well, well..."

"Well, what?" Charlemagne questioned. "What are you doing here?"

"What am I doing here? What are *you* doing here?" Director Black questioned. "If I hadn't been here, then the Chinese government would have complained to the Committee and you'd have been in a heap of trouble. Charles, what are you doing?"

"I'm on a simple adventure – nothing grandiose..."

"You were in a firefight with the People's Liberation Army!" Director Black explained, "no less, in the middle of Myanmar at an abandoned temple!"

"They're Chinese?" Charlemagne questioned. "What are the Chinese doing in Burma?"

"Myanmar," Director Black corrected, "and it's none of your business. What have you taken? What's in this temple?"

"Nothing," Charlemagne stated.

Director Black looked at him.

"Nothing," Charlemagne repeated with annoyance. "You can search us all you like, but there was nothing in this tomb!"

"We will be searching you, and afterwards, we'll be taking you straight back to Canada where you'll have a lot of explaining to do," Director Black stated. "Come along now..."

Charlemagne looked at her, upset, and then turned around to wave to the others to come out. Miklos, Lukas, and Dr. Vidkunsen exited from the temple and went down to join Charlemagne. Once they had joined him, the four of them followed Director Black to the rear of the V-TOL where a pair of men in black stepped forward to search them while the director went to confront an elderly Chinese man in a general uniform that had arrived from the helicopter that had landed nearby. The man cursed at her in Chinese. Director Black was accompanied by a G-man in black who helped translate. Charlemagne looked at them as he spread his arms out to be searched. He then looked forward and sighed.

Act 1, Scene 2

Tristan held Diana around the waist as the couple danced together in the gymnasium of Lord Phoenix Secondary School to the tune of soft music in the background. Several other couples, dressed in formal attire, could be seen around them and the lights of the gym were cast dark. The gymnasium had been converted into a ballroom with a chandelier dangling from the center and an array of the school colors, red and black, spread out from wide ribbon strands. The stage, where the DJ was positioned and had been playing high-beat music, was decorated with balloons in the same color along with lights cast in a red tone. Towards the opposite-side of the gym from the entranceways there were tables with food and drinks. At the rear of the gym, facing the field, there was a large banner that read, 'Prom Night 2020.'

Diana wore a dark reddish-purple slit dress that went just above the ankles with a slit on the right that exposed her right knee. Her lower legs and arms expressed their light fair tone and her skin was smooth and clear. She wore matching-pointed short heel shoes and a diamond white gold necklace alongside pearl earrings. At her right wrist was a gold bracelet. All fine jewelry that had been gifted to her over the sum of almost three years. Her dark brown hair had been straightened and brought around her shoulders on the right-side. Her eyebrows were fine, thin and plucked, and lower eyelid highlighted with in a light dab of black mascara to bring out her dark blue irises that started lovingly up to Tristan's greens.

Tristan was dressed in a black blazer with a pure white handkerchief from the right breast pocket. He wore a matching dress shirt underneath a black vest, and his trousers were slim, black and went just to his pointed black dress shoes. The top of his collared shirt was open, exposing his chest, glimpses of his thin gold-chain necklace as well as his tender neck that expressed his tanned, fair orange-like skin inherited from his mother like his dark orange-blonde hair. Tristan's hair had been neatly trimmed and cut to less than an inch in length on the sides, and just about two inches in length at the front and top. His hair was styled to point slightly to the right-side. Tristan was clean-shaven. His physique was similar to how it has been in the course of the last four or so months with a minor difference unlike in Tristan's eyes, which appeared more serious, more mature – not tired, but still with the same dark tone around them that he's had since he was young. Tristan continued to look at the love of his life.

Diana looked to her side as she looked at her classmates who had all but snubbed them. She saw Maia Grayson with Peter Huxley, who had flown from Harlech amidst the shutdown of universities and schools over a minor pandemic that has swept the world. There was also Vivian who was with Aaron Phillips – the couple had been dating since the start of November. Diana saw others from her small graduating class, but she also noticed the distinct lack of presence of her best friend who she had not heard from since Halloween. Moira had left the school district and town as a result of her father's death during the uprising that none remembered except Diana, Tristan, and Charlemagne, to live with her mother in Edmonton. Diana let out an empathetic sigh and embraced Tristan, resting her head on his shoulder.

Tristan noticed the shift in Diana's emotion as he looked at her with concern. He then looked out as they continued to dance for another two minutes until he brought them apart. He looked at Diana.

"Why don't we ditch this place and head on home?" Tristan questioned. "I can tell you're uncomfortable and to be honest, nobody wants us here."

"I don't care about them…" Diana replied with a sigh, "but you're right. It'd be better off if we bounced."

Tristan took Diana's hand and the couple left, out the doors of the gym, and into the halls of their school where they shifted their hands so that their arms were locked. Diana continued to rest her head on Tristan's shoulder in this position as they passed through the halls. At the end of the corridor, there was a photographer set up to take pictures of the dates, but the couple had already had their picture taken, so they continued down the hall to reach the entrance into the school.

There was a minor chill in the early spring night, but there were no clouds in the sky and the moon was bright. Diana shivered at the cold air and Tristan gave her his blazer so that they could continue through the front gardens to reach the parking lot where Charlemagne's sedan was parked. There was a slight frost atop of the car windshield. Tristan unlocked the car and opened the door for Diana so that she could step in. He then went around to open his door and start the engine. The couple sat in the car for a brief five minutes as the windows defrosted. A minor chill could also be felt in the car, but it soon passed with the heat from the radiator and seats.

Tristan brought his hands around the heated steering wheel and then hit the switch to cause the windshield wipers to clear the water that had been formed by the melted frost. Once the windows were clear, Tristan shifted gears and pulled out to drive home. Diana sat in her chair, head back and looking out her passenger seat window as they drove across the quiet lands of St. Allan's Fields and then crossed the Nattau River to reach the west bank. From there, Tristan drove around and came through the gates of the manor and then downhill to come into the garage.

Once the couple was inside, Tristan shut off the engine and looked to Diana.

"Well, how was that?" Tristan questioned.

"Was what?" Diana replied.

"Prom?"

"It was good," Diana responded. "I mean, it's a once in a lifetime event, and I'm glad we did it... especially as a couple and not as best friends."

"I think we did it as both," Tristan said, smiling at her and then kissing her on the cheek, "and you know, Charles isn't supposed to be home for another week, so..."

Diana smiled at Tristan with a slight look of disbelief. He gave a light laugh and opened his car door. Diana opened her door before Tristan could come around, but when he did they instead joined hands to return upstairs. The couple kissed as they entered the elevator and then parted as the elevator reached the top. They walked through the kitchen, dinette, and living room only to stop as the library door opened from the other side. Diana's smile lowered slightly and turned to a slightly embarrassed and shy appearance.

Charlemagne waved to them. He was dressed in his traditional suit and looked tired.

"Hello, children!" Charlemagne greeted. "I bet you weren't expecting to see me!"

"N-no," Diana responded. "We weren't... What brought you home so soon?"

Charlemagne briefly explained his trip to Burma, encounter with the Chinese, and then his encounter with Eleanor Black of the Global Defense Project.

"Needless to say, my calculations were wrong and I'm in the midst of recalculating the location based on the information I have," Charlemagne stated before pausing for a moment as he looked to Tristan. "Tristan, if I were to have a sample of your blood, I could send it off to the best scientists at my disposal and be able to put an end to all this. All I'd need is a small sample – no needle required."

"No," Tristan denied. "I told you, my mother didn't want anyone to know what was left behind – it's brought too much pain, and even then, she's encrypted it so that it couldn't be translated. It'd be pointless and we'd only be dishonoring her if you were to attempt to look into it."

"While I believe your mother to have been a smart woman and that whoever ordered the attack on you for your blood last November is having an equal of a hard time, if you won't help me, then I will have no choice but to respect that decision out of respect to you and your mother," Charlemagne replied with a sigh. "I will continue to search on my own – in fairness, it's been more exhilarating that way while your mother's secrets are like the final answers to a crossword puzzle that I shouldn't be looking at and instead attempt to solve on my own."

Charlemagne let out another sigh. He looked at the couple as they continued to hold hands. He had an equally timid appearance on his face as Diana.

"How was your prom?" Charlemagne questioned at a shift of tone, attempting to be supportive of the couple's relationship. "Did Ms. Quinn take a photo of you two before you left?"

"Yes, and it was good…" Diana replied, smiling.

"It's only about a quarter to eight," Charlemagne said, looking at his watch. "Is it over already?"

"Yeah," Tristan answered. "It is."

"Huh," Charlemagne remarked, "well, we're lucky as a county to not have been struck by the coronavirus crisis that has hit the rest of the world... I've been monitoring myself, just checked my blood as well as the other's, but it appears that we will be safe as long as we are careful. All Cabernet Industries non-essential travel has been brought to a halt and most workers that can are working from home. The company has been doing well, but that can't be said for the rest of the world economy... We're in for some dark times ahead, and it's times like these that I'm gracious of my grandfather for setting our home in these sacred lands."

"Yeah," Tristan replied.

"Anyho, I will be in my study if you need anything," Charlemagne replied, waving to them and then going back into the library.

Tristan looked at the door as it shut and then looked to Diana with an apologetic look.

"Well, there goes tonight's plans," Tristan stated, shrugging. "What can you do?"

"What does Charles knowing about our relationship have to do with what we do in the bedroom?" Diana questioned. "The doors are closed and our rooms are connected. He won't know if we're together or not."

"Are you joking? Ever since we returned from the states, I've been paranoid about him roaming the north wing of the house. I'm pretty sure he's been listening and he gave me a strict talk about what boundaries we'd need to have when we returned."

Diana looked at Tristan with disbelief.

"The rules are rules, and I don't want to disrespect old Charles," Tristan concluded.

"Okay then," Diana replied. "What then? What are we going to do?"

"We're not deviants," Tristan stated. "We've been doing other things as a couple other than having sex for the last two years. Come on, let's go to Scruton Creek if you want to be alone. We can take Zephyr."

Diana looked at Tristan with a smile.

"Okay, but let me either get changed or get a coat…" Diana replied.

• • •

Tristan rode Zephyr with Diana holding him from behind across the field behind the manor and all the way to Scruton Creek. Behind Tristan, he had strapped a longbow and a small bag of arrows, but this wasn't the same longbow as the one that Finn had crafted. Diana changed out of her dress and into some simple clothes to brave the late winter cold. She wore some jeans, a t-shirt, and her black leather jacket. Meanwhile, Tristan wore dark blue soccer sweatpants and his dark grey hoodie sweatshirt. Once they had arrived at the river bank, the couple hopped off and Diana allowed Zephyr to roam while she went to a rock and sat down. Meanwhile, Tristan went to the edge of the creek and looked forward.

All around the surrounding area, targets had been made with holes in them as they had been used. Tristan had made a makeshift target course for him to practice shooting arrows. There were targets everywhere, from below on the rocks across the creek, to above the opposite cliff-side and in front of trees, behind bushes, and anywhere Tristan could reach. Tristan dropped the bag of arrows onto the ground and picked one up. He then brought his longbow around from his back and held it to start shooting. He let an arrow go and saw it hit a target across the creek. The targets Tristan had placed were made of plastic and were standard red-white bullseye targets – some came in sheets while others were circular and stuck into the earth on poles.

Tristan lowered the bow and picked up another arrow. He then looked over to Diana.

"I know why you became upset," Tristan said to her. "You started to think about Moira, didn't you?"

Diana sighed and crossed her arms.

"Yeah…" Diana replied. "I- it didn't feel right being there, even though I was with you, but with her gone. I haven't talked to her since that night on Halloween when we were in the warehouse – that night when the mercenaries and then that supersoldier attacked us, and then he possessed her to attack you."

Diana gave another sigh.

"I wish I could tell her that it was all real, and that her father didn't die attempting to stop a riot, but during an uprising that saved all of our lives…"

Tristan shot another arrow. He then picked on up and looked at Diana.

"It's unfortunate," Tristan stated, "but what can you do?"

Diana shrugged.

"I'm glad she's at least safe and perhaps away from this town… but then again, with the pandemic hitting all the urban centers… the world doesn't seem like a safe place."

Tristan shot another arrow and looked forward with serious eyes.

"No, it's not."

"And it's not like we're safe either," Diana remarked. "The Protection Squad won't save us. The Global Defense Project won't save us. I'm surprised we haven't been attacked in the last four months since we got back from the U.S."

Tristan shrugged.

"Zimmerman got what he wanted from me," Tristan said. "I figured we're of no use to him anymore, but to be honest, we're the only ones we should rely on to save ourselves. If the time comes, I'll be ready for that bastard... I'll protect you, Diana. I promise."

Tristan shot another arrow. Diana looked at him with uncertainty. She looked to the side and brought a hand to her forearm as she looked to Zephyr.

"Who'll protect you?" Diana asked.

Tristan looked to her.

"I can protect myself."

"And what if you're not around to protect me?" Diana then asked. "What if Charles or the Protection Squad aren't around to protect me – like when I disappeared into the forest and was kidnapped by the Mysterious Stranger?"

Tristan looked to the ground. He picked up an arrow and readied to fire it. Tristan had no answer. He misfired his arrow and hit a boulder by the creek. Tristan clenched a fist as a result of that misfire.

Act 1, Scene 3

Diana looked forward, out of the window of her apartment and onto the streets of Keswick. There was a heavy downpour across the city and the streets were quiet due to the severe acute respiratory syndrome coronavirus that had infected the town. She could not see a single person and all that could be seen was the rain, the reflection of the nearby structures and incandescent lights in the wet streets, and stormy clouds above.

From a distance, Diana could hear the noisy chatter of her neighbors through the thin walls of the apartment building. She was alone in her unit, parents gone, Charlemagne and Tristan nowhere to be seen. The apartment was neat, furnished with an austere expression, but furnished. Diana turned around from the window and heard a knock on the front door. A chill fell upon her.

Diana moved from the couch where she was knelt on to look out the window, and stood up to go answer the door. She opened it and saw that it was empty. Diana stepped outside and onto the front porch of the manor, looking around the outside. The exterior of the manor was dark and there was no more rain. There were no lights on around the front gates and fence, and there weren't even any lights coming from the other side of the river, from the town, or any of the farms. Diana looked around and went down the steps to the top of the causeway to look around as if she was looking for someone. She held a worried expression on her face.

"Moira?!" Diana shouted, but no response came from anywhere.

Diana looked around for another moment and then returned up the steps to re-enter the manor. She closed the door behind her and then looked around the foyer. There was a different atmosphere in the manor. The lights were off and it was dark – darker than usual and it appeared as if the manor had been abandoned for years. The wallpaper on the walls had been torn and the rug in front of her was crooked and dirty. The manor was dusty and the furniture was off. Some windows were shattered and a flash of lightning briefly lit up the room. Diana proceeded to wander right, into the halls of the manor.

Through the right archway, Diana found herself on the second-floor in the north wing of the house. She looked down the corridor that led to her room and saw that it was longer than it typically was. Diana proceeded to walk down the hallway to return to her bedroom, looking outside through the windows of the hallway to see a forest outside. She walked and walked, and when she reached the end of the corridor she entered her room and closed the door behind her.

Diana looked around her room. The blinds were shut as was the door to the bathroom. She brought herself away from the back of the door only to notice that despite her attempt to shut it, the door did not close. Diana brought her hand to the doorknob and attempted to close it, but for some reason, the door was slightly too small for the frame it was in, leaving a gap between the bolt and the wall, making it impossible to truly close the door or even lock it. Diana maintained the door as it was and stepped back, hitting someone behind her and jumping with slight fear and surprise as she saw him behind her.

The Mysterious Stranger looked down at her, neon green eyes piercing through the eyeholes of the gas mask and brows tense as he looked at her with anger. Diana attempted to escape from him, but he grabbed her by the arm, clenching hard against her wrist. She proceeded to hit him in the chest, but his chest was firm almost as though it were made of metal, but at the same time it was soft as it was muscular flesh. The Mysterious

Stranger produced a knife from his jacket and brought it down upon Diana, piercing her shoulder – the same shoulder that she had pierced with a harpoon.

Diana jumped forward with a frightened moan, sitting up from her bed as she awoke in the darkness of her room. She quickly turned on the light on her bed-side and looked around, panting. Her room appeared to be normal, as she had left it before she went to sleep with the blinds closed, curtains shut at the French window, and her door to the hallway and bathroom closed. There was a warm appearance to her familiar room. She looked at the objects on the shelf above her dresser, at the same mementos with an addition of a purple candlestick from the Convent of Our Lady's Maidens. Diana also looked at her desk and saw the time to be almost two o'clock in the morning. In front of her clock was her latest read, *Beowulf* translated by J.R.R. Tolkien, and beside it her laptop.

Once Diana had become one with reality, she took a deep breath and lay back down. She brought a hand to her face and ran another through her sweated hair. Her face and body was wet. Diana closed her eyes and covered her eyelids with a hand, a thumb and finger at her temples. She then removed her hand and lay on her side, turning off the light and then closing her eyes.

"Hail Mary, full of grace..." Diana began to recite. "The Lord is with thee..."

Diana proceeded to finish reciting the Hail Mary prayer, and when she was finished, she repeated the prayer again and again until she took a deep breath. Diana opened her eyes and readjusted the blankets around her before closing her eyes with a light smile on her face to fall asleep again.

Meanwhile, in the other bedroom in the same wing, Tristan sat at his computers with the lights off in his room. His eyes were bloodshot and dry as they stared at the computer screen before him with focus. He sat with his back against the leather office chair of his desk with a hand around a glass bottle and the top at his lips. Tristan raised the bottle and drank from it, drinking the yellowish-clear liquid that caused him to become further inebriated. He drank the rest of the contents of the bottle and then sat it down on his desk where there were three other empty bottles. Tristan then let out a sigh and brought his head back to rest his neck against the top of the chair. He looked up and over to Finn's longbow. He then turned, looked over to his dresser on his right where there was a picture frame with his aunt and uncle, the parents that raised him, and a picture of his mother and father, taken from the convent, Sophia and Maxim, the parents that hadn't raised him, but loved him nonetheless. The picture was from when they were approximately his age if not younger in Rome, and next to this photo was a recent one taken at the monastery, which was of him and his mother in the snowy monastery gardens.

Tristan looked at them with sadness. A tear fell down the side of his face and he stood up. He walked over and looked at the pictures. He then brought a hand at either side of the dresser and tilted his head down.

"Father, if you can hear me, please say something…" Tristan muttered under his breath. "I know you're watching… you sent me to her, and you knew who I was deep down… Please, I feel so alone… I want to hear from you again… Why won't you talk to me?"

Tristan stopped talking to himself and looked over to the Vulgate, an early edition of the Holy Bible in Latin, which he had taken with himself from his mother's cell. He opened it and left it open. He then walked over to the foot of his bed, fell onto his knees and then turned around to face the Bible. He then lowered his head and brought his hands together as his mother had shown him. Tristan then made the sign of the cross.

"Our Father, who art in Heaven, hallowed be thy name," Tristan recited. "Thy Kingdom come, thy will be done… On Earth as it is in Heaven…"

Tristan finished reciting the Our Father prayer and when he was done, he continued to hold his hands together.

"God, what is the point of this all? Why do you make me suffer? What did I do to deserve such a life? I didn't do anything to deserve all of this… My parents didn't do anything to deserve to die – neither of them! What…"

Tristan stopped himself. He brought his hands apart and straightened his back, looking forward with watery eyes. He then stood up and turned his back.

"What's the point…" Tristan remarked. "There's no point in anything…"

Tristan grabbed the bottles from his desk and brought them over to his dresser where he hid them in the lower drawer. He then took his sweatshirt off, closed his computer screen down and sat atop of his bed. He rubbed his eyes and then pulled the covers over. He climbed inside and kept his eyes open as he looked over to the opposite-side of the room. Tristan looked forward and began to weep. He clenched the pillow next to him as he expelled his emotions for up to ten minutes, and when he had settled, he looked forward for another minute. Tristan then closed his eyes and without issue, he passed out into a deep sleep.

Act 1, Scene 4

Charlemagne passed his secretary as he walked to his office in downtown Allabrese. He was dressed in his grey business suit with his coat folded over his arm. The time on the clock on the right stated that it was almost a quarter to two o'clock and the limited daylight outside, masked by the dark grey clouds and torrential rain, said that it was afternoon. Charlemagne looked towards his desk and saw a cardboard package labeled with safety warnings that the contents inside may be radioactive. He looked at the package and stopped in front of the doorway into his office. He then looked behind, closed the door, and hung his jacket behind it before continuing forward. Charlemagne walked to the package atop of his desk and saw a letter above. He took the letter, opened it, and read the note inside that said:

'Charles, the renovations at Cabernet Towers are on schedule and we can anticipate the new laboratories to be open this autumn at the earliest. Sadly, the same can't be said for the main headquarters as it'll take a long time before we can patch over the crater in Champion Plains and even then, start construction on a new facility. At the latest, we might have a new facility by 2025 from what the project managers have told me.

On another note, the package I sent you came from the dig site where construction workers were able to find the items inside buried in the crater. Naturally, it carries a harmless amount of radiation, but radiation nonetheless so it's been packaged in a lead container. All I could think about what that mysterious man that you met after the Halloween party last October who disappeared on us, but perhaps you'd know more about what this is and what its use might be. Best regards, Barry.'

Charlemagne finished reading the note and then dropped it besides the package. He quickly opened the box and saw the squared lead container inside. He removed the top of the container and dug his hands inside to take out three thin silver-like necklaces with small black rocks attached to them. Charlemagne looked at them and held them in his hands, which quickly began to tremble as he looked at the necklaces with fearful eyes.

"My God…" Charlemagne remarked, "… it. It's all true then… Tristan was right."

Charlemagne brought a hand to his forehead as he began to breathe faster. He dropped the necklaces back into the container and moved over to take a seat in an armchair before his desk. Charlemagne's shock soon passed as it turned to a hopeful smile and an emotional laugh of relief. His eyes soon began to glisten and his expression dropped again to one of sadness and regret. Charlemagne brought his hands to his eyes and leaned forward. He then jumped at the sound of a knock. Charlemagne spun around and looked over to his door.

"Come in," Charlemagne remarked, walking over to his desk to pick up the box and drop it behind his desk. "Come in."

The door opened and Mr. Huxley walked in. He closed the door behind him.

"Ah, Richard," Charlemagne greeted. "How can I help you?"

Mr. Huxley walked in and went behind an armchair, bringing his arms to the top and leaning forward on it as he looked at his friend and boss with attentive eyes.

"Well, how'd it go?" Mr. Huxley questioned.

"Disappointing," Charlemagne replied, sitting down at his desk and bringing his hands together. "I spent less time than I hoped to spend in Asia due to issues with the local government, the Chinese government, and as a result, and in combination with the current COVID-19 crisis, was forced to cut my trip short. Not that it mattered, seeing as the Naga Temple was empty – typical of a Buddhist temple, so I'm forced to retrace my steps and start again."

"Not that, Charles," Mr. Huxley remarked, banging a fist atop of the armchair and straightening up. "I'm talking about your appointment with Dr. Moore. Isn't that where you went just now?"

"Oh, that's right," Charlemagne remarked, dropping his expression and standing up.

Charlemagne paced to his left and brought his hands behind his back. He said no more to Mr. Huxley. Mr. Huxley looked at him. Charlemagne turned his back on him and looked outside to the storm that fell.

"Charles…" Mr. Huxley questioned in suspicion. "What happened? Is everything alright?"

Charlemagne's hands began to tremble again. He held a serious, deep frown on his face as he looked outside. There was also a hint of sadness in his eyes. Charlemagne brought his hands from around his back and looked at them.

"Unfortunately, Richard, it is bad news," Charlemagne remarked. "Although the scans aren't definitive, so I'm told, they've scheduled me for a biopsy later this week…"

"Biopsy? For what?" Mr. Huxley asked.

"Cancer," Charlemagne clarified. "There is a growth in my right arm, and by the size of it, it's possible to spread within weeks into a melanoma and infiltrate other parts of my body…"

"My God," Richard replied in shock, looking at his friend. "I'm… I'm so sorry, Charles. W-what can be done? Radiation? Chemo?"

"Amputation – if it were an option, would be ideal, but not at this point... it's too late for that," Charlemagne replied, shaking his head and bringing his arms down onto his desk as he leaned forward. "I've been so... focused on other projects – my tours in Europe and now this hunt, that I've neglected this important warning from Judith – that the early work of the fusion reactor left us exposed to an invisible form of radiation. Luckily, Barry was able to look into his own health in a timely manner even though he was in perfect health and they found nothing, but next to Judith and others that have been contacted, I was one of the few that was closest to the source of radiation. I... I've had this coming for me for quite some time now, and it's fitting... It's all fitting – what a fitting end for me..."

"Don't talk like that, Charles," Richard responded. "You're not going to die from this. There are treatments and it sounds like there are more tests that need to be done before it is definitive..."

Charlemagne looked away and to the side. He straightened out.

"If it wasn't going to be cancer, it would have been Parkinson's," Charlemagne replied. "My family is predisposed... It took my great-grandfather, and I'm sure it would have taken my grandfather as well... I'm only disappointed that it's so soon..."

Huxley was speechless. He shook his head.

"For now, this news stays between the two of us," Charlemagne remarked to Mr. Huxley. "Am I understood? There will be no official statement made to the press. There will be no talk about my health anywhere, to anyone. Not to Mr. McGarrick. Not to Mr. Gilberts. Not to Mr. Heavner. Not even to your wife. Please, Richard. And last, but not least, not to the kids… At the best, at the size it is, I may have a year to live, perhaps a little more…."

Huxley nodded. The two then stood in silence for a brief minute.

"What are you going to do then?" Richard asked. "Other than attend your appointment for this biopsy? Is there a treatment plan? Chemotherapy? Radiation?"

"Not yet," Charlemagne responded, turning his chair and sitting down so that his body was positioned to his left. "I'm… I'm looking into my options… For now, I already have a will and testament written out, updated less than a couple of weeks ago…"

"Charles," Richard interrupted, "forget about the 'What if you die,' and instead focus on attempting to beat this… You've been through so much. I refuse to believe that you, in all your brilliance, will succumb to such a fate. You're Charlemagne! Enough with this pessimism, and…"

"I need to be prepared for the worst, Richard!" Charlemagne remarked in a bold and strict voice. "If I were solitary and in a right state of mind, I would be motivated to beat this, but I have two children to think of in my care who will be devastated to hear this news and later come to terms with the possibility that I may die. I have to think about what will happen to them, who will take care of them, who will protect them, and then there's who will take care of this company, and all the sort… If you were in my position, I know for sure, as a father, you'd be thinking of your wife and children foremost…!"

Huxley flinched and held a shameful expression. He nodded.

"Right," Richard replied in an embarrassed, but professional tone, "I'm sorry, Charles."

"I know, if my life were different, and I was with Manon and Finn… I'd be thinking of them foremost…" Charlemagne said in a solemn tone, "… after all, they are my only regrets in this life. The fact that I abandoned not only her, but the two of them, and for Finn to have been put into such a home, to be turned, and placed in a position of peril where he consumed himself. If I had the knowledge and willpower I had now… they would be safe, Finn would be alive, and I would fall asleep and awake with Manon at my side… Hell, for all we know, I could have come to adopt Diana and Tristan in this same timeline… Diana for sure, and with the lunacy of my brother, Tristan in due time. What an ideal, realistic world that would be…"

Charlemagne looked outside.

"Instead, if I hesitate for even a minute, Zimmerman's achievement and triumph over the innocent people of this world will be my final regret – and a grave one at that! That sick, rootless shell of a man… I won't have him tear this world apart out of his own greed and pride! Do you hear me?!"

"Of course, Charles, but if you want to ensure Zimmerman is kept in check," Mr. Huxley remarked, "it'll have to start with your health and ensuring you are able to live long enough to see it through. We serve no purpose in passing on our struggles to our children. We have to end them ourselves."

Charlemagne looked over to his friend and did not respond. Instead, he nodded and then looked down at the box on the ground where the necklaces were. He let out a sigh and stood up. Charlemagne buttoned his blazer, looked to his friend and cleared his throat.

"Right, I need you to do me a favor," Charlemagne said in a shift of tone. "I need you to have a casket and space at the town cemetery reserved."

"Charles…" Huxley responded.

"Not for me," Charlemagne interrupted, raising a finger at him, "but for a friend that passed away last Halloween… It'll be an empty casket burial and I'll send you the details of the inscription for the tombstone later."

"Yes, Charles," Huxley replied.

"Thank you," Charlemagne said, nodding to him, "now if you'll excuse me, I'll be leaving early. All of this talk has left me riled up and I need to be alone in my study at home. If you need to reach me, please ensure that it is an emergency."

Act 1, Scene 5

Charlemagne left his office several minutes after Richard Huxley had left. He had put on his coat and left the space with a briefcase in hand. He quickly passed Trudy, retrieved his umbrella from a rack near the elevator and then took the lift to the main floor. Once there, he then passed through the lobby to exit onto the street. Charlemagne took out the umbrella in one hand and carried his briefcase as he proceeded down the sidewalk and around the street corner to reach his car.

A black van could be seen driving down the road. Charlemagne stopped to look at it and then turned around as another black van appeared from around the other side, screeching to a halt. Charlemagne lowered his umbrella and fluttered it towards a man in a black suit that approached him from in front. However, a man reached from behind and brought a sack over his head, blinding him as his briefcase was taken from him and he was handcuffed. Charlemagne struggled and yelled. He was lifted from his feet and hauled into one of the vans. He then heard the door of the van shut. The black van soon sped off as Charlemagne thrashed around.

"Is this some sort of sick joke?!" Charlemagne questioned. "After the service I perform for this organization, this is how they treat me?! Tell Ms. Black that this is beyond low!"

The agents in the vehicle were silent at Charlemagne's outrage. The van continued to drive for another few minutes until it stopped for a moment. The car then continued to drive at a light pace before coming to an absolute halt. From here, the door of the van slid open and Charlemagne was dragged out and brought onto his feet. He was forced to walk forward and then thrown into a chair where the bag was removed.

Charlemagne looked before him and saw Director Black.

"Eleanor, what the bloody hell is this?" Charlemagne questioned. "Kidnapping me? What for?"

"Charles, calm down," Eleanor responded. "I'm here on unofficial business to warn you of a grave danger…"

Director Black moved out of the way and pointed a remote to a screen behind her. Charlemagne looked around to his surroundings. He was in some sort of warehouse – possibly even the warehouse used by the militia, but Charlemagne showed doubt in his face as he looked around and then forward again to the start of a slideshow. The title of the first slide read, 'An Analysis of Zimmerman Corporation Activities, 2017 – Present.' The van was parked nearby and there were only about three agents with them. Director Black changed the slide to the next, which showed a management tree of the structure of Zimmerman Corporation with Audric Zimmerman at the top of the hierarchy. The Chief Executive Officer of Zimmerman Corporation was listed as Cynthia Violet Dulles. A small board of directors listed various people, most of which Charlemagne had no idea of with the exception of Mrs. Dulles' husband, Franklin Ames Dulles.

"The Global Defense Project has been monitoring the activities of Zimmerman Corporation in accordance with the FBI since Zimmerman toppled what was formerly known as Fitch Corporation," Eleanor stated. "A small American research and development firm, which later became one of the largest manufacturing and technological firms in the entirety of the United States. The FBI has been interested in the sudden mass wealth of Mr. Zimmerman who seemingly came out of nowhere and won his wealth as a stock broker, believing him initially to be a tax evader, but later to be a stock-market manipulator – however, their investigations have proven none of that."

Director Black changed the slide to show the headquarters of Zimmerman Corporation in New York City at the Rockefeller Center. The image showed the base of the skyscraper with the golden statue of Prometheus behind the ice rink in the middle of a fountain. The entrance of the skyscraper had been refitted to bare the logo of the company. Director Black changed the slide again and came to one that showed Zimmerman Corporation's financial growth in the span of the last three years.

"Not much is known about Mr. Zimmerman's early life, and our agents inside haven't been able to learn much about their overall operations," Eleanor explained. "However," she added, changing the slide to one of the harbor in Alexandria, Egypt, "what happened two years ago with the so-called 'underground race' for $50 million dollars peaked our interest, especially into the worth of this…"

The slide changed to display the Amulet of Ra, or the fake variant rather, that was on display in the Cairo Museum.

"From the intelligence we've gathered, Zimmerman is interested in this artefact, and…" Eleanor said, changing the slide to display an artistic depiction of the second orb within a scepter, "this artefact… wherever it may be. Our sources say that while the Amulet of Ra was safeguarded by Queen Hatshepsut, this one was found by King Ramses II and passed on to Alexander the Great, but you know this already, don't you, Charles, because you were in Egypt during this time…"

The slide changed to show the Tomb of Alexander the Great in Siwa. The slide then changed again to show a map of all of Asia from the Near East to the Far East.

"The Global Defense Project does not have a specialty in archeological research. In fact, we've had to finance our research to multiple institutions, who have been able to produce less than we hoped," Eleanor said, pointing from Egypt to around China with a laser pointer, "but what we do know, as you should know as well, is that the artefacts secured in the Tomb of Alexander the Great had been pillaged during the Roman Era and made its way into the east where it was traded by merchants, and disappeared into the area…"

The slide then changed to more focused map of East Asia with Burma, Thailand, Vietnam, China, Korea, and Japan in view. China stood in the middle of the map.

"And that brings us to the now," Eleanor remarked. "Less than twelve hours ago, our correspondence with Zimmerman's elites informed us that a small entourage had arrived in China despite the current sanctions against the country during the global pandemic in pursuit of the second orb for whatever it is worth. Our agent informs us that Zimmerman is close to locating the orb in a tomb of a former emperor in the Shanxi region."

The slide changed to show the Shanxi region in central China, to the west of the Hebei region where Beijing was and south from Mongolia.

"We don't know what Zimmerman's intentions with the orbs are. We don't know what worth they hold. All we know is that Mr. Zimmerman holds them in high regards, and our encounter in Burma told me that you know something that I don't know," Eleanor stated. "Now, I'm not asking you to share what information you might have on the orbs, or what worth they might have. My instructions as Director of the Global Defense Project is to safeguard the world order and status quo – Zimmerman is a threat to that status quo and the Committee believe him to be a threat to the New World Order. That being said, the Committee would never authorize me to contract you, which is why I'm here on unofficial business."

"Go to hell," Charlemagne responded as the slideshow finished. "If you think, after the lies and deceit in the last months, that I'd work with you to defeat Zimmerman… You'd have to be pretty daft!"

"Charles, please…" Director Black expressed, "with your knowledge, and my unlimited resources, I am prepared to authorize for you to travel to East Asia as a representative of the United Nations, allowing you to fly overseas amidst the current pandemic in order to find this artefact. You will have not only diplomatic immunity, but the protection of my most elite troops who will be prepared to defend you as you come into inevitable contact with the Huntsman mercenaries. I can provide you with whatever you want that your fortune cannot purchase, and the treaties do not permit you to own. You have a blank cheque…"

Charlemagne crossed his arms and looked at her.

"I don't trust your bosses, this 'Committee,' because in my own opinion and the opinion of my grandfather, they are a bunch of parasites, and I don't trust you because you *lied* to me about what happened in this town," Charlemagne remarked. "You had me believe for four months that I had been manipulated, brainwashed by Maxim Bauer who instead laid down his life to save all of whom I love. You deceived all of the townspeople, and for what? To maintain the 'status quo?' To hell with the status quo and the New World Order! All of that you defend, I despise, my dear! I want nothing to do with it…!"

Director Black rolled her eyes. She turned off the projector and walked to a foldable table to set down the remote and shut down her laptop. She then pressed her hands against the table and tilted her head over. Director Black shook her head.

"I thought we could work together as we did to return those aliens to their mothership," Eleanor remarked. "I thought we had a common goal, and I took a risk in going behind the back of the Committee… Charles, I understand that we are not friends and that ever since you signed the treaties, I have become a nuisance and a burden towards you. I am not sorry however..."

Charlemagne looked at her.

"I trust your judgement because you have never lied to me. In fact, you cannot lie to me..." Eleanor went on and said. "If you believe Zimmerman to be indeed a threat to the world, then you will take my offer. If you do not, then I will not care because it means that you do not believe Zimmerman to be a threat to anything including yourself. You know that, under the current regulations, you will not be able to handle Zimmerman on your own or recover this artefact in due time. So, I will ask you once more with this in mind: Are you in?"

Charlemagne continued to look at her. He sighed and looked aside. Charlemagne then looked back at her and nodded.

"Fine," Charlemagne caved, "but under a few conditions. For a start, I will take your offer of diplomatic immunity, but our destination will be for Japan where I will meet with some of my technicians with Cabernet Electronics. I have been unable to meet with them due to the current pandemic and they have recently finished a piece of technology that may be able to assist in an important piece in my research. Secondly, I will not accept protection from the Guardians, but instead request the rearmament of the Protection Squad as they were before October – this is an unconditional article of our agreement."

"You can travel with your 'Protection Squad,' but Guardians will travel with you as well," Eleanor replied. "We will also provide weaponry and supplies so that you can 'rearm,' not as though you haven't been doing that in secret anyway..."

Charlemagne looked at her with a serious expression.

"However, in order to draw suspicion from the media, you will travel with your children to Japan. After you find what you need, they will be escorted back to Canada before you venture towards China. As a diplomatic, and due to the current pandemic, you will not need to make official visits, meetings, or give any speeches (thankfully…) but the nature of your visit will be purely touristic, hence why your children will be asked to come as it will cast too much suspicion if you are without them. Am I understood?"

"Very well," Charlemagne replied, "as long as we are in agreement that there is no need for them to be dragged into the bloodshed that will inevitably unfold and are kept safe."

Act 2, Scene 1

Diana and Tristan sat in the business class of a commercial airline that had been rented out for the use of their trip with Charlemagne and the Protection Squad to Tokyo, each with pillows at their heads as they had attempted to sleep through the last two hours of their flight. The couple sat together at the right-side of the airplane while Charlemagne sat with the twelve operatives that were part of Charlemagne's private guard for himself and the children. Miklos, Lukas, Maris (Lacplesis), Brandan, Viggo, and Björn traveled alongside three fairly new recruits, Gottfried 'Hagen' Wittman and Adrien 'Renaud' Doriot, who were hired after the deaths of Olivier and Naimon in France, and Diego 'Sid' Ezquerra who was hired after Igor was taken out of the team and transferred to the organization's counter-intelligence division in Harlech. Hagen and Sid were both young, in their early twenties, while Renaud was slightly older and in his late twenties. Each of them had fair skin, but Hagen had medium-blonde hair and lighter skin, Renaud had medium-brown hair, and Sid had dark brown hair. They were dressed, like the others in the unit, in formal suits. With the exception of the pilot and co-pilot in the cockpit, these were all of the occupants of the plane that was travelling for the capital of the small island nation of the noble Japanese people. Diana and Tristan continued to rest until sunlight peaked from the horizon and into the fuselage window, waking Tristan with ease to look out.

After ten-hours from Harlech to the grand metropolis that was at least thirteen times the size of the former city they had departed from, they had arrived. The plane flew over the sea where the couple could see the polygonal coastline and flatland that stretched beyond where the city rested upon. Various structures were spread throughout in all sorts of rectangular shapes and sizes, but there was a uniform greyscale in them that met with the moving vehicles on the roads and the occasional patches of greenery. There were many skyscrapers, especially at the center where among them, a tall, pointed tower stood among them with a flashing red light at the top. The skyscrapers were lit with the twilight horizon in the background as the sun rose onto the land of the rising sun.

The airplane began to make its descent over the water and reach a space of green land by some harbors. The size of the skyscrapers began to become of notice as the plane moved closer to sea level from the high altitude it flew from. At the same time, as the plane continued to fly forward, the breadth of the city was seen to be immense as it stretched from each direction in the horizon. The plane flew past the harbors and went over the sea before reaching another patch of green land where the runway could be made out below them. The airplane flew over the tarmac for a split moment before touching down, causing the vehicle to shake for a brief moment and then slow down.

Tristan looked ahead and the saw the large airport, which was bluish in appearance because of the many glass windows that covered it. There were various other airplanes parked around, and in comparison to Harlech International Airport, the Tokyo airport was larger and more spacious. At the end of the tarmac, the airplane turned around and continued to drive down as it slowly came to a halt. In the distance, Tristan could see a triangular structure, small as it was far away, with a red-white color scheme. Behind this tower, and the various skyscrapers, were mountains with one mountain in particular pointed upwards among them. The mountains were like shadows against the skyline. Once the plane came to a halt at a terminal, Tristan unlatched his seatbelt and stood up with Diana to leave.

Charlemagne led them out of the plane and into the airport with their luggage. Diana looked around as they travelled, rolling her luggage behind her as they travelled along a corridor. Above them was a sign in various languages with English among them, standing distinct from the two others, Japanese and Mandarin. The airport corridor was quiet. Diana looked at various commercial advertisements on the wall, seeing them to be mostly in Japanese. She could also recognize some commercial brands half the time as some were entirely foreign to her. Charlemagne brought them through the airport and towards a gate where they were stopped by customs.

There, Charlemagne presented the papers given to him by Director Black, which included a visa to travel to Japan on diplomatic business on behalf of the United Nations, and medical receipts for each of them that stated they were negative for SARS-CoV-2. The twelve of them waited for a brief moment until they were given the clear and permitted through. Diana observed the customs officers to be polite and respectful as well as professional in appearance and deportment. Charlemagne led them to the exit of the airport and then outside where they saw a convoy of black vehicles parked on the curb of the arrivals causeway.

A small team of agents waited for them to approach and they were backed up by a small squad of Guardians, dressed in urban camouflaged tactical armor and armed with a brand of assault rifles Charlemagne did not recognize. At the front of the convoy was a large van, similar to the one that Diana recognized two years ago to be lurking in Harlech and the one that Charlemagne recognized as the one he was forcibly taken into last week. Behind this vehicle was a small limousine and then two SUVs. The windows of the cars were tinted. An agent opened the door for them to enter the sedan with their luggage.

Charlemagne turned around and spoke with Miklos. Miklos then turned around and spoke in German with his team. The team split up into groups of three. Miklos, Lukas, and Brandan walked with Charlemagne and the kids to the limousine while the others went to the SUVs. Charlemagne and the Protection Squad helped the kids into the limousine. Afterwards, an agent closed the door behind them. The cars then proceeded to drive. Charlemagne remained in silence for almost ten minutes.

"All this protection makes me feel like Charles is the President of the United States," Diana remarked.

"It's all necessary," Charlemagne replied, "even if I tried to only have the P.S. with us. The stakes are as high as ever. Ms. Black insisted on her own lackies being here, however, and the deal we struck was that my men protect me on Cabernet property and at the hotel, while the Guardians and her agents protect us on public property. This way, Miklos and his men will have access to firearms and will be permitted to open-carry."

"They're not open-carrying now, are they?" Tristan asked.

"No," Miklos replied, "our liaison with the G.D.P. said that our weapons would wait for us at the hotel and that we'd have all that we'd need."

Charlemagne looked out the window as the others talked. He held a pensive appearance.

"I'm not expecting them to satisfy their needs," Charlemagne stated. "In fact, I'm expecting them to annoy us, which is why I didn't want to work with them."

The convoy of vehicles continued to drive through Tokyo. Diana looked out the tinted window as they passed through the streets of the city. She noticed a small amount of pedestrians, male and female, from young adults to elders. Almost all of them wore face-masks and held their heads up high as they walked with confidence. The pedestrians were well-dressed, well-groomed and neat, and they were homogenous. In fact, as fate may have it, Diana noticed that the capital of Japan was strictly Japanese in contrast to Paris or Harlech. The convoy continued to drive through the metropolis as it woke up, reaching the East Shinjuku district.

Diana saw that in addition to the people being well-dressed and groomed, the streets were clean and there was almost no trash or litter in sight. Even the richest district of Harlech, Stoneridge and Camross, didn't compare to the cleanliness of the streets. Diana moved her eyes from the streets and to the shops and then up the towers that surrounded them. Once Diana had an eyeful of the surrounding, she moved away from the window and kept her eyes in the cabin of the limousine for a moment.

The convoy soon arrived at their hotel, driving up a causeway and then parking in front of the hotel doors. An agent opened the door for them, and Charlemagne stepped out with his luggage before helping the kids. Once everyone was set, all twelve of them walked up the steps and came into the sleek, modern hotel lobby to reach the check-in desk. In the middle of the lobby was a black pond with a golden pot in the middle sprouting a golden tree. The pond was elevated and water fell from each side, gently. Behind the fountain were steps that went to the check-in desk with grey pillars at the side. The lights at the side of some white armchairs and couches were rectangular beige boxes, and the ceiling above them was composed of wooden beams. The walls were of smooth black stone bricks and floor of a medium-grey marble. The wall behind the check-in desk was a white screen with a sliding door that went to some offices behind. The entire hotel had this sort of neo-Zen appearance, which was futuristic, but appropriate. Behind the desk, a woman with latex gloves on her hands and a face-mask over her face entered through the sliding door to check them in. Once they were signed-in, with a cute and happy expression, smiling through her mask, she bowed as she presented their card keys to their rooms as she welcomed them to Tokyo. The convoy, agents, and Guardians did not accompany them as they travelled to the elevators and went to their room.

Charlemagne distributed five card keys to five different rooms for the Protection Squad and then gave a spare key of the two that remained to the kids for their suite. At the top floor, the twelve of them exited and entered a corridor where they split up, two to a room, except for Miklos who had his own room. At the end of the hall, Charlemagne led the kids into their own suite, which was a small apartment with a view of the city around them and Tokyo Tower in the distance. Before them was a small lounge, and behind the lounge was a dining table that went to a kitchen. At the side of the kitchen was a corridor that went to one of the bedrooms. There were another two bedrooms, including the master bedroom on the other side. The floor of the main room was composed of a beige stone. The walls were a lighter shade of beige, and the ceiling was white. There was a slight curve in the windows over the living room, which addressed the skyscrapers sort of round shape. Behind the dining room, or space, was a more linear set of windows, and in the kitchen space there were no windows, but the walls were linear as well. Above the living room was a circular chandelier set of lights. The doors to the bedrooms were sliding doors. Charlemagne looked around and left his luggage in front of the master bedroom door.

"Tristan and I can take the bedrooms here," Charlemagne remarked to Diana. "Diana, you can have the bedroom behind the kitchen. I believe it is more spacious and has a bathroom of its own."

"Okay," Diana responded in a slightly timid voice.

Diana went to her bedroom with her luggage and opened the sliding door to look inside. The bedroom was large and had a small space with couches and armchairs on the side, behind a set of windows that looked out. On the right of this small sitting room was a glass sliding door that went to a balcony. In front of the bed was a bench that looked to a flatscreen TV on the wall. The carpet in the room was a dark blue and the lamps on the nightstands were squared lampstands similar in design to the lamps in the foyer. The walls of the room were blackish behind the bed, but beige in the rest of the space. On the other side of the bed was a door that went into a bathroom. Diana set her luggage on the bench and then went to the bathroom. Afterwards, she returned to her room and looked outside. The penthouse was at least two-hundred meters or so above the ground and gave a view of a large span of the city which went on into the horizon in a totality of skyscrapers and structures. Diana turned around as she heard someone else step into the room.

Tristan stepped in and looked around.

"I think this room is the master bedroom," Tristan remarked. "It's at least larger than Charlemagne's room or mine."

"It's obvious that Charles wanted us to be separate," Diana replied, sitting down atop of the armrest of a couch. "Doesn't that bother you a little?"

"Not really," Tristan responded, picking up a remote and going over to an armchair.

Tristan turned on the TV. The TV turned on to display a news channel with all of the writing on the screen in Japanese script and news anchor as a Japanese woman with dark brown hair set up in a double bun. Tristan changed the channel and turned to a game show. He then changed the channel again and came to a Japanese cartoon, or anime. He continued to flip through the channels before looking to Diana.

"So, what's your impression so far?" Tristan asked, turning off the TV and resting into the armchair. "I'm enjoying this…"

"If there wasn't a pandemic at the moment, I'd be pretty happy to, but other than that, unlike Paris, Tokyo's met my expectations from what I'd expect from it…"

The couple turned to the door as Charlemagne knocked on the side. He then poked his head in.

"I hope everything is well for you two," Charlemagne said. "Tomorrow, I have a meeting with executives at Cabernet Electronics not too far from here, but right now I'm going to take nap to try and adjust to the time zone. I suggest you do the same with the melatonin I gave as I'm not sure how long we'll be in the country – not that you have a school to return to now that the province has cancelled all public lessons."

"Okay…" Tristan replied. "I think I might try to nap a little – I've barely slept."

"Good," Charlemagne responded. "Miklos and his men are in the five rooms behind us, but unfortunately, they aren't permitted to leave the premise. I'm going to have to ask that you don't leave until I wake… please?"

Diana and Tristan looked at each other. Diana then looked to Charlemagne.

"Yeah," Diana replied in slight resignation, "I think we can keep that promise."

"Thank you."

Act 2, Scene 2

Later in the evening, Diana and Tristan exited from Diana's room and made their approach to the front door as Charlemagne sat atop of a stool at a kitchen counter. Charlemagne had his laptop on his right and his journal on his left. He held a pencil in one hand and also wore his reading glasses. He looked to them. Diana was dressed in her leather jacket and Tristan in a dark blue, almost dark grey light jacket with no hood. Diana wore a white shirt underneath with light blue jeans. She also wore sleek brown leather high-top shoes. Tristan wore sneakers and medium-blue jeans. Diana also had her purse and had tied her hair back in a pony tail. She looked to Charlemagne with confidence, while Tristan looked ambivalent if not nervous.

"Where are you going?" Charlemagne questioned.

"We're going out," Diana firmly answered. "Tristan and I want to eat out, together – to have a date. We're both hungry, and we've been indoors all day. I don't see any problem with this."

"Except for the fact that there is a pandemic at the moment and the three of us have had a run-in with an assassin who has likely homed in on our location, which is why we're travelling with such a large security detail."

"Tristan can't get sick – he has a super-immune system, and you told us that this SARS virus was artificially modified to contain aspects of HIV, which I'm immune to, so the way I see it, the both of us don't have to worry about the pandemic," Diana argued. "If you're worried about us being kidnapped by that assassin, then send some Protection Squad members to spy on us."

Tristan looked aside and then back over to Charlemagne.

"I doubt we'll see him again," Tristan remarked in a brooding tone. "He only wanted me for my blood, and he got what he wanted. Diana and I don't matter to him anymore."

Charlemagne crossed his arms. Diana looked to Tristan and held a slight look of relief as he chipped in.

"He may have gotten your blood, Tristan, but the two of you matter to me, and that being said, he wouldn't look twice to kidnapping either of you to get to me," Charlemagne remarked. "Besides, the Protection Squad aren't allowed to watch over us outside of the hotel and Cabernet properties as I told you this morning, but as a matter of fact, I wouldn't put it past Ms. Black to send a small detail to watch over you if you were to leave."

Charlemagne uncrossed his arms and returned to placing his hands over the keys of his laptop.

"If you're going to leave, then make sure your phone is kept on, Tristan, at a high volume," Charlemagne stated. "And don't even think of removing the SIM card again. I'll know next time, and I won't hesitate to send the Protection Squad after you the moment I know."

"That won't happen again," Tristan replied in annoyed tone.

"Thanks, Charles," Diana responded, moving Tristan away before he started to get into an argument with Charlemagne.

The couple left the suite and proceeded to walk down to the elevators. Charlemagne froze as he sat at the countertop. He then set down the pencil in his hand and removed his glasses, pinching his temples with one hand and closing his eyes for a moment as he sighed. Charlemagne then picked up his phone. The couple made it to the elevator and Diana pressed the down button to call the lift.

A door behind them opened and Miklos stepped out to walk over to the elevator. He was still in his suit, although not in his blazer, which revealed the holster around his torso that carried a firearm. He also did not have his ear-piece. He stopped behind the couple and looked at them.

"Sorry, but Charlemagne wants me to see you out," Miklos stated. "Don't mind me."

Diana looked at him with a light smile.

"We won't," Diana replied as the elevator door opened.

The three of them stepped in. Diana then looked at the many buttons and studied them for a moment to see which one went to the main lobby. Miklos rushed them and pressed a button for them. The doors then closed and they travelled down. Once at the main floor, the three of them walked to the main doors where the convoy was parked with the Guardians loitering at the front entrance. Miklos escorted them to the front door and then stopped there.

The couple walked out and looked over to the Guardians sheepishly as they left the property, not turning back as they went to the sidewalk and proceeded down and into the town. Diana took Tristan's hand and continued to walk with him, slowing down their pace as they went a fair distance from the hotel. She turned around once they were a fair distance away and didn't see anyone behind them, stalking them or watching over them. She then looked around, at the many windows of the skyscrapers around and saw that it was very quiet along the street, but this quiet nature did not last as they reached a street corner. The couple stopped at the large street corner of what was Shibuya City

Diana looked around and took in the vibrant lights of the commercial signages, billboards, and advertisements. The street intersection was large as the road before them was a major artery through the town with a large crosswalk at either side. The street was unknown to them as they could not make sense of the signposts, but they could make sense of some of the commercial brands that were in English. Diana looked around for another moment before taking Tristan right, across and with the current of people who were going east.

Despite the pandemic, there was a moderate amount of people out, and those that were out wore facemasks to cover their mouth and noses, and some even more latex gloves at their hands. The lack of either on Diana and Tristan, in addition to their fair-skin, made them stand out from the crowd. The couple made it to the other side of the street and looked at the street corner where there were three shops beneath the structure with various signs, unlit, but in Japanese script advertising the shops for whatever it was they were selling. Diana and Tristan continued to walk down the major street, going slightly uphill at a low angle. In addition to the moderate amount of people out and about, there was also a fair bit of traffic.

Ahead of them was a white skywalk between two structures. The skywalk connected to a tall white structure on the left, which was connected to some sort of shopping center further ahead with a sign that said, 'Lumine 2' in Latin letters, and on the right was a train station of some sort named Shinjiku Station. The sidewalk stretched out in front of the station as they passed underneath the skywalk and continued to walk east to each a crosswalk in front of the train station.

Once the traffic had passed and sign changed for pedestrian traffic to pass, Diana and Tristan walked across the major street to reach the other side and come up to the front of the mall. There were less signs in this area compared to where they had started from, but the area was well-lit nonetheless and looked modern. The structure at the other side was not in fact an entrance into a mall, but another entrance into the train station. The Lumine 2 shopping center was further ahead.

The couple continued to walk down the street, passing the actual entrance into the shopping center, which was a tall structure that was several stories tall. Next to the complex was a small plaza with some stairs that went down to a street underneath the main road, which turned to an overpass. In this area, there were a lot more shops with signs and billboards with small roads with lots of pedestrians walking about at either direction. The couple reached this area and walked down, walking past all the various shops for almost five minutes, looking at the individual restaurants about until they came out and reached a small plaza surrounded by various larger commercial buildings at another large road. The two went around the plaza and crossed a large intersection with an X in the middle that went to an entrance of a mall, or promenade where vehicular traffic was restricted and pedestrians could walk along and pass even more shops. This area was even more well-lit with even more signs, neon lights, and advertisements as it was a sort of bazaar. The ground was of a smooth small stone and there were trees in the middle. The pathway was wide and went through the block to reach another street at the other side, approximately a hundred meters on.

Diana and Tristan walked about, looking at the individual shops where various local foods were being sold; more than simply sushi, but an array of local foods of a variety of noodles from soba and udon in soups of oden, sukiyaki, and nikujaga. There were also rice-based foods served with sides of fish, pickled vegetables, or boiled vegetables. A variety of seafoods could be seen as a part of the cuisine of this island nation, served raw, deep-fried or grilled. They didn't stop at any of the shops to dine, but instead continued to the other side which reached a major road. Diana and Tristan stopped here before a crosswalk where they looked out and embraced the surrounding.

The area around them was distinctly atmospheric of what it meant to be in modern Tokyo with the LED light signs, neon signs, and large billboards around, on glass skyscrapers looking down at them. There was a large crowd of locals around them, patiently waiting for the traffic sign to change and allow pedestrians to cross. After the sign changed, the couple walked with the other civilians to reach an LED gate that read in English, 'Godzilla Road' in vertical writing at the side with a small emblem of the cinematic monster. Behind the gate was another promenade with various shops going to a hotel at the end of the street. The shops along this promenade were less so small businesses, but major stores and restaurants. Beneath the hotel at the end of the walkway was an entranceway across the street to a cinema.

The couple continued to walk around Shinjuku City in Tokyo until Tristan had stopped at a food stand after seeing some of the food being cooked. There, they ordered and paid for some food and then took the food with them to a park where they quietly ate together away from the mass of people. By the time that they had finished eating, a small drizzle of rain began to fall down. The couple threw the containers into a nearby rubbish bin and proceeded to walk out of the park when the rain began to become heavier. Diana stopped suddenly as she looked to Tristan whose hair was beginning to flatten out.

"I came prepared," Diana remarked, rummaging through her small purse to take out a small extendable umbrella.

Diana opened the umbrella and Tristan took the handle into his hand to cover them as they continued to walk through the park. Once they were out, they looked around back at the brightly lit city and returned to roam the streets. They stayed within the limits of Shinjuku City and proceeded to return to the hotel when Diana found an alleyway with various small shops with their own signs and lights. Diana led Tristan down the alleyway until they reached an entrance into a small club advertising a kimono show in a couple of minutes with tickets still available.

"How much yen do we have?" Diana questioned Tristan.

"Lots," Tristan replied. "Do you want to buy tickets?"

"Yeah," Diana enthusiastically answered. "Let's wait out this rain and see this."

"Okay," Tristan responded, lowering the umbrella and shaking it before opening the door for Diana.

Diana walked and came to a small ticket booth where they paid for two tickets. The couple then walked down a set of stairs to enter the basement of a moderate-sized theater with seats spread around the club at tables. There was a bar at the back of the club with local men in business suits drinking, and some local men at tables. The club was quiet and looked to a stage that was empty at the moment. Diana presented their tickets to a young man at a booth at the bottom of the stairs. He then led the couple to a table and presented them with some drink menus.

Tristan looked around the club and saw a peculiar symbol behind the bar. The symbol was distinct from the logo of the club and in gold. The symbol was similar to the standard yin and yang symbol, but contained three heads instead of two. Tristan's attention turned from the symbol as a waiter brought a tray with some water to the table and set it down. Within a couple of minutes, the lights in the dim club dimmed even more and brightened over the stage as the show was about to begin. Tristan looked at the stage with intent.

A sort of string music filtered into the room through a set of speakers in a mystical tune. The stage began to become covered in a light haze of artificial fog before a group of eight women dressed silk kimono dresses knelt down at the center of the stage with their hands raised so that their arms covered their faces. The women were young and their faces were powdered slightly so that their skin was brighter than it typically was. They wore lipstick and had mascara outline their eyes to bring out their beauty. Their hair was tied back in a bun with a single strand along the right-side of their faces. At their feet were a type of wooden sandal. The dresses, each in a different color, had patterns on them, mostly floral patterns, and these dresses went to their ankles and to their wrists. A large belt was wrapped around their waists, and at the top of their hair was a single flower. The music elevated and the women stood up, fanning their arms out in a traditional dance before spreading out as a group across the stage.

The women moved their arms out and in, and then fluttered them like birds. The arms of their dress contained large flaps that extended down as they extended their arms out. The women brought their hands together, raised high and in front of their faces and then twirled around in unison. They then twirled around once more in the other direction before bringing their right hand up and then their left hand up to wave them like the gentle sea waves. The music developed a mixture of local instruments to develop a flavor of music that described the ancient spirit of Japan. The women came together once more with their backs to the audience, fluttering their left arm out with their smiling faces and then back in again. They then spread out again, producing fans from within their sleeves and taking them out to cover their faces.

Diana watched with intrigue as the show continued, eyeing the central dancer, a woman who was chosen because she was of course, the most beautiful of the group of dancers, and the woman looked at Diana with a serious face. The woman continued to dance, taking her attention away from Diana who felt a bit of shock at the woman's glance that caused her to lower her small smile and look away from the woman and drive her attention to the other dancers who continued to smile as they danced. The women began to flutter their fans like the wings of the butterfly, shaking their hands by their wrists as they did so and bringing the fan up and down as they squatted down and then stood back up again in a smooth motion. Diana crossed her arms and continued to watch the dancers, looking back at the lead dancer who had stopped looking at her.

At the end of the performance, the women turned their backs at the audience with their fans raised and then slowly turned back to them, with the front row kneeling down while the back row of four stood. The group then posed and the music came to a halt. After a brief minute, the women in the front row stood up and the eight of them shuffled off stage.

Diana and Tristan clapped with the rest of the audience. The couple then remained silent as the music transitioned for the next dance in the performance. Diana sat uneasy with her arms crossed again as she looked to the stage, while Tristan flipped through his phone to check a message from Charlemagne. Diana then looked to the stage again as the music transitioned for the next performance in the show, which took them into the rest of the night at this small club.

Act 2, Scene 3

Diana lay asleep in her room later in the night when the couple returned from their date in the city. She had closed the curtains of the large windows that looked out to the city and had fallen asleep in the center of the large bed, sleeping on her stomach with her arms and legs stretched out. Diana slept in a manner in which her head was on its left-side and her arms were wrapped around the sides of the pillow.

Suddenly, the shatter of glass from within the suite caused Diana to wake up and raise her head towards the shutter door exiting her room. She turned onto her back and looked properly towards the door, keeping her body up by her elbows before sitting up and then getting out of bed. Diana wore a white satin nightgown and walked barefoot to the door. She brought her hand to open the sliding door, but froze her hand at the handle as she felt goose bumps rise over her arm. She turned her head slightly to the right and then looked over to the exit to the balcony as she felt a rush of wind from outdoors.

Diana saw, behind the glass door, the Mysterious Stranger standing menacingly with his arms at his side, looking in to the room. The assassin appeared tall before her in his boots with his eyes seeming to glow a bright neon green as he wore night vision goggles. Diana let out a brief scream as she saw him and then immediately attempted to open the sliding door and exit into the suite. She came down the short corridor and heard the Mysterious Stranger barge through the glass and screen of the sliding door after her. Diana stopped in the main room of the suite as she noticed a group of mercenaries in the far corner near the bedrooms of Charlemagne and Tristan.

The mercenaries had a similar appearance to the Guardians she had seen yesterday, with a blackish-blue hue to their uniform. They wore night vision goggles over their eyes, which caused them to look at Diana with artificial neon green eyes back at her as they turned their attention and raised their weapons to her, causing her to stop. The mercenaries spoke in a strange tongue, an almost alien-like language as they pointed at her and shouted out.

Diana let out a scream and then turned around as she saw the Mysterious Stranger come after her with a large dagger, tearing the wall as he ran after him. Diana quickly unlocked the front door and exited through that, coming into the corridor outside which was lit in a reddish hue by the lights above. She went to the individual doors of each of the Protection Squad members, banging loudly, going from door to door, before escaping towards the elevator and then turning around to see the Mysterious Stranger come after her. The assassin walked slowly towards her with the Guardians behind. Diana brought her back to the elevator door and then peered to her left to see a fire exit door. She quickly went for the door, pushing against it, and then proceeding to run down the concrete steps as fast as she could. Diana heard the alien shouts of the Guardians from above, echoing down as she continued to go down each staircase.

At the twentieth floor, Diana stopped as she noticed a squad of Guardians climbing up to her location, which forced her to divert and exit on this floor. Diana ran down the corridor of the twentieth floor and came to the end of the corridor where there was a glass door that went out to a rooftop plaza. She quickly pushed against the door and came outside. The rain continued to pour down and Tokyo was around her with all its skyscrapers. There was a low fog that roamed around the buildings, but the area was brightly lit. The floor of the plaza was wet, but miraculously, Diana did not slip as she ran around looking for an exit to escape from her impending doom.

The Mysterious Stranger made his approach, breaking through the glass window that looked into the plaza from the hotel corridor and walking onto the patio. Diana took steps away from the Mysterious Stranger as he went to her. The Guardians filtered around and took position to block any potential escape, and within seconds, Diana was trapped in the corner of the patio with its glass fence keeping her from falling over. She fell down onto her bottom and looked on with horror as the Mysterious Stranger approached her. A crack of lightning could be seen in the background. Diana looked past and saw a space between some of the mercenaries. She pushed herself forward and attempted to slide past the Mysterious Stranger in a quick bolt, but he was faster and grabbed her by the arm. The Mysterious Stranger picked her up by her waist and raised her up.

Diana let out another screech as she clenched her body, and with a simple toss, the assassin threw her over the side of the building, causing her to fall with gravity before jumping forward in her bed as she awoke with another yelp. Diana panted and took a deep breath, closing her eyes, and letting out a sigh.

"Dammit," Diana remarked, punching the bed with her right fist. "Dammit, dammit, dammit," she repeated, continuing to slam her fist with each say of the word.

Diana laid back and brought her hands to her face. She then sat up again and began to rummage through the drawer of the nightstand. Inside was a book on Buddhism and nothing more. Diana closed the drawer and then laid back down, looking up to the ceiling for a brief moment until she decided to get out of bed and walk to the bathroom.

The clock on Diana's nightstand read that it was little over three o'clock in the morning. Diana ran some water in the sink and washed her face. She then looked at herself in the mirror before exiting, turning off the bathroom light, and then returned to sit atop of her bed. Diana looked around the room and looked back towards the sitting area, the window, and then around to the door to the patio balcony. Diana then looked to the sliding door out of her room and stood up to leave.

Diana walked out of her room and entered the main room of the suite where she stopped at the end of the corridor from her room and looked around the darkened space. She looked to the back and towards the doors into Tristan and Charlemagne's rooms, pausing for a moment before she calmly walked over to Tristan's sliding door and opened it. Tristan lay in bed, without a top on, but the lights off with his right arm flexed and grabbing the top of his head. He had earphones plugged into his phone and ears, and was listening to music as he looked to the ceiling with a somber face. Tristan immediately noticed a shift in the room as the sliding door opened and Diana walked in. He looked up and over to her, supporting himself with his right hand to look at her with surprise as she walked in. Tristan turned off his music and removed his ear-pieces.

"Diana," Tristan whispered, "what are you doing?"

Diana stepped forward and looked to him as she grabbed her left forearm with her right hand. She looked sheepishly at her boyfriend.

"I had a nightmare," Diana confessed.

"Oh," Tristan replied, hiding his phone under his pillow. "Okay."

Diana went around to the other side of Tristan's bed and climbed in. She then moved over to Tristan and brought her arms around his waist as he laid on his side with his back to her. He kept his right arm flexed and under the side of his head, cushioning his head. Tristan felt that her hands were cold in comparison to his warm body, but it didn't bother him. Diana noticed the difference too and as a result, held on gently before settling in. She embraced him and pressed her right cheek against the top of his back, just below the back of his neck with open eyes to the ceiling. The couple sat in silence for almost five minutes with their eyes open until Tristan closed his and took a deep breath. He then opened his eyes again.

"What did you dream of?" Tristan asked. "Your mother?"

"No," Diana replied, closing her eyes. "I dreamt of the assassin."

Diana held on to Tristan more tightly.

"He tried to kill me – he almost killed me, but I woke up."

"Oh…" Tristan responded, looking around without focus as though he was thinking.

The couple resumed into silence for another five to ten minutes. Diana's grip softened in that time. Tristan sighed.

"I've missed this," Tristan confessed, feeling Diana's leg with his left arm. "Have you?"

No response came.

"Diana?" Tristan questioned, looking over to see that she had fallen asleep.

Tristan gave an awkward and then looked back forward before him. He sighed and closed his eyes, falling asleep soon enough with Diana's arms around him to sleep a short sleep.

Act 2, Scene 4

The next morning, Diana, Tristan, and Charlemagne were driven by their security detail from the hotel in Shinjuku City to the business center of Tokyo, Marunouchi, where Cabernet Electronics headquarters was located. Diana looked out of the tinted windows of the limousine and noticed that the district was very similar to Central Harlech with its skyscrapers, streets, and shops, and lack of large billboards, neon lights, and commercial advertisements in comparison to Shinjuku. The sidewalks contained small plots with thin trees. There were a lot of men, older men in particular, dressed in suits walking about, some with briefcases. There weren't a lot of regular civilians in this area, although it was not all simply business as at the bottom of some of the large skyscrapers one could see luxurious brand shops and high-end restaurants. The district was definitely quieter than where their hotel was. Diana looked over to Charlemagne who was not dressed in his standard plaid suit, but instead in his business suit. Tristan was dressed in a simple suit, unlike the one he wore to their prom, but a simple one with a blazer, dress pants, and white dress shirt with no tie, open collar, and black leather shoes. Diana wore a simple springtime lavender lace dress with low-heels and had her purse at her side.

In the cabin of the limousine was Miklos and Lukas, each in their own suit. Charlemagne was reading a newspaper with English print as they drove through the city. He had a briefcase next to him. The sun was bright and clouds had dissipated, but it was not entirely warm – only when one stood out in the sunlight could they feel the warmth of the sun, such as when the car arrived in front of the Cabernet Electronics headquarters, and the group exited to look towards the entrance. Cabernet Electronics was a smaller structure compared to some of the skyscrapers they had seen and sat at six floors tall with the entire façade composed of glass windows and the logo sat atop on the roof. The facility was on the outskirts of Marunouchi on a large plot of land surrounded by a tall iron fence, which was in the midst of a perimeter that contained hedges and a neatly trimmed lawn. From the main road, a causeway extended from the entrance gates and wrapped around before going to an exit gate. From the entrance, there was an offshoot, similar to the offshoot of Cabernet Manor going to the garage, which went around the right-side of the building. Once everybody was out of the car, the limousine and rest of the convoy drove off.

Diana looked to the entrance of the headquarters and saw a small team of executives at the entrance, standing tall and straight. In the midst of them was an older Japanese man in his late-fifties or early sixties with balding black hair and thick-rimmed black glasses. Charlemagne went towards him as he bowed to Charlemagne. The two then shook hands.

"Welcome to Tokyo, Mr. Cabernet," the man spoke in a clear English. "We are pleased to have you here."

"Thank you, Mr. Morimoto," Charlemagne responded, shaking the hand of another man in a lab coat. "Hello, Dr. Nakashima."

Dr. Nakashima was a younger man with black hair and rimless glasses.

"Welcome, Mr. Cabernet," Dr. Nakashima replied.

Once Charlemagne was finished greeting the executives, he walked with them into the main lobby of Cabernet Electronics where a row of staff had lined up to bow to Mr. Cabernet as though he were royalty. Diana and Tristan lingered behind, estranged to whole arrangement. The main lobby of the headquarters consisted of modernist architecture, large and slick blue floor tiles, large grey paneled walls, and the sort. From the entrance, they walked to a small, but large nook at the side where there were several elevators. There, they stopped. Charlemagne spoke with the executives and then turned to the kids.

"I have to attend an important meeting now," Charlemagne said to them. "Dr. Nakashima is going to give you a tour of the facility behind the offices where some of our most important products are made."

"*Hai*," Dr. Nakashima responded with a light bow.

The Protection Squad had split into three groups, one of the three groups remained at the entrance, while the other two were split between the kids and Charlemagne. Miklos, Lacplesis, and Volger stayed with Charlemagne while Lukas, Brandan and Hagan stayed with the kids. Of the two groups that had now formed, the executives left in an elevator before another was called for the tour. The Protection Squad walked in with the kids and Dr. Nakashima, and they then went to the second-floor where they exited and proceeded to walk down a platform that looked down to the lobby past some glass railings.

"Do you know what Cabernet Electronics does for Cabernet Industries?" Dr. Nakashima questioned.

"No idea," Tristan replied. "Make electronics?"

"Yes," Dr. Nakashima responded, "but in a more general sense, we replicate some of the most advanced computers that Cabernet Technologies and their scientists have developed, which are at the frontier of what is available in the world. They are not just consumer electronics, but as you say in English, they are 'state of the art' computers used for research and industrial purposes. They are the computers that are put in airplanes, boats, and cars as well as other devices, including our recent pursuit in robotics and cybernetics, but those are not developed in this plant. Below, we are putting together motherboards to create computers that run a type of Cabernet operating system used by various separate companies and educational institutions because of their high-quality and superior processing power. All of Cabernet Industries uses this O.S., including Cabernet Forestry, Cabernet Extraction, and Cabernet Construction. Mr. Cabernet designed the system himself, but the upgrades to the motherboards have been made by other scientists, including myself, the Chief Engineer of Cabernet Electronics."

At the end of the platform were a set of doors that went down a short corridor with windows looking to the right-side of the building where various cars were parked along that extension of the causeway. At the end of this corridor, Dr. Nakashima scanned his ID along a proxy card reader and then opened a set of doors, entering another platform that looked below to a large space inhabited by a multitude of autonomous machinery and some workers that wore a type of white hazmat suit, but without a headpiece as they instead wore hardhats and facemasks. Sparks flew from where some robotic arms were working. Dr. Nakashima took them to the end of the platform and then proceeded to walk the corner and as they continued around the perimeter. In neat rows around the factory space were assembly lines of circuit chips. Dr. Nakashima took them all the way around and then back into the office space where he led them to an elevator.

The elevator door opened and they travelled down to the sub-basement where they proceeded to walk into a sublevel space beneath the main factory floor. In this area with a low, but suspended ceiling, there were various machines lined in a row with additional workers in similar garments checked and ran some of the machines. The room was considerably cool as the air was conditioned.

"Most of the circuitry is made by some of the robots we've designed. For example, the arms you saw upstairs, but also these smaller machines," Dr. Nakashima explained, showing them some machines that were punching into green circuit boards. Dr. Nikashima then turned to the next aisle and said, "However, there is only so much that the robots are capable of…"

In the next aisle, there were dozens of seats where workers, mostly women, were sat along an assembly line, placing individual components onto circuit boards as they ran along a conveyor belt. A square robot rolled down the aisle carrying a crate with components for workers to restock on pieces they ran out of. The factory space stretched across the large room where at the back there were workers boxing items. Dr. Nikashima brought them to the end of the assembly line where the workers, mostly men moved the items onto palettes, which were then taken to a shipping area where gates were open with delivery trucks parked at their rear.

"The computer components manufactured here are either taken upstairs to be put together and to create the computers, or to other plants where they are put together to create specialized computers such as the ones used in Cabernet-brand cars, airplanes, or other machines such as our robots. Overall, the tasks are split between humans and the robots who provided a considerable amount of assistance to the workers who take care of the more important aspects of the job."

Dr. Nikashima then exited the factory and went into a sublevel of the office space, which was a sort of maintenance tunnel with bright tubular LED lights in the ceiling. The floor was grey and there was a mess of pipes on the right-side and a grey matte floor below them. The ceiling was not suspended in this area, but there were various vents stretched above, running the air conditioning. Dr. Nikashima took them towards a set of blast doors and waved his ID at a proxy card reader.

Diana and Tristan walked in with the doctor and Protection Squad to enter another open space, but considerably smaller and less cramped. The area was a sort of workshop or laboratory, and in the corner was a doorway, which Dr. Nikashima took them to. He waved his ID at the proxy card and opened the metal door to bring them into a dim room where there were approximately four rows of large metallic rectangles, which looked like cabinets with metallic devices stacked inside displaying bright blue lights. The room was cooler than the lab. Diana and Tristan looked down the corridor.

"Do you know what these are?" Dr. Nikashima asked, walking over to one and placing his hand on its side. "These are supercomputers – specifically, this is the most advanced supercomputer in the world, designed by me to assist Mr. Cabernet with a special task of his to decrypt a code he had trouble with. Computers like these are the end-product of what is produced upstairs."

"Charles is using a supercomputer to decrypt the code in the nanomachines…" Tristan remarked with an unhappy face. "Why?"

Dr. Nikashima looked to Tristan.

"You will have to ask him yourself," Dr. Nikashima responded. "All I have is my task – I know nothing of the details. I do not care about the details. I only care about the task."

Tristan continued to frown as he looked at the computers. Dr. Nikashima looked at his watch.

"That is the end of the tour, but it went quicker than I expected," Dr. Nikashima remarked. "I am now to bring you upstairs to the company bar where we will have a sushi lunch with Mr. Cabernet, Mr. Morimoto, and the others."

• • •

Diana and Tristan ate in a sort of restaurant at a bar where they were served freshly-made sushi from a company chef who was working in an open kitchen nearby. Dr. Nikashima had left the kids in the care of the Protection Squad, who were sat nearby at a booth, eating together. Tristan poked at his sushi until Charlemagne arrived, alone with his own security detail. Diana looked to him.

"Ah, children, how was the tour?" Charlemagne questioned, looking to them. "Did you learn lots?"

"Yeah, it was very educational," Tristan responded in a sort of grudge tone. "I learned that you have a supercomputer downstairs attempting to decrypt the code used by my mother to scramble the notes stored in the nanomachines in my blood."

Charlemagne held a frown as he looked at Tristan. He went around and sat down next to Tristan.

"I thought you were going to find the scepter without taking my blood," Tristan remarked. "You were going to find it yourself…"

"The times have changed," Charlemagne confessed, "and like I told you in my last trip, I came to a dead-end because I had made a miscalculation. In truth, there was only a 0.001% chance that I could have been right, and that isn't good enough because time is not in our favor anymore. Zimmerman is in Asia – China specifically, in search of this final orb, and the pair of you know of the dangers of the orb. You've seen them in action just as I have."

Tristan looked to Charlemagne.

"You… You believe what happened last October happened?" Tristan questioned.

"Yes," Charlemagne confessed. "I do – your father, Tristan, was a hero that saved us that night, and we're not here because

I needed to pay a visit to Cabernet Electronics on goodwill, but because in this building there is a machine that can give us an advantage in the search for this orb. However, I will need your help and a sample of your blood to get there. Can you do that for me?"

Tristan held the chopsticks in his hands firmly. He held a serious face and closed his eyes. He then let out a sigh and opened them.

"Okay," Tristan replied. "You can have a sample of my blood."

Act 2, Scene 5

Tristan rolled down his sleeve upon having a syringe take a small vial of blood from his arm. Charlemagne took the vial to a machine in Dr. Nikashima's workshop and proceeded to set off to separate the contents of the vial from the leukobytes, to the rest of the contents of the bright red liquid. Charlemagne brought them down to the workshop immediately after the kids had finished their lunch, skipping his own meal to set off to work. Tristan sat around, patiently waiting for several hours as Charlemagne worked, while Diana had been taken upstairs by Lukas and Brandan to get some shots of the adjacent city with her camera, which she had brought in her purse. Charlemagne reviewed a series of long sheets of papers, attached to each other, which had just been printed out by a machine in the workshop. Tristan looked attentively over to them before looking over to Miklos and Lacplesis who were by the exit to the lab.

The Protection Squad had been divided into three groups of two, one with Diana and two securing the perimeter, and a group of three in the labs. Dr. Nikashima worked with Charlemagne alongside several other trusted engineers, all of whom were oblivious to the larger task at hand. Above, on the rooftop of the electronics company, Diana looked out to the Tokyo skyline and took pictures with her camera while Lukas and Brandan stood nearby. The skies were still clear, although the sun was now halfway above the sky and started to set as it was midafternoon. Once Diana had finished taking pictures, she left with Lukas and Brandan to return to the penthouse of the structure, which was a maintenance room with various machines. The Protection Squad called for an elevator to take them back down below and then entered with Diana.

The elevator made a slow descent back into the sublevel of the corporate building until it suddenly halted midway. The lift shook and the lights flickered before shutting off. Diana hugged the corner while Lukas and Brandan positioned themselves in front of her as they produced flashlights to provide some light and they kept their other hands at their holsters. In the workshop, the lights flickered and then shut off, resulting in some backup lights to be turned on and create a dim atmosphere. Tristan and Charlemagne looked around while Miklos immediately took his radio and prepared his handgun for combat.

"Charlie-One to Charlie-Two, is the package in check?" Miklos questioned.

Lukas hesitated for a moment before replying, "All in check, but we're stuck in the elevator on the third floor."

"Copy, I'm sending Charlie-Seven to assist," Miklos responded, looking to Lacplesis. "Go and see if you can open the shaft door. I'll hold here with Holger."

"Understood," Lacplesis replied, leaving the room.

Diana crossed her arms as Lukas and Brandan proceeded to attempt to open the elevator shaft door. She looked above and saw an emergency hatch that was optional for them to open and escape from. Her ears then twitched as she heard a patter of footsteps above them.

"Charlie-One to Charlie-Nine," Miklos radioed. "Is all good along the perimeter?"

"All is good," Björn replied. "No dangers spotted."

"Copy that," Miklos remarked, turning to Charlemagne. "It's probably just a fault with the power then."

"I'll contact the engineer at the plant," Dr. Nikashima said, producing his own radio and speaking in Japanese.

"All units, radio check," Miklos ordered.

Each unit, from Charlie-Two, skipping Charlie-Three and Four, and going to Charlie-Five, skipping Charlie-Six, and then going from Charlie-Eight to Charlie-Twelve who responded with a copy. Once the entire Protection Squad was accounted for, Miklos turned to Charlemagne with a nod. Charlemagne nodded back to him.

"All units, remain vigilant. We are on a cautionary Level Two," Miklos announced. "Stand-by for further instructions and keep your eyes peeled."

"Copy," Björn replied.

Charlemagne looked around the room and kept a hand to his side and another over a counter he had been working on. Tristan looked nervous, but looked to Miklos and Holger with confidence. He then looked over to Charlemagne who was extremely serious. Maris soon arrived at the elevator shaft and helped Brandan and Lukas out along with Diana. Charlemagne closed his eyes and then opened them as heard the radio go off again.

"Charlie-One, this is Charlie-Seven. I've met with Charlie-Two and the package is secure," Lacplesis remarked. "We're returning to your location as soon as possible."

"Copy that," Miklos replied.

"Come on," Lacplesis said, taking point, "we'll take the fire exit."

Lacplesis proceeded to lead them down the corporate office corridor on the third floor, leading them to an open area which exposed them to the top-most platform that looked down to the main lobby. Diana looked around suspiciously, as if she was looking for someone around them. She then jumped as she heard a grunt come from behind her. Brandan had disappeared with his handgun on the floor. In another second, he fell down from above, landing hard against the tiled floor, falling from a beam from above.

"There!" Lacplesis shouted, opening fire.

"Man down!" Lukas yelled. "Charlie-One, we have sighting of a hostile target from the main atrium."

"Copy that," Miklos responded. "I'm sending Charlie-Eight to respond."

"Copy," Lukas replied.

Diana watched as a shadow ran across the beam above them and then escaped through a glass window onto a metal awning outside. The P.S. attempted to shoot at the shadowy figure, but it escaped without a trace.

"Charlie-Nine, the target has moved outdoors," Lacplesis remarked. "Keep your eyes open."

Maris moved over to Diana as he looked around and above him. Lukas went to Brandan and assessed him.

"Copy," Björn replied.

"He's breathing, but he's out," Lukas said, standing up and looking around. "We'll have to move on. Charlie-One, Charlie-Five is out. Recommend immediate emergency evac ASAP."

"Copy that," Miklos responded.

"Come on," Maris encouraged, looking back over to Lukas. "We need to get her downstairs now."

Maris yelled out and Diana flinched as she saw to small, circular, but sharp objects fly from above and hit him in the left shoulder causing blood to squirt out. He fell to one knee and then looked up to shoot his pistol towards a beam where another shadowy figure had appeared and then ran off, crashing through a glass window and escaping from their sight from around the other side of the building. Lukas quickly went to Maris. Diana looked at the objects more closely and saw them to be throwing stars. Maris grunted as he tried to remove them before standing up with trembling legs.

"Charlie-One, Charlie-Seven is wounded," Lukas stated. "We need another medevac for him."

"Understood," Miklos replied. "What is the state of the package?"

"I'm going to deliver her to you myself," Lukas responded. "Double-time."

Lukas went over to take Diana's hand, but as he stepped towards her, a shadowy figure jumped down from above and landed behind. Diana's ears twitched as it happened, but before she could turn around, she felt an arm come around her waist as she was lifted up into the air. A plumage of smoke quickly erupted at where the two had stood and she was hoisted into the air. Lukas opened fire as the figure brought Diana up to a ledge near some windows that went onto the roof of the factory.

Diana struggled with her captor and Lukas landed a revenge shot into the left shoulder of the figure. Diana elbowed the figure in the side and escaped from his grip, running through the window and onto the roof to escape.

Charlemagne listened from the basement as Lukas updated him and Miklos, saying, "Target on the roof of the factory. We've lost the package!"

Miklos looked to Charlemagne.

"We need to go and help," Charlemagne said, taking his handgun from within his suit and loading a magazine. "Send Viggo and Lukas to the roof; we'll sweep the factory floor."

"What about Tristan?" Miklos questioned.

Charlemagne looked over to Tristan who was listening. He then looked over to the door to the supercomputer room. Charlemagne went over to the door and waved to Tristan.

"Come here!" Charlemagne shouted to him.

Tristan looked at him.

"Now!" Charlemagne hurried.

Tristan walked over as Charlemagne opened the door.

"Stay here until it's clear," Charlemagne said to him, pushing him in.

"Wait, what?" Tristan questioned, resisting.

"I don't have time to argue with you, Tristan," Charlemagne replied, pushing him back. "We need to go and save, Diana…"

With those words, Tristan conceded and allowed Charlemagne to push him in and close the door. Tristan, in a burst of rage, kicked the side of the supercomputer behind him.

"This isn't fair!" Tristan yelled out. "This is just like what happened in Metz!"

Charlemagne then went to Miklos.

"Let's hurry," Charlemagne said to him, turning to Dr. Nikashima. "Do not let anyone into this room. Understood?"

"*Hai*," Dr. Nikashima replied. "I'll see the power restored as soon as possible."

Meanwhile, Diana rushed over the various obstacles on the roof as she ran to the opposite-end from the shadowy figures behind her. She vaulted over airducts and jumped up the steps of platforms to reach the end where she looked around and saw that it was a three-story fall. Diana's feet trembled as she saw the height. She then looked over to left-side where there was a large rubbish bin with various cardboard recyclables. The bin was next to freight containers, which were stacked so that she could jump down to the tallest with ease. Diana made her way towards the container and looked down at the two-meter jump below. She took off her low-heels and then jumped down, going down another container and then jumping into the recycling bin to move around and then climb down a ladder on the side.

Diana came to the asphalt of the shipping and receiving area of the factory and then ran towards the garage doors, down the concrete ramp and towards the entryway where she saw Hagen. Hagen immediately jumped down and ran to her as he saw her. He then took his radio as he took Diana with one arm and brought her over to a set of stairs that went into the back of the factory.

"Charlie-One, this is Charlie-Ten," Hagen remarked. "I've secured the package at the shipping area."

"Copy that," Miklos remarked. "We're nearby."

Hagen took Diana indoors where she was soon reunited with Miklos and Charlemagne.

"Are you okay?" Charlemagne questioned.

"Yeah, I'm fine," Diana replied, hugging him.

"Come on, let's get you to Tristan and hold out in the workshop," Charlemagne said.

"Good work," Miklos commended Hagen. "Remain at your position and keep an eye out for suspicious activity."

"Copy that," Hagen replied.

"Charlie-One has secured the package. Charlie-Two and Charlie-Eight, what's your status on the rooftops?"

"Rooftops are clear," Lukas replied. "What are your orders?"

"Spread out and search the area for any hostiles," Miklos replied before turning to Charles. "I'll phone our contact with the G.D.P. to have the cars brought out."

"Thank you," Charlemagne replied, escorting Diana out with him back into the sublevel corridor.

Charlemagne opened the door into the workshop and then took Diana to the supercomputer room where she was let in. Tristan, who was sat down at the side of the supercomputer he had kicked, stood up and took her into his arms.

"Stay here until all is clear," Charlemagne said to them. "We're going to search the area for any more of those hostiles while we wait for the G.D.P. to get us out of here."

Neither Diana nor Tristan responded. Charlemagne closed the door. The couple hugged each other while Charlemagne went over to Miklos who set his phone down.

"They're on their way," Miklos replied.

"Good," Charlemagne responded.

Diana and Tristan stood in the darkness of the supercomputer room, hearing only murmurs from the other room.

"Are you okay?" Tristan questioned with hands at the side of Diana's face.

Diana nodded and then proceeded to cry. She buried her head into Tristan's chest and began to sob.

"I can't do this anymore, Tristan," Diana remarked. "I just can't."

Diana cried and cried while Tristan stood awkwardly and simply held her. His ears began to twitch as he heard motion from above. He parted from Diana and turned around, looking above before becoming dizzy. His hands began to tremble. He grabbed the side of the supercomputer and looked around the side. In the middle of the aisle was a canister that was emitting a faint cloud of gas. Tristan immediately turned around and went to the door. He began to bang on it.

"Charles! Let us out!" Tristan yelled. "They're here!"

Diana looked around the corner and saw the canister. Her ear then twitched as she heard a figure jump down from the suspended ceiling from the other aisle behind Tristan. Tristan turned around and saw the figure. The figure looked at him and held a katana sword up, preparing to strike at him before pointing it straight at him. Tristan froze. Diana then looked to her side as another two figures jumped down from the ceiling. One of them shouted in Japanese, pointing to Diana, causing the other to grab her. Tristan immediately reacted and jumped for her, taking her other arm.

"No!" Tristan yelled out.

A figure engaged Tristan and took him down to the ground. Diana struggled with her captor again, but she was at a loss of energy and the more she struggled, the faster she lost consciousness. Tristan looked above him as a figure stood over him with his sword pointed at his neck. Tristan breathed sharply, but remained conscious though weak. However, with a sharp blow to the face, Tristan lost consciousness just as the door opened and Charlemagne and Miklos busted in. Charlemagne saw the figure and raised his handgun to shoot at them, but the two that remained put away their swords and then jumped away with back handspring jumps, around to the furthest aisle. Charlemagne and Miklos went to the aisle and turned around with their pistols pointed. A figure jumped up into the ceiling and then disappeared from their sight.

Charlemagne pointed his pistol with intent to shoot into the ceiling, but Miklos stopped him and said, "Too dangerous."

Charlemagne nodded.

"Come on," Miklos then said, guiding him out of the room.

Miklos left on his own as Charlemagne stopped to assess Tristan.

"Go on," Charlemagne said. "I'll catch up in a second."

Charlemagne quickly assessed Tristan and saw that he was breathing and simply knocked out. Tristan came too quickly and looked at Charlemagne.

"W-what happened?" Tristan questioned.

"Stay here," Charlemagne told him before leaving.

Charlemagne left the server room door open as he went with Miklos out of the workshop. Miklos looked around the corridor as he listened to the movement in the shafts.

"This way," Miklos said, leading him down the hall and towards the steam plant.

Miklos quickly opened the door and busted in. The room was small and two-stories tall, similar in appearance to the boiler rooms on the ships they had been on. The ninjas could be seen at the other side of the room, exiting from the vents and then rushing behind the machinery. Charlemagne saw one with Diana around his shoulders. She was unconscious. Miklos opened fire, but they escaped into the compartmentalized room.

"Move your men here – lock this room down," Charlemagne said with a growl. "They won't leave this room!"

"Copy," Miklos replied. "All units, proceed to the sublevel of the corporate office ASAP."

Each unit proceeded to copy. Tristan soon appeared at the front door within a second.

"Watch this door," Charlemagne ordered him. "If anyone attempts to pass, then shout."

"Okay…" Tristan replied.

Charlemagne and Miklos then went forward with their pistols. Tristan stayed at the door and soon enough, Hagen arrived followed by Lukas and Viggo, and then Björn, Sid, and Renaud. By the time they were all here, Charlemagne and Miklos were at a nook in the plant and looking down at a manhole in the ground, which had been opened.

"Looks like we know how they got in," Miklos remarked, kneeling down at the manhole and shining his flashlight down. "My men will search below. Sceafa, take Hardrada, Hagen, and Renaud. Sid and Holger, check on our wounded."

"Come on, Charles," Miklos said, taking him away. "The G.D.P. should be here by now. We need to get you out of here."

Charlemagne nodded and they regrouped with Tristan at the entrance of the plant. Tristan looked at them with curiosity.

"Did you find her?" Tristan asked.

"Come on, Tristan, we're leaving," Charlemagne instead said.

"W-what about Diana?" Tristan instead asked.

"The Protection Squad are looking for her, but we need to leave," Charlemagne argued with him in an annoyed tone. "Come on."

Tristan walked away and with the adults as they returned to the workshop. Charlemagne appeared frustrated. He went to the papers with the decrypted information and took them into his briefcase. He then closed the briefcase and looked to Miklos. Tristan stood near the doorway with his arms crossed.

"I'm leaving this in your hands, Miklos," Charlemagne announced. "I'm also leaving Tristan in your hands. If your men cannot find her in the tunnels below, then contact Mr. Heavner and escalate the situation to him. He will take over per regulations, while Tristan will be placed in isolated-care in the manor under constant watch and protection of the Protection Squad. Twenty minutes after I leave, call a taxi, escort Tristan to the airport, and take him back to Harlech. By then, if Diana is recovered, then have your team watch them under constant supervision at the manor until I return. If not, contact Mr. Heavner to have him safeguarded at once. Do you understand?"

"Of course, Mr. Cabernet," Miklos replied, "but what about you? Who will protect you?"

Charlemagne sighed.

"I'll have to travel with the Guardians," Charlemagne replied. "It's the only manner and arrangement that can be made so that I can find this stone before Zimmerman. All of this is a clear distraction from my main quest – to keep me from competing with him. I can't let him get ahead of me, and I have to find this orb to end this nonsense once and for all. I have what I need here."

Miklos' cellphone rang. He picked it up and listened. He then closed it and looked to Charlemagne.

"They're here," Miklos said to him.

"Good," Charlemagne replied. "Let's go then."

Charlemagne put his handgun away and grabbed his briefcase. He then left the room with Tristan and Miklos, going to the stairs to come to the main floor. Tristan said nothing and only walked with them. They then stopped outside of the corporate office were the convoy was parked with the Guardians and men in black spread out. Charlemagne looked at them and then turned to Tristan.

"Farewell," Charlemagne said to him. "Please, be safe and don't do anything rash."

"I want to come with you," Tristan stated. "I don't want to hide like a coward. I'm stronger than that. If Zimmerman's taken Diana, then I want to be with you to help."

"Tristan, enough!" Charlemagne shouted at him. "You are to stay with Miklos and that is that. I won't have any more arguing from you, because I've had enough. Diana's been kidnapped…!"

"I know, but why should I stick back when you get to go on! I can help you! She's my girlfriend and I need to find her! I know that Zimmerman's behind this, so please, let me come! Zimmerman killed my mother. He killed my aunt and uncle. I won't let him kill the love of my life as well!"

"You can help by remaining at home," Charlemagne stated, looking at him seriously and calming down. "Goodbye."

Charlemagne proceeded to walk off. Tristan stepped forward. Miklos grabbed him. Tristan yanked Miklos' grip off with all his might and sped walked to Charlemagne.

"Let me come!" Tristan argued.

Charlemagne had reached the limousine and was about to close the door as he stepped in. Tristan grabbed the handle on the opposite-end and pulled at it. The two struggled for a brief moment until Charlemagne knocked Tristan back.

"Enough!" Charlemagne yelled. "Quit acting like a child and do as your told!"

Charlemagne stepped out of the vehicle, slammed the door shut and grabbed Tristan by his forearm.

"You're to stay with Miklos!" Charlemagne shouted, bringing him away from the car.

"I don't want to," Tristan argued as Miklos took his other arm. "I want to help! Why can't I help?!"

Charlemagne stopped and pointed his index finger at Tristan's chest, and shouted, "Because I won't have another child die because of me!"

Tristan looked at Charlemagne, stunned, the three of them had stopped three-quarters of the way to the main doors of the corporate office. Charlemagne and Tristan looked at each other angrily.

"If I let another child of mine fall because of my own negligence, then my God...! I won't be able to handle that, Tristan," Charlemagne confessed, lowering his tone. "I've already lost Finn, and I might lose Diana – please don't let me lose you too."

The two continued to look at each other as Tristan did not respond. Instead, the three of them were overcome with a sudden blast from the convoy of vehicles as the limousine suddenly erupted into a large fireball that rose up. Tristan, Charlemagne, and Miklos were knocked over by the blast and they felt a heatwave rush past as the other vehicles detonated next. Charlemagne moved over to Tristan to cover him from the shrapnel that would soon fall. They stayed huddled for almost two minutes until the situation settled. A fire bell from the office sounded and sirens could be heard. Charlemagne and Tristan looked over to the wreckage as pieces of metal fell over them.

Tristan saw several Guardians and men in black on the floor, knocked back by the blast and dead on the floor. Charlemagne helped Tristan onto his feet, but he did not stop looking at the blast zone. Charlemagne attempted to get Tristan's attention, shaking him.

"Tristan," Charlemagne repeated, holding his hands at his shoulder. "Are you alright?"

Tristan looked at Charlemagne.

"He's in shock," Miklos stated. "I'm going to go and help any survivors."

"I- I'm fine," Tristan finally said, looking back over to the blast.

"Wait, Miklos," Charlemagne interrupted, forcing him to come over. "A gun, please."

Charlemagne motioned him to hand him a handgun.

Miklos took a handgun from a holster in his jacket and handed it to Charlemagne by the handle. Charlemagne checked the gun and then took out the magazine and unloaded the chamber.

"Miklos, I'm going to take Tristan to the hotel instead," Charlemagne said. "We're not safe… as we are, we're not safe," he repeated, looking to Tristan who had small cuts on his face. "Find Diana, and then find us. I'm going to take care of Tristan myself and find this orb."

"Yes, Charles," Miklos affirmed before leaving to help any survivors.

"Here," Charlemagne said, handing Tristan the handgun and clip. "You know how to use this. You know how to handle it. You know how to fire it. Pray that you don't have to do any of those."

Tristan took each into his hand. Charlemagne then looked to the curb of the office as a fire engine arrived.

"Hide that, quickly," Charlemagne ushered him.

"Yeah," Tristan replied, hiding them both.

"Come on," Charlemagne then said, getting him to walk with him away from the office and down the causeway as firefighters arrived. "We're leaving."

Charlemagne could see police nearby on approach. Ambulances had already arrived. They left the property and stepped onto the sidewalk of the city streets. The two travelled away from Cabernet Electronics and Charlemagne walked with a hand on Tristan's shoulder to guide him as they proceeded to walk into a crowd of bystanders that looked on as they disappeared into the public.

Act 3, Scene 1

Charlemagne and Tristan sat in the carriage of a high-speed bullet train they had taken from Tokyo. Two days had passed since the events at Cabernet Electronics, and upon their return to the hotel, they took their essential items and left the rest for the Protection Squad to pick up at a later date. Both Charlemagne and Tristan had abandoned their suits and opted for civilian clothes. Tristan wore a hoodie and jeans alongside a baseball cap, while Charlemagne wore a dress shirt, sweater underneath, and a coat along with a pair of jeans. Remarkably, Charlemagne had also shaven his moustache, although in the two days that had passed, he had a minor stubble. Nonetheless, his appearance had almost changed entirely. Charlemagne and Tristan seldom spoke to each other in the two days they had spent.

At the moment, Charlemagne read a newspaper while Tristan looked out of the train window before looking to Charlemagne.

"Why am I here?" Tristan questioned. "With you?"

Charlemagne looked back at him.

"What changed your mind?" Tristan asked.

Charlemagne folded the newspaper and sat it at his lap. He looked to Tristan.

"I had escaped a sure death when you pulled me from the car at Cabernet Electronics," Charlemagne said to him. "Had you complied with what I said, I would have entered and been in the epicenter of the blast. I quickly realized then that the Guardians were not a safe option, and since I could not travel with the Protection Squad due to the G.D.P., the only other option was to take you with me and disappear. It was the safest option for the both of us."

Charlemagne looked around the carriage of the train, looking at others suspiciously, but they were all minding their own business. He took his newspaper and opened it.

"We're traveling to Osaka so that we can travel to China through Cabernet Fisheries. I phoned Mr. Heavner before we left Tokyo to explain the plan, and he said he'd arrange for items to be left at an arbitrary hotel under an alias. An agent will leave the hotel room unlocked for us to enter. There shouldn't be any problem of someone raiding the hotel – Japan is a homogenous society of social trust and cohesion. There shouldn't even be any trouble of any enemy agents intercepting them. From there, we'll sneak into China – I should have enough money to last us a week and fund an expedition into Gansu."

"Gansu?"

"I've been reviewing the notes your mother left in you," Charlemagne explained. "This Bishop Williamson described the location of the scepter of Alexander the Great to be in the tomb of a Dragon Emperor. The tomb of which was constructed according to two points along the Great Wall of China in this region. Although he knew where the scepter was, he never had the time to go and find it."

Charlemagne paused for a moment as someone passed them. He then looked around his chair to get a better look of the person before looking back at Tristan.

"The notes left behind by this Williamson are remarkable," Charlemagne admitted. "They recount much of my curiosities, even explaining the location of the Amulet of Ra from the get go, and so much more."

The P.A. in the train carriage went off and a soft-spoken Japanese women announced something that was not understandable to either Charlemagne or Tristan, but they picked up the word 'Osaka' from the blurb.

"There's also more to this tomb…'" Charlemagne said, looking aside and out the window. "According to legend, the tomb of this Dragon Emperor is guarded by a dragon that looks out for pillagers and robbers. Within the tomb, there is also a fountain that collects the tears of the dragon, and these 'Dragon's Tears,' are said to cure any ailment and heal any wound… Of course, how much of this is true, and how much of it is symbolic fiction, I'm not sure, but nonetheless, we have to move quickly and quietly…"

Tristan looked at Charlemagne suspiciously. Charlemagne proceeded to stand up as the train slowed down and they arrived at their destination.

"Get your things," Charlemagne said to him. "We're here."

Tristan looked out his window and saw that they had arrived at the station platform. He grabbed his backpack from the seat next to him and moved behind Charlemagne who put on a face mask. The two of them walked out of the train and proceeded to follow and stick with the crowd of people as they exited the station and came to the streets of Osaka. Tristan followed Charlemagne as he got to a taxi cab.

Osaka was a city similar to Tokyo, given that it was the second-most populous metropolitan area next to the capital. From the train station, Charlemagne had the cab driver take them to their rendezvous hotel, which was a long distance from where they were. The cab took them through the heart of Osaka, through a commercial district before going into a quieter, more industrial area where there were dockyards and warehouses. Once at the hotel, Charlemagne paid the cab driver and left the car with Tristan.

Tristan looked at the run-down structure before them, which was a large contrast to the sort of hotels they had stayed in in the past, especially the motel he stayed in last November with Diana during their misadventure. In contrast to the rest of the city, which appeared much like Tokyo in its novel and modern fashion, the structure before them looked to be of the early last century and was composed of bricks. Charlemagne led Tristan into the lobby of the hotel, which was small and a little better in atmosphere than the exterior. Tristan and Charlemagne took their luggage upstairs where Charlemagne found the room Mr. Heavner had reserved for them.

The two walked into the hotel room and then closed the door behind them. There were two beds for them and a single window that looked out to the railyard along the harbor. Above each bed was a large briefcase. Charlemagne opened his and found a fishermen's uniform as well as a series of documents, including a fake passport, license, and yuans for their travel to China. Charlemagne looked at his passport as he sat on his bed, and read his alias from now on. Tristan went to his briefcase and looked inside. Alongside the documents and uniform, there were magazines for their pistols and some survival equipment, including a water canteen, emergency blankets, lighters, and a Cabernet GPS with an emergency beacon option. The two sat atop of their beds as they looked at their respective passports.

"Michael," Tristan read, looking at his new passport. "What a lame name."

"It's an alias," Charlemagne replied. "It's not supposed to be an attractive name."

"What's yours?"

"Gabriel," Charlemagne answered. "Gabriel Shepherd from Reading, United Kingdom. If I'm correct, you're my son – Michael Shepherd from Mississauga, Ontario, so the narrative of our relation is by blood. Your mother died in childbirth and I have sole-custody of you. You have a sister, Mary, but she's not with us at the moment."

"What now then?" Tristan questioned, putting his things back into the briefcase. "What do we do now?"

Charlemagne looked at his watch, then to Tristan and said, "Tomorrow, we board a Cabernet Fisheries vessel for Dalian, and from there, we make our way to the Great Wall of China to find the Tomb of the Dragon Emperor."

Act 3, Scene 2

Diana slowly opened her eyes and looked forward to the medium-brown camphor hardwood floor to the white street ahead of her. She lay on a futon in the corner of the room and sat up, looking around. There was a gentle chirp of birds outside as well as a rush of wind against trees. A small amount of light filtered into the bedroom from small and wide windows above. Diana was dressed as she was, in her lavender dress and bare feet. She didn't have her purse, her camera, or any of her belongings. She rubbed her eyes and felt groggy. Finally, Diana stood up and went to the sliding door of the house she was in and entered a narrow corridor.

The walls of the house were of a traditional Japanese home. The floor was made of rice straw. She walked to the end of the corridor and entered a room where there was a woman was knelt down at a square pit in the middle of the room where there was an open fire, or *irori*. Over the fire was an iron hook with a kettle attached to an iron rod. The kettle was suspended over the fire. In the pit, there was also an iron grill at the side where there was some food being prepared. Diana looked at the Japanese woman and saw that she was young, perhaps ten years older than Diana, and dressed in a kimono.

Diana and the woman looked at each other. The woman was not stunned to see Diana, but appeared to be mildly surprised, but not as surprised as Diana. The woman spoke to Diana in Japanese. Diana did not understand her. She looked around the room and saw that there was a low table, or *chabudai*, with six cushions, or zabutons, two at the far-ends and two at either side. Behind the table were open doors that looked out to a courtyard garden. Diana stepped back and proceeded to walk the other way of the corridor. She entered a foyer and came through a set of open doors to reach a porch at the entrance of the home, which looked onto another small Japanese courtyard with cherry trees in bloom with their pink leaves. Diana left the porch of the home and stepped down onto the gravel path that went around a pond and came to the gates of the walls of the house.

From the gates of the house, Diana looked below to a small village with rice fields around. The house that Diana found herself in looked to another elegant home at another hill across from the current hill she was at. The entire village was surrounded by these forested hills. At the left-side of the village was a medium-sized river that flowed through. Diana's head spun as she looked around her. She then jumped at the sudden appearance of two shadowy figures that made their appearance from seemingly nowhere, but likely had jumped from atop of the walls off from either side. Diana froze as they pointed their katanas at her and spoke in Japanese.

Diana looked at the hooded figures and saw that they were Japanese males in an outfit that made the figures appear like ninjas. They were entirely black with hoods that only exposed the area around their eyes. The shoulders of the outfits were padded and they wore gauntlets on their forearms with spikes that stuck out. At their chests was a black metallic chest piece. Underneath the chest piece was a black tunic that went down just midway to the thighs. Below the chest piece was a black belt tied around the waist, and then below the belt was an additional piece of armor at the groins. The pants of the ninjas were baggy and tucked into the tall boots of the figures. One of the ninjas yelled at Diana in Japanese, intimidating her and causing her to sweat. Diana raised her hands as though to surrender.

The cloaked figures moved in and each took one of her arms to bring them back. They tied her hands behind her back and then pushed her to move forward, down the hill. Diana walked submissively as they took her through the quiet village where various onlookers, women and children, looked to her for what she was to them, a foreigner and a spectacle. The ninjas took Diana uphill and to the house on the opposite side from where she had awakened at. The gates of this place were larger and the front garden larger too as they came to a porch where they helped her up the steps and into the foyer. From the foyer, the cloaked figures brought Diana through the house until they reached a large room with a large open space.

The room was rectangular with entrance on the wider side. An arcade surrounded the margin of the room, which created a sort of balcony. On the opposite-side from the entrance, there was a platform where a man sat atop, cross-legged, and in a black cloak similar to the one worn by the ninjas. The man was elderly and had a fine-trimmed beard. He was bald and looked seriously from his throne down to Diana. Diana then noticed another ninja at his side, but without his face veil. The boy was young, perhaps Diana's age, with short black hair and a serious glance upon him. His arms were behind his back and he kept his sword at his side rather than behind him. The boy stood at the right-side of the leader of the village.

The leader proceeded to speak in Japanese. The boy stepped forward and looked to Diana as the old man looked to her as he spoke. Once the old man had finished speaking, the youngster translated what he had said for Diana to hear in perfect English.

"Outsider, you are asked by Daimyo Oishi Kiyoshi of the Oishi Domain, to identify yourself," the young warrior demanded.

Diana trembled and replied softly, "D-Diana Cambridge."

The old man said something briefly.

"Louder!" the youngster translated.

"Diana Cambridge," Diana stated. "My name is Diana Cambridge."

The old man proceeded to speak.

"Ms. Cambridge, you have been arrested and brought before the Daimyo to be questioned on your relation to the demon known as Audric Zimmerman, whose spirit has been sensed within you by one of our agents in Tokyo where you were abducted from. How do you plea?"

"What? I'm not related to Audric Zimmerman?!" Diana replied. "What on Earth are you talking about?"

The old man spoke.

"Who was your father?" the boy questioned.

"William George Cambridge," Diana answered. "My mother was Scarlett Anastacia Wright. How could I be related to Zimmerman?"

The old man spoke again.

"Who was your father's father?" the boy then asked.

"I- I don't know," Diana answered. "My mother told me that my dad was abandoned as a child and raised in a foster home. I have no idea of anything beyond my own parents. There's no way I'm even remotely related to him. Both my parents were only childs, and Zimmerman's like, thirty-years old? He couldn't be my father if that's what you're thinking of as well…"

The boy translated what Diana had said to the old man. He then looked at Diana with intent. He spoke something, but the boy didn't translate it. From the tone the man spoke, it sounded like an insult. The old man stood up from his seat and stepped down from his throne. The boy stayed where he was as the man went towards Diana and then proceeded to walk around her. Diana stood awkwardly as the man made several laps around her, eyeing her and then returning to his throne to sit down. He then began to speak. The boy looked to the grandmaster and then to Diana.

"The Daimyo extends his apologies to you, Ms. Cambridge, for startling you and putting you through the hardship that you have experienced in the last day. We will provide transport for you to return to Tokyo, but in the meantime, you are welcomed as a guest to the home of my nephew, Oishi Shinji, who would be delighted to take you in for the night as a guest to his home."

Diana looked at the daimyo and then to the boy. The boy stepped forward while the ninjas that had escorted Diana to the castle proceeded to untie the ropes behind her back to free her. Diana was now stunned and confused. She rubbed her wrists and then looked to the boy.

"I'll take you back to the place you were sleeping at," the boy said, walking forward.

Diana walked timidly behind him. They came to the foyer of the castle where they stopped. The boy turned to Diana and looked at her. He held a serious glance like the grandmaster.

"Wait here," the boy said, leaving through a set of doors.

Diana waited in the foyer. There was a modest chill in the room. The boy later returned with a female who was dressed in a kimono. She carried a set of clothes, towels, and a set of wooden slippers.

"Before we leave, it would be preferable if you were to bath and change from the dress that you are wearing," the boy asked. "This woman will take you to a bath and then I will take you to my home."

"Okay…" Diana said in a timid voice.

Diana left with the woman and went through the castle to reach a moderate-sized room with stone floors, but the same wooden panel walls of the rest of the castle. In the middle of the room was a small pool of hot water. The women gave Diana the clothing, towels, and shoes, and then bowed to her. Diana was then left alone for her to bathe.

Once Diana was finished, she changed out of her dress and into the kimono they had given her to wear. She also wore the shoes. Once she was ready, she stepped out of the room where the woman had been waiting for her. The woman proceeded to escort her back to the foyer where the boy waited for her. The boy looked at her and then began to escort her back to the house where she had awakened at. Diana looked around the village as they walked together. The two didn't speak to each other.

Once through the gates of the house, the boy stopped at the steps of the porch, or *engawa*, but allowed Diana to go in.

"Please remove your shoes before you enter inside," the boy cautioned.

"Okay…" Diana replied in the same timid voice, removing her shoes. "When will I get to go home?"

"Tomorrow," the boy replied. "We have only one car that goes out and it left already. We won't be able to take you home until tomorrow. You can stay here until then."

"Your home?" Diana questioned.

"Yes," the boy answered.

"Okay…" Diana replied.

"My mother will take care of you, but she doesn't speak English, so don't bother asking her for anything," the boy stated.

"Alright," Diana replied, scratching her arm. "Wh-what is this place?"

Diana looked at the boy.

"It's better not to ask questions," the boy simply replied. "We'll take you back to Tokyo tomorrow. Stay here and don't wander around."

"Okay…" Diana replied in her timid voice once more, watching the boy off.

Diana then turned around to look at the home before giving off a sad sigh.

Act 3, Scene 3

Tristan and Charlemagne stood on the main deck of a Cabernet Fisheries crab fishing vessel alongside several other fishermen. They were dressed in the standard uniform among Cabernet Fisheries, which included a blue rubber raincoat that covered the pelvis to midway over the thighs, and wide rubber trousers and tall rubber boots. They also wore thick rubber gloves. The logo of Cabernet Fisheries was on the right breast of the coats. Tristan and Charlemagne watched from their positions as a net was dragged from the bottom of the ocean and up the stern of the ship and down an aisle where it brought the catch of the day, and laid them out.

The workers set off to untangle the net and proceed to distribute the crabs into plastic containers. Tristan looked at all the small crabs that were caught in the single net and saw some small fish that were caught as well. He started to sort the crabs as he was instructed to, by size. Charlemagne sorted through his share, but stopped as he picked up a crab with a rounded abdomen. He showed it to the supervisor of the fishing crew.

"Where do we put the female crabs?" Charlemagne questioned.

"By size," the Chinese man replied. "Put here."

Charlemagne flinched as the man told him to put the female crab with the others.

"I thought it was policy to release female and juvenile crabs," Charlemagne questioned.

"You put here," the Chinese man said again.

Tristan looked over to Charlemagne. He did as he was told and didn't argue.

Once the haul was sorted, the net was cast out to sea again and pulled in with another catch. Likewise, these were sorted until there were plenty of crabs and the ship could continue its sail to Taipei to deliver its catch.

Later in the evening, after the crew had dinner, Tristan and Charlemagne sat down at a table in the crew quarters while the others sat amongst their own. Charlemagne drank some tea as he wrote in his journal. Tristan simply quietly sat with him, thinking to himself. Charlemagne scratched his thin beard that had formed in the last two days. Tristan scratched his cheek. He only carried a very thin stubble with hairs that were less than a millimeter in length, unlike Charlemagne whose hairs were more than a centimeter long.

"Do you think Diana's alright?" Tristan questioned.

Charlemagne looked to Tristan. He then continued to write in his journal.

"I believe, that if we are correct about who captured her, they won't think to harm a hair on her body," Charlemagne stated, "and if he is responsible, then the Protection Squad will find her and they will rescue her. I have absolute confidence in Miklos and his team to rescue her. Perhaps then, it'll be fate that our paths cross once we arrive in China."

Tristan didn't respond to what Charlemagne had told him.

"How long will it take us to get to Dalian?"

"Two days at most," Charlemagne surmised. "We're travelling at about fifteen knots. It's about seven-hundred or so nautical miles from Osaka to Dalian, but once we arrive, we should be free to leave the boat and push on."

Charlemagne looked to the crew as they cheered and played a game between themselves. He tapped his pencil on the table and then looked back to Tristan.

"You know, it bothered me how this vessel has been neglecting the provisions put in place by Cabernet Industries," Charlemagne stated in a slight whisper. "Cabernet Fisheries has a strict guideline to preserve the local population of spider crabs by releasing the young and females so that they can continue to reproduce. I know there are no such regulations in Japan or China, but the rules are in place for an environmental reason, to conserve the species. If I wasn't so desperate to arrive to Dalian without issue, and if I wasn't Gabriel Shepherd and instead Charlemagne, I would have taken issue with this blatant corruption in my own organization."

Charlemagne then sighed. He looked to Tristan.

"One day, Cabernet Industries won't be mine," Charlemagne stated. "I was twenty-seven when I became Chairman of Cabernet Industries. My father had resigned from the position, pressured by the Board of Directors because of his poor leadership, but he was happy to leave. I've worked with the company for more than twenty-five years, but never have I been to so many of our subsidiaries like I have on this voyage. I thought I wasn't naïve to believe that there wasn't active corruption within the organization, because I knew that corruption existed even within the ranks of the company, but not actively… I thought we had a handle on it all. Today, I was proven wrong…"

Charlemagne closed his journal and looked to Tristan.

"I'd hate to think that there was someone at Cabernet Electronics who informed Zimmerman of our arrival," Charlemagne said. "I'd hate it even more to think that there would be someone within the Protection Squad who is working against me, but greed exists. All it took for Allodia's fiancé to betray his own morals was a fair sum of cash… Why not one of my own?"

Charlemagne paused for a moment as he looked aside. He then looked back to Tristan.

"Anyways, I digress... What I meant to say with all this, is that one day I won't be alive, Tristan. You and Diana are all that I have placed my time and energy into – who I have invested in, so it's only logical to assume that Cabernet Industries and all of its subsidiaries, including the foundation, will be yours to control when that time comes. Have you thought of this?"

Tristan hesitated to answer.

"It's crossed my mind before," Tristan admitted, "but to be honest, with the fact that Diana doesn't know what she wants to do with her life job-wise, I kind of just assumed that she would take over – I hoped actually."

"You're bothered that she doesn't seem to have a direction in life?" Charlemagne questioned.

"A little..." Tristan replied. "I mean, I'm happy that she took up being a lifeguard after the races, especially since it's helped her adjust to the community, but she can't be a lifeguard forever, and she knows that. Ideally, I'd be fine if Diana didn't want to do anything but read and take care of our kids while I took care of them all as a provider, but... she'll be bored by that especially once the kids grow up. To be honest, I've always envisioned our future together to be independent from Cabernet Industries, especially financially independent, because I wanted to start our lives together on our own."

"An honest goal," Charlemagne commended, drinking some tea. "You have no obligations to take care of my family's legacy – neither of you do. In my will, I'm obligated by law to divide my estate between you and Diana. If neither of you wish to take control, then I ask that you pass it on to Allodia... if she is still alive at the time that is. If not, I have confidence that the two of you will make the right choice."

Charlemagne went quiet for a moment.

"When I heard last year that I had a son, I had a glimmer of hope that the Cabernet family would continue on through him," Charlemagne admitted, "but alas…"

Tristan looked down to the table.

"We've never talked, the two of us alone, like this, in a long time," Charlemagne stated. "Ever since Finn died, we've been more or less antagonistic of each other, haven't we?"

"I don't hate you," Tristan replied. "I told you that I don't blame you for Finn's death."

"I never said that either," Charlemagne remarked. "I'm only stating the fact that we've been opposed to each other."

Tristan didn't respond. Charlemagne sighed.

"If I can ask," Charlemagne said, clearing his throat. "What was my son like? If it isn't too much of a burden to you that I have you recall…"

Tristan looked to Charlemagne and into his eyes. Tristan's face grew solemn and sad.

"He was…" Tristan said, hesitating for a moment, "eccentric, but deep-thinking and dignified. He would sometimes go on in tangents when he'd speak, speaking in monologue about his passions without giving you a chance to say anything until the end. He was very passionate, especially over his beliefs. He had a deep-heart and was empathetic to all to an extent."

"He sounds like his mother," Charlemagne replied with a sigh. "I envy that you got to spend time with him rather than me, but at the same time, I'm happy that you were in his life of all people, and that the two of you held an affinity to each other to become the friends you were. Thank you."

Tristan didn't respond. The two went quiet for a moment. Charlemagne opened his journal again to continue writing.

"When the time comes, I'll take charge of Cabernet Industries," Tristan stated. "I'm not saying this because of this conversation we've had, but because it was my honest intentions, in the least, to repay you for all you've done for us."

Charlemagne looked to Tristan. He then continued to write in his journal, keeping his head down.

"You simply do as you believe you should, Tristan," Charlemagne said to him. "If you wish to take charge of the company, then do so, but don't let it distract you from your own vocation or from Diana, and your future children."

"Diana and I don't intend to have kids for at least another ten years," Tristan said with a smile. "Even then, by the time they're grown, I can see myself taking charge of Cabernet Industries at a time when I'm older, naturally, when you feel fit to resign."

Charlemagne diverted his pencil down, drawing a prolonged line through his book as he heard these words. His hand began to tremble. Charlemagne cleared his throat.

"Yes," Charlemagne repeated. "When the time comes, but don't forget what I've said – focus on what you want to achieve, Tristan, and remember to place Diana and your children as your foremost priority."

Charlemagne closed his journal and stood up.

"I appreciate the talk we've just had, but I believe I'm going to retire for the night. I'll see you in the morning."

"Yeah, okay…" Tristan remarked, watching him leave.

Tristan sat at the table slightly puzzled by their interaction. He sat at the table alone, crossing his arms and pressing them against the table. He stayed there in his own thoughts as the fishing vessel continued to sail over the East China Sea.

Act 3, Scene 4

Diana sat at the *chabudai* in the in the kitchen of the home where Diana ate with the boy who spoke English and his mother. The boy, as Diana had deduced, was Shinji Oishi, the nephew of the elder of the village, or Daimyo. Diana had learned this by how his mother had been referring to him as Shinji. Diana ate a meal of rice, fish, and miso soup with Shinji and his mother. Shinji's mother was a polite and nice woman who often asked Shinji to ask Diana if she wanted anything else, wanted more food, and saw to it that she was well. Diana observed the pair and saw that Shinji was a strict, short-tempered boy who never raised a smile unlike his mother who appeared to always be smiling. Diana wore the same kimono that she had been given at the village. Shinji had changed out of his uniform upon his return from the castle and was dressed in a navy blue male kimono and baggy trousers.

Shinji's mother began to speak to Shinji as the meal came to an end. Shinji spoke back to his mother in his typical annoyed tone. His mother replied to him in a strict and annoyed manner. Shinji forced himself to turn to Diana. Shinji's mother continued to speak and then he translated.

"My mother would like to tell you a story that's often shared to the females of the village," Shinji said to her. "You do not have to hear the story if you do not want to."

"No, that's alright," Diana replied, looking to Shinji's mother and nodding. "You can tell the story."

Shinji responded for Diana in Japanese. The two then bickered for a moment before Shinji's mother went on. Shinji translated.

"There is a popular tale told to the girls in the village of a woman named Mochizuki Chiyome, who was the wife of an esteemed samurai, Mochizuki Moritoki, who died in battle. She was placed in the care of her husband's uncle, Takeda Shingen, who was the leader of the Takeda Clan. During this time, Japan was divided and in a civil war between many warlords. Shingen approached Chiyome to recruit women and create an underground network of *kunoichi*. The women would be trained in the art of *ninjutsu* while also employing certain distinct characteristics of the female form in order to achieve the war efforts needed by the clan. Chiyome, who descended from the Koga Clan of ninjas, accepted this task and recruited various women who had no place in the world. In Japan, a women's role was as the backbone of the family, but where women have no family or children and when their land is threatened with no one to save them, it is permissible to take arms and fight – this was the creed of these *kunoichi*. The women that were recruited included prostitutes, orphans, lost and abandoned children, and victims of the civil war; widows like Chiyome. They were trained to be information gatherers, verifiers, seductresses, messengers, and when necessary, assassins for the clan. They achieved their roles well, especially since they were all trained as *miko*, or female shamans, that allowed them to travel across the lands despite the ongoing wars without suspicion. The women, who were trained in the art of war, resided in the Takeda Dojo. The lesson is important for the young girls so that they can understand what is expected from them if their village needs of them, because although the men are sworn to protect the village, the women are also expected to do what they must if they are needed."

Shinji paused to drink from his soup. His mother continued to speak in a happy tone. Shinji finished slurping his soup and looked back to his mother and argued with her. He then sighed.

"The Takeda Dojo is a sanctuary not too far from this village where the tradition of the kunoichi continues much like how the shinobi continue to protect and reside in this village. The women of that dojo embrace a pious lifestyle, but are trained in the art of ninjutsu to defend the village if the time ever comes again. They haven't seen action though since the end of the American-Japanese War when many women who were left orphaned or widowed due to the careless bombings of our cities were recruited to wage an insurgent war against our captors. Their fame comes not only from the story of Chiyome, but also from their perfection of the techniques of meditation to achieve a state of consciousness where one is able to train through the mind and learn what usually takes months, but is able to be done in hours and days. For over seventy-years, the dojo has been quiet as Japan has been at peace with others, although we are not free. The main reason the *kunoichi* was born alive during this period was because of the decimation of the war that left the *shinobi* unable to defend the lands at a full strength, but that has changed and we are as strong as ever."

Shinji finished the tale and continued to slurp his soup. Diana looked at him and then to the mother.

"How familiar," Diana simply muttered, "but then again, maybe not so similar."

Once dinner was over, Diana was restricted from helping to clean the dishes. She spent some time in the garden until Shinji came around. Diana turned around to look at him as he loomed behind her.

"We will take you home early in the morning," Shinji said. "It is best if you get some sleep now."

"If this is such a secluded village, how come you know English so well?" Diana questioned. "Who taught you?"

"I learned English when I went to school abroad," Shinji replied. "It was part of my own training to be taught of Western ways."

"You know of the Western way of life then?" Diana questioned.

"I'm familiar," Shinji simply said.

"And you prefer this village over the cities?" Diana asked.

"Yes," Shinji answered. "This village is my home and my ancestors are tied to the soil I walk on every day. I would do them a great dishonor if I were to abandon the village for the shallow intricacies of the material way of life brought by our occupiers at the end of the last war. I see no purpose and thus no desire to leave this village for that world. My people are here, and I have never seen a happier people than here or similar villages. I am the descendant of a noble line of samurai who have poured their blood into this village. It would be shameful and selfish to abandon all that... and that is what is taught and encouraged in the West; to be greedy; to consume and consume. It disgusts me."

"All of Japan's modernity was brought by the Americans who have changed your way of life..." Diana said.

"They've killed Japanese society," Shinji stated. "The bloodshed of Americans against the Japanese never ended after the American-Japanese War when they shamelessly invited themselves to a continent that is not theirs. The only thing that disgusts me more than the American way of life, is the Japanese who praise the Americans for creating the Japan of today or those that respect them as a greater adversary when they didn't fight, but massacred us. They had no honor. The only comparable embarrassment to that was in the politicians of what you refer as the Meiji Restoration who displaced the samurai and industrialized our society, inviting peasants into the army, but that was again not the fault of the Emperor, but of the Americans whose greed forced us to trade with them when Matthew Perry arrived here with guns pointed to our people. And these are our allies?"

Shinji scoffed.

"What is this village about then? You don't seem to enjoy anything," Diana remarked.

"We live simple lives here," Shinji answered. "We enjoy each other. We live for each other. We would die for each other, and the Emperor, who we have sworn loyalty to."

"So, you praise the Emperor even though he was also responsible for the society you have?" Diana questioned.

"You do not understand the significance of the Emperor to our people, you outsider!" Shinji yelled. "He is a god to our people, the descendant of the noblest of lines as he descends from Amaterasu, the sun-goddess. For centuries, the emperor has ruled through other men out of his divine command. The Emperor is exempt from the actions of these inferior men, such as the politicians under Emperor Meiji or politicians of today. In Japan, there has always been a Shogun and the Emperor, even if the Shogun have not existed since the Tokugawa before the Meiji, but this only marks that descension of Japan as we have not been ruled by a wise man ever since, perhaps, Tojo who defended Japan against the bloodthirsty Americans."

"You really hate Americans then, don't you?"

"I do not hate American people, although I despise a great many of their lifestyles. I despise the American government and all likewise regimes who have placed economics and the material over what is more important."

Diana looked back out to the garden. The evening air was warm. She could hear cicadas chirping and there was such a lack of polluted light in the skies that she was able to see the web of stars above her. Diana stood up and passed Shinji who continued to stand behind her. She went to her room, but stopped as she got to the bedroom door. Diana looked to Shinji, but hesitated to speak.

"About the story your mother told," Diana said. "Would it be possible for an outsider to learn as those women have learned?"

"The idea of such a thing would be unthinkable," Shinji replied. "The dojo has a sacred tradition where their talents are only required when it is needed from them to do what is necessary at a time of war. Even then, a spirit to endure suffering and overcome adversity is needed. A spirit whose principle guidance is the greater good. A spirit of determination. A spirit of discipline. Even if an outsider were to contain these, I do not see them willing to take an outsider in, not without permission from Daimyo Oishi."

"Your uncle?"

"Yes," Shinji confirmed. "Did you think that you were to take this training?"

Diana didn't answer.

"How fast is the process?"

"You cannot complete the training, so don't even think of it," Shinji stated. "I will not speak of it anymore with you."

With those words, Shinji passed Diana and left. Diana stayed in the hallway for a moment longer before she slid the door open and then closed them behind her. She then retired for the night, removing her kimono and entering the futon. She brought the covers over her and then blew out the candle that lit her room. In a short time, she fell asleep.

Act 3, Scene 5

Diana stood at the end, or start, of a dirt road at the edge of the village, carrying a makeshift bag that held her lavender dress. She stood alone and watched the white pickup truck from afar as it slowly made its approach towards them. Diana watched the truck carefully before turning around. Beyond the road was a short path they had walked through the rice fields and went back into the village. The pickup truck was between one and two minutes from them. Diana kept a frown as she looked at the truck again and then turned around, returning up the path and entering the village again. She walked through and went to the base of the hill to the castle, made her ascent, and then walked through the gates and into the garden. Diana removed her sandals at the entrance of the palace and then walked up the steps to go to the throne room where the daimyo was seated.

Shinji looked at Diana, surprised to see her again. The daimyo looked down at her as he rested his hands at his knees. He spoke in Japanese.

"The daimyo asks what it is that you think you are doing by making an appearance in his court unannounced," Shinji translated. "We provided you transport to return to the capital – leave at once or be punished."

"I wish to be trained in the art of ninjutsu under the maidens of the Takeda Dojo," Diana demanded. "Last night, I had heard the tale of Mochizuku Chiyome and the service she paid Japan. You brought me here, believing that I was related to Audric Zimmerman, a man you described to be a demon – and I will agree with you that he is certainly a devil, but he is also a common enemy of ours."

"Go away," Shinji argued without translating.

Shinji's uncle shouted at him. He then proceeded to translate.

Diana went on to explain Zimmerman's interest in two particular orbs. She spared the details of the powers of the orbs, but explained Zimmerman's interest to obtain these orbs, the quest in Egypt surrounding the amulet and then the current quest to obtain the scepter of Alexander the Great.

"If I return to Tokyo, I will most likely attempt to return to my guardian, Charlemagne de la Cabernet, who is in search of the scepter to nab it before Zimmerman does, but we face a difficult issue. We are vulnerable and weak. Last year, we were attacked by a man I've come to dub 'The Mysterious Stranger' because we do not know his identity. He attacked us during our vacation in France, attempted to kill my guardian, and then later kidnapped me. Luckily at this time, my guardian and his band of mercenaries later rescued us, but these were different times, and our government has placed restrictions on our abilities to defend ourselves. To make matters worse, last year, when my boyfriend and I were alone and travelling in the United States, we met this mysterious stranger again, and he kidnapped me again. My interest in being able to learn this valuable skill is more than to just stop getting myself kidnapped and to defend myself, but to defend the ones that I love against this agent of Zimmerman's who I haven't stopped having nightmares of where I'm helpless and powerless to fight against him. Please, I beg of you to assist us, if not give myself the means to help myself. Please."

Shinji finished translating Diana's plea. The daimyo then stroked his beard and thought. He looked at Diana with intent.

"The path to become a warrior," the daimyo said to Diana in a broken English, "is a difficult one, child. And for a woman, the transformation of mind and body is irreversible."

"I am willing to do whatever is necessary," Diana interrupted.

The daimyo raised a hand.

"You have come to my castle, interrupted me in my court, and made demands of me? You have disrespected me? You expect me to permit you to be trained by the kunoichi in the sacred art of ninjutsu?" the daimyo asked, increasing his anger. "And the spirit, it must be already bold and hardened!"

"What do I need to do to prove myself worthy?" Diana questioned.

The master looked at her and stood up. He shouted out something in Japanese, and four ninjas jumped from above and landed in the arena before the throne with their swords drawn. The master shouted something else in Japanese, and the ninjas disarmed themselves and put their swords away. Instead, they readied their fists.

"If you wish to train with us, then show us what it is that you possess," the master stated before shouting in Japanese.

Shinji looked to Diana with worry. The ninjas moved in. Diana raised her fists, but was quickly kicked to the ground. Diana looked up and saw another ninja move in to strike her. She moved out of the way and hid behind a pillar. She held her hands up. The ninjas were cautious and kept a fair distance from her as she looked at them. One of the ninjas shouted something in Japanese, and the four of them encroached on her. Diana sucker punched one in return, hitting hard, but the others took her down. Shinji looked away as they beat on her.

Diana's eyes lit up with fury and she grabbed leg of a ninja and attempted to bring him down. The others caught on and hit harder against her until one picked her up and tossed her to the ground. Diana fell against the floor with a hard slam and was left to lay there. She breathed carefully and was conscious, but kept her eyes closed as she embraced the pain silently. Her nose bled. The master looked at her for less than a minute before sitting down again. He shouted something in Japanese, and a couple of ninjas moved in. They then stood back as they saw Diana move. Diana pushed herself off the ground with one arm, the other kept around her stomach, and she stood up. The ninjas moved in again, more quickly, ready to pick her up, but she hit back at one of them, forcing the others to go in and knock her down again. Diana fell back and didn't move as she breathed sharply.

The master shouted something in Japanese and forced the ninjas to back off. He stood up and stepped down to look at Diana. He then stepped over her and proceeded to leave. Shinji attempted to join him, but stopped as he reached Diana, seeing her to move again. He looked at her as she attempted to pick herself up from the ground. The master looked at her.

"P-please…" Diana begged to him.

The master spoke in Japanese to Shinji. Whatever it was that he said, Shinji was shocked by it, which caused the master to yell at him and force him to comply. He helped Diana walk and the two walked out of the throne room and down the hall where she was taken to rest in a room. Shinji then left Diana on a bed, looked at her grudgingly, and then left the room. A woman later entered and washed her face. Diana lay on the bed for several minutes where she slowly fell asleep.

Diana opened her eyes hours later and saw Shinji stand in front of the door to leave the room. He frowned at her.

"My uncle wishes to see you," Shinji stated, "when you are feeling better."

Diana nodded and got out of bed. She walked with Shinji out of the room and back to the throne room where the daimyo was sat at his thrown, looking down at the two of them as they arrived. Diana looked to the daimyo as he began to speak and then to Shinji briefly as he sighed.

"The daimyo was impressed by your determination earlier this morning, but wishes to explain to you the following: once you follow the path of the warrior, there is no turning around. You cannot expect to be the same person as you once were, because that person will not exist anymore. The path of the warrior requires that you face your fears and overcome them – it will never end, but it will become easier with time as you build strength. Most importantly, there is no quitting or option to resign once it starts. The only resignation is by death. Do you understand?"

Diana nodded and then said, "Yes."

"*Hai*," Shinji translated.

The daimyo continued to speak in Japanese.

"Tomorrow, at sunrise, you will make the journey by yourself through the Koga Forest with only your wits and a sword. You will make the journey and go to the Takeda Dojo where the daimyo's niece, Oishi Rei, will await you to begin your training. Do you understand?"

"*Hai*," Diana agreed.

The daimyo made a last remark in Japanese and then threw his hand for them to leave.

"You will remain in the castle until sunset," Shinji said. "Your journey begins tomorrow."

Act 4, Scene 1

The next morning, Diana stood at the outskirts of the hidden village, but on the other side from where she would have departed from yesterday. She was dressed in a uniform similar to Shinji's and the other ninjas, fit with her own breastplate, but without a hood as it was pulled back. Her hair was tied in a ponytail and she was given only a wakizashi, or short sword to arm herself. The short sword was presented to her by Shinji and she attached it to her belt as he instructed her to. Shinji then looked to her.

"This is your last chance to fallback," Shinji warned. "The journey is difficult and it is not guaranteed that you will see me again."

Diana simply looked back at him and then over to the daimyo as he arrived on horseback. He looked down to Diana with a solemn face. He spoke in Japanese.

"Outsider, before you lies the Koga Forest where the ancient shinobi of our ancestors once trained to hone their skills in ninjutsu. There will be no exam other than the journey you will take, in which failure will necessarily result in your shameful death. You take with you only the clothes and sword we have given to you – the dojo you are required to go to is a hike away, travelling north. Go forward and meet your destiny."

Diana bowed and then turned around. She stared across the small meadow of grass that separated herself from the road she was on to the forest ahead. She then proceeded to make her first steps forward and towards the forest. Diana looked to the sun in the east, on her right, as she walked and continued to walk straight to enter the forest. The forest was dense, but the trees were tall and sunlight could filter through and make it to the soiled ground. Diana walked along until she came to a stream.

The stream was clear and ran against a stony surface. Ahead, westward, there was a small cascade from where the stream poured out via rapids. Diana went to the spring and drank some water before she continued along. Diana took her sword out as she walked and looked at it. It was made of a slick steel and was shiny. She could see her reflection on the steel. A reflection of the sunlight bounced off the blade forcing her to squint. She put the sword away and continued to walk. There was a rustle of leaves above as the wind blew past. The echo of the stream behind her could be heard.

The day soon turned warm as she continued to hike along, easily with no weights on her back but the heavy chest piece that covered her torso and the groin plate. She walked and walked, ensuring that she continued to head north as she checked the direction of the sunlight on occasion, and by mid-day, she began to slow down her pace and stop at another stream. The day was warm and slightly humid.

Diana washed her face and then felt her stomach grumble. She looked in the small creek, but so no fish to attempt to catch. She also couldn't see any birds around either, or even any bushes producing any sort of flowers or berries. Diana stood up and crossed the creek, wading through the shallow waters, and then reaching the other side where she continued to hike.

"Come on," Diana spoke to herself. "Charlemagne had me read that book for a reason. I can survive out here, even for a night... I just need to find some food..."

Diana continued to walk through the forest, reaching a hilled area that required her to climb. She pushed off the ground with every step, furthering her altitude to come to the top of a hill and then come back down again as she continued straight. Diana stopped for another break at another river and looked out for fish to possibly catch, but she couldn't see anything.

Instead, Diana could hear a hissing sound come from a bush. She stood up and looked over, hand at her sword, and bent her knees to see a small snake slither out of the bush and go into some tall grass. Diana looked at the snake uneasily.

"I can survive without food for a couple of days," Diana remarked. "I'll just keep drinking water and... possibly die..."

Diana sighed and continued on. The sun proceeded towards the horizon as the day was to come to an end. By the time it was clearly evening, Diana stopped in a small clearing and proceeded to collect tinder, kindling, and fuel so that she could build a fire as she was taught to. Her knife was too thin to act as a hatchet, so she was forced to collect debris of sticks and some dried leaves. To start the fire, Diana found some rocks to hit against the side of her brand new sword, sending sparks into the leaves and igniting a fire. Diana smiled as the fire started. She fed it some kindling and built the fire until it was a modest size to keep her warm.

Once the fire was secured, she fed it some fuel and then laid down on the ground to look up to the twilight sky. She flexed her arm behind her head to prop it and felt her stomach grumble as she looked to the stars. She held a saddened look on her face.

"What am I doing?" Diana questioned. "I can't do this... What do I know? I know what I've been taught on the streets, and... What the G.D.P. taught me in two days... Neither is enough."

Diana adjusted the hood of her uniform to conceal her head and keep her arms at her side as she lay on the ground. She continued to look up.

"Tristan... I hope you're safe. I hope you're not worried... I know you're strong though – stronger than me. I need to be strong too, like you. I need to do this for us... I won't let the

Mysterious Stranger attack us ever again. I won't let myself be kidnapped ever again. This is our only hope…"

Diana turned her back to the fire and cushioned her head with her arm. She closed her eyes and soon fell asleep in the midst of the Koga Forest, ready to continue her journey tomorrow when the sun rose.

Act 4, Scene 2

Charlemagne and Tristan stood at the side of the fishing vessel as they made their approach towards the Dalian harbor on the early morning of what would be their third day at sea. By now, Charlemagne's beard had amassed a fair length, while Tristan continued to appear as he was three days ago. Charlemagne was more or less unrecognizable to his former self. The boat made a gentle approach to the harbor where it moored. Charlemagne and Tristan awaited for the boat to dock properly so they could leave. They stood with their satchels behind their backs and waited patiently.

Tristan's ears soon twitched as he heard the sound of a whistle. The ramp was brought to the side of the ship and a small group of three uniformed officers boarded the boat, shouting in Chinese to the crew. The supervisor presented himself and spoke in Chinese to the officers. They wore navy blue uniforms with caps. They were armed with pistols and appeared to be either police or customs officers. Charlemagne felt uneasy. He put a hand in his coat as Tristan and he looked at the officers.

The supervisor of the fishing crew shouted to the crew in Chinese, then Japanese, and finally English, "Everybody in line. The boat is going to be searched for contraband. Prepare to present your identification!"

Charlemagne and Tristan looked at each other. They walked towards the end of the line and got their passports ready in their hands as well as their forged work permits. A Chinese man led the team of officers and looked at the identification of each worker, asking questions in Chinese, which were translated by the supervisor of the boat.

"What's really going on here?" Tristan asked Charlemagne in a hush. "Are they looking for us?"

"Not likely," Charlemagne replied. "Remember when we crossed into Allabrese during the lockdown, and we thought they were looking for us, but they were looking for the militia? Possibly a similar situation – don't get paranoid."

Charlemagne removed his hand from his jacket and looked to Tristan.

"Where's your firearm?" he asked in a hush.

"In its holster, in my jacket. Why?" Tristan questioned.

Charlemagne sighed.

"At least it's not in your bag – pray they don't do a body search," Charlemagne replied.

The officers soon approached Tristan. The team lead looked at Tristan disgustingly and took his passport and permit into his white-gloved hand. He opened the passport and then looked to the passport. He then spewed some words in Chinese to be translated.

"What purpose does a Canadian boy have in China? Can't you find work in your own country?" the supervisor translated.

"Cabernet Fisheries pays well," Tristan answered.

The supervisor translated.

The customs officer gave off a laugh and replied in Chinese.

"What is he saying?" Tristan asked, looking to the supervisor.

The customs officer shouted at Tristan in Chinese and slapped a hand across his face. Tristan staggered back and brought a hand to his cheek.

"Hey!" Charlemagne shouted, stepping towards the officer that hit Tristan.

"He said what a miserable place Canada is to China, where its youth are forced to work like slaves like his ancestors before him. He also says for you to not speak out of turn and know your place."

The two other officers with the team leader intervened and kept Charlemagne back, forcing him onto his knees. The team leader produced a baton and raised it in a threatening manner as he shouted in Chinese. He put Tristan's passport and permit into his jacket and then took Charlemagne's from his hand. He looked through them and then put them into his jacket as well. He then shouted in Chinese to his subordinates and got them to raise Charlemagne onto his feet. They proceeded to search Charlemagne, patting him as they did a personal search, checking his limbs, and legs, and then his body, stopping at the left of his torso where they felt something. A female Chinese officer shouted to her supervisor who then produced his pistol and pointed it to Charlemagne.

Tristan looked on with fear as the gun was pointed to him. He raised his hands. The Chinese authorities continued to shout at them with their weapons drawn. They spoke into radios. Even the supervisor was shouted at. Tristan and Charlemagne were soon forced onto their knees by reinforcements who disarmed them and then arrested them. Tristan felt his face become smothered against the steel of the surface of the fishing vessel as they handcuffed him. He was then brought to his feet and pushed forward to walk off the boat and be thrown into the back of a police van with Charlemagne. Tristan stood up and sat down as soon as the doors shut.

"Dammit..." Charlemagne remarked, lying on the floor and sitting up.

"It's never any easy getting through customs..." Tristan remarked, spitting on the floor. "What's going to happen next?"

Charlemagne looked to Tristan and sighed.

"Well, if I'm correct, they'll accuse us of being enemy spies, possibly interrogate us for what our purpose is, and so on...

Come to think of, we've been so set off from society that they could have been searching the ship for anyone feeling ill…"

Tristan didn't respond.

"Are you okay?" Charlemagne questioned.

"I've just been detained by the Chinese authorities, but other than that, I'm peachy," Tristan replied in a sarcastic tone. "Maybe they'll quarantine us."

"It's a possibility…"

The van drove for almost twenty minutes until it stopped and the doors were opened. Tristan and Charlemagne were yelled at in Chinese while uniformed men with respirator masks went in and pulled them out. The two were thrown to the ground within a parking garage and then forced onto their feet to walk into a cell block where they were brought to a room with two cots and a toilet in the corner. The Chinese closed the door behind them and left them in the room alone. The room was bright and the walls and floor were similarly composed of a greyish-white tile. Each of them stayed in the room, handcuffed, and soon received a couple of women who swabbed them and assessed their vital signs. They did so with face masks on, wearing gowns, and under supervision of two armed officers with assault rifles. Once they were done, the four of them left them alone where they stayed for close to two hours.

At the end of the two hours, the doors opened and two armed men with assault rifles entered while a uniformed officer who appeared to be a higher rank, with no mask, spoke in Chinese in an angry tone. He pointed to Charlemagne who was then pulled out while Tristan was left in the cell room. Charlemagne was escorted through the compound and its bland corridors until he was brought to a similar room like the cell, but with a table in the center and chairs on either side. Charlemagne was pushed in and forced to take a seat while the senior most officer sat down.

A Chinese woman in a suit entered the room and stood at the short-side of the table. The senior officer put Charlemagne's passport on the table alongside the permit and the driver's license that was recovered from his belongings on the table. He then spoke in Chinese.

The woman translated what he said, and said, "We have been in contact with the Canadian Embassy who have not been able to verify your identity. Who are you and what is your business in China?"

Charlemagne hesitated to speak for a moment. He then sighed.

"My name is Charlemagne Phillipe de la Cabernet, Chairman of Cabernet Industries, and owner of the name and all its subsidiaries," Charlemagne stated. "Please do not harm myself, or my son, and instead, please verify our identities. We are travelling under classified business, under direction of the United Nations, which I cannot speak of with you. Please speak with your superior and get into contact with the Party who will be able to verify our business in your country."

The senior officer was not pleased by this response and slammed a fist on the table. He shouted at Charlemagne in Chinese.

"The People's Republic of China is not subservient to the United Nations. If you are spies of the U.N., then you are enemy spies to the People's Republic. What is your business in China?"

Charlemagne repeated what he had to say before. The senior officer slammed his fist again and asked once more. Charlemagne repeated.

"So, if you will not tell us what it is that you are doing in China, then we will have a word with the boy you claim to be your son," the woman translated.

"Leave him alone," Charlemagne grunted as the senior officer stood up.

"What is your business in China?" the woman translated.

"I told you, that is classified business. Contact your senior officials and get into contact with the United Nations to escalate my presence – I will not be harassed by a petty officer because it will reflect poorly on you when it comes to light who I am, and how I have been treated."

The woman finished to translate what Charlemagne had said. The senior officer simply looked down at him, huffed, and then left the room with the translator. Charlemagne stayed in the room, handcuffed for close to an hour without any stimulus. He simply sat hunched over and deep in thought.

Tristan later looked up and over to the doors of the cell as they opened, expecting Charlemagne to be brought back, but instead, Tristan was dragged out and brought to a separate interrogation room. The woman proceeded to translate what the senior officer, the same officer that had interrogated Charlemagne, said to Tristan.

"The Canadian Embassy cannot verify your identity, Mr. Shepherd. Who are you and what is your business in China?" the woman translated.

Tristan looked down at the passport, the permit, and the driver's license. He then sighed.

"My name is Michael Shepherd, and I've travelled to China to work with Cabernet Fisheries," Tristan said in a neutral tone.

The senior officer chuckled. He then spoke.

"You do not need to tell us this story again, because your father in the other room has already told us the truth. We only need to hear it from you as well…"

Charlemagne's ears twitched as he could hear the mumble of the officer. He stood up and moved over to the wall to see if he could hear better, but it was still mumbled and incoherent. Tristan looked at the senior officer. Tristan's face was red and slightly swollen from where he had been hit. He looked at the officer angrily.

"My name is Michael Shepherd," Tristan stated. "I'm here to work for Cabernet Fisheries."

The senior officer frowned. He leaned forward and looked at Tristan in the eyes.

"Tell me again," the woman translated.

Tristan stared back at the customs officer. He then repeated what he had to say. The senior officer shook his head and shouted out in Chinese. The door opened and two officers entered with stun rods in hand. Tristan saw them and then looked back to the senior officer.

"Do you wish to say the same thing to me now?" the woman translated. "I already know from your father, so do not say those words in vain. What fisherman carries a firearm? You are spies sent by the United Nations, aren't you? Admit it."

Tristan's face went flush. His breathing became sharper. The senior officer shouted in Chinese.

"Admit it," the woman translated.

Tristan shook his head.

"No, that's not true," Tristan said. "We're not spies. That is not true."

The woman translated. The man gave off a pitiful response. The officer ignited their stun rods and stepped forward. Tristan flinched as he saw them approach him. Charlemagne looked confused as he could only hear a glimpse of what was occurring, but then he heard a bang. Tristan heard the bang too as it was against the door into Tristan's interrogation room. The senior officer asked the officers to halt for a moment as he stood up. The woman did not translate.

The door opened and another woman spoke to the senior officer in a rushed manner. The senior officer listened and then left the room with the two other officers and translator. Tristan's heart rushed and he panted as though he had just run a mile. Charlemagne then turned around as he heard the door to his room open. He looked and saw the door open, filtering light in, and a woman in a black suit entered and looked to Charlemagne displeasingly. Charlemagne looked back at the woman in her medium-brown hair and fair skin with an equally displeasing appearance. She shook her head at him while two officers entered the room to remove the handcuffs from Charlemagne's hands.

Charlemagne rubbed his wrists and looked to Director Black and said "What are the chances we run into each other, Ms. Black? In China no less."

"You're lucky I was in the area," Director Black stated, "looking for you no less after you disappeared on us in Tokyo… Why don't you have a seat, Mr. Cabernet? We have some catching up to do?"

"And Tristan?"

"Tristan is safe – we won't let the Chinese harm you or him," Director Black replied. "This is the second time I've had to save you from the Chinese. That's twice you owe me, so how about you take a seat and let's talk? You're still on the clock, so you're not in trouble, for now…"

Act 4, Scene 3

Diana opened her eyes and pushed herself off the ground as she looked around the temperate forest she was in. The fire had burned out on its own. Diana continued to look around suspiciously before looking up to the sky. Snow fell from above, but not around her. The snowflakes didn't touch down the ground and therefore didn't stick. The trees around her seemed different as well. They were coniferous, evergreen trees that were tall, taller than the ones she had seen in England, and perhaps as tall as ones she's seen in the pacific northwest. Diana brought a hand to her stomach as it rumbled. Her legs also mildly shook as she stood.

"You should eat," a feminine voice said in Japanese.

Diana looked around, a hand at her short sword as she looked for the source of the voice.

"Who's there?" Diana questioned in Japanese.

Diana then paused.

"How come I can speak Japanese?" Diana then questioned herself. "How come I can understand Japanese?"

"Because I presented onto you, the gift of the language of my people," the voice replied. "My name is Oishi Rei, high priestess and grandmaster of the Takeda Dojo."

"I'm... I'm in a dream?" Diana questioned, looking at her gloved hands.

"You are physically unconscious, but your mind is awake in this world I've constructed so that you can complete the training beset before you," Rei stated. "Here, you can learn the skills that you will then be able to use in the physical realm, but while time flows in that world, time flows faster in this world. You will only age, physically, however, as fast as time flows in the physical realm."

"How come I can't see you?" Diana asked, looking around for the source of the voice.

"I'm in your head," Rei stated. "We will meet later... but now, you must eat and harvest from nature, the energy to demonstrate your skills."

"There's nothing to eat in this forest," Diana complained. "It's barren."

"Not exactly," Rei replied. "I seem to remember you passed an opportunity to eat yesterday, believing that you'd get to eat when you arrived at the temple."

Diana then pivoted her leg and turned to the right. She heard a hiss.

"You've got to be kidding me," Diana remarked. "You want me to eat a snake?"

"A warrior does not argue what his meal is going to be, but eats for the nutrients that may aid him," Rei explained.

Diana looked to the shrubs and withdrew her short sword. She then approached the shrub with careful steps. Diana paused.

"What if the snake bites me? What if it's venomous?" Diana asked. "If I die in this dream, do I die in real life?"

"If you die in this world, it will not go well for you," Rei simply said.

Diana continued to approach the shrub.

"How venomous can a little snake be?" Diana questioned.

Diana stepped into the shrub and then jumped back as a large viper raised its head and hissed at her. The snake then lunged towards her, biting her in the thigh. Diana fell backwards and shouted out in pain. She cried out and cried out for minutes.

"Do you see the error that you made?" Rei questioned. "In the physical realm, lessons like these are harder learned, and for good reason.

The wound and pain in Diana's thigh soon dissipated and she found herself on the ground, looking up to the bright sky. Diana stood up as she heard a hiss. She took out her short sword and held it, looking over to the bush.

"Approach with caution and mind the reflexes of the snake," Rei said. "They are fast and nimble, much as you should be."

Diana took a careful step forward. She saw the eyes of the snake poking out from the bush, looking at her.

"If you take another step, you are going to find yourself bitten again, and my patience with you will shorten and force me to leave you in agony to seriously think of what you did wrong," Rei remarked. "Put your sword away, and think of something else."

Diana frowned and put her sword away. She then took a step back and looked around. There was not much to use. Diana looked to the creek and then eyed a boulder. She went to it and picked it up. It was heavy and weighed close to forty-five pounds. Diana took the boulder over to where the snake was, but stopped at the limit of her footprints. She then threw the rock, hitting the snake and crushing it with a terrible hiss. Diana then drew her sword and went over, seeing the bloodied impact. She quickly sliced the head off the snake and kicked it aside. Diana detached the rest of the body of the snake from the other side and picked it up, frowning and looking at it with displeasure.

"Can I eat this?" Diana questioned.

"Of course, it is food," Rei stated. "Although not an ideal meal, when forced to survive, venomous snakes can provide nutrients for you to carry on. However, they are fast as I said, so do not think to yourself that you can outspeed them."

Diana took the snake over to the firepit and proceeded to prepare it and the fire for her to eat. Once she was fed, she stood up and looked up to the sky.

"What now?" Diana questioned.

"You need to travel north to reach the temple," Rei stated. "What are you waiting for?"

Diana did not argue and simply started to hike again. She travelled through the mystical forest, stepping over the tall plants and fallen debris as she walked at a gentle speed.

"At this rate, you will never reach the temple," Rei stated. "Pick up your speed…"

"Isn't that a waste of energy? I can only run for so long, but I can walk for a lot longer," Diana argued.

"Nevermind that," Rei stated. "Simply run."

Diana didn't argue and picked up the pace, but did not sprint or even run. At best, she jogged, jumping over the debris until she paused at a fallen tree that required her to crawl under. Diana got down onto a knee.

"Do not break your pace," Rei complained. "Sweep under, and move on."

Diana stood up.

"Turn around, and try again."

Diana turned around and ran back a short distance, and then onwards to reach the fallen tree and slide underneath before continuing. Diana jumped over the knee-high debris in the forest, and continued to meet with fallen trees for her to slide under. Ahead, she began to some fallen debris with a slot in the middle. Diana reached it and attempted to vault over, but her head hit the side of the large trunk above.

"Flip," Rei stated. "You must flip through. Again."

Diana recovered from her crash and stepped away from the tree.

"Run from this position, and show me a flip," Rei demanded.

Diana did not argue and simply ran. She then jumped up, twisted her body, but landed on her bottom.

"Again, but this time, land on your feet," Rei stated. "I will guide you through…"

"It'd be a lot easier if you were physically here to help," Diana muttered, turning around.

"It'd be a lot easier if you held more confidence in yourself," Rei replied. "Now, run forward and prepare to flip. I will tell you when…"

Diana ran forward, back towards the debris. She passed the midway mark and began to slow down as he reached the debris.

"Keep your pace," Rei stated. "Forward."

Diana continued on.

"Jump forward," Rei said as she was about to reach the obstacle. "Turn your body to the side and lift yourself up. Tuck your legs in and hold them until your feet face the ground, and bring them out."

Diana did so, and passed through the obstacle without touching either the top of bottom.

"Keep on," Rei stated. "It is like the snake that we must be nimble as we travel and stop for nothing as we make our escapes…"

Diana continued through the forest with Rei's voice speaking to her. She continued to run through the forest, jumping, flipping, and sliding. Eventually, Diana was brought to the top of a hill where she looked below to a clearing. Diana saw the movement of some figures below. She got down and laid low, watching ahead at the people that were travelling below. They were armed with rifles. Diana recognized one of them. He had brown skin and long dark hair. The other was a female with even longer black hair and darker brown skin. Diana continued to watch them as they disappeared into the forest.

"Follow them," Rei told Diana.

"Why?" Diana questioned.

"You recognize them," Rei stated. "You understand they are not good people. I am instructing you to follow them, but remain hidden. Their firearms would easily kill you."

Diana looked down and saw the short slope was steep. She stood up.

"Jump," Rei instructed.

Diana jumped down and landed below.

"Now, stay low as you run," Rei told Diana, "but remain conscious of what you may step on… One bad step, and you're stealth is broken.

Diana crouched down and ran forward, looking down to avoid stepping on a stick or anything else that could attract attention. She then looked forward, looking around for the targets.

"You've lost them," Rei stated. "You had a simple task of following them, and you lost them."

Diana said nothing. She instead went to a tree and hid behind it. The communitarians could be seen ahead. Diana could see the faces of Nirvana and her son, River, as she remembered them from last year. They were discussing amongst themselves, but Diana could not hear what they were saying. Once they were done talking, they continued through the forest. Diana noticed that two of the communitarians were carrying on two sticks, some sort of killing, wrapped in a grey blanket with blood dripping down.

Once they were a fair distance, Diana continued to follow them, looking down to mind her steps, but looking up to keep an eye on the group as they walked through the forest. Within a couple of minutes, Diana could begin to hear the sound of some crying and wailing in the distance. She continued through and stopped as the group stopped and met with another two communitarians. One of them, Svante, was beating on a young woman with fair skin with the other. She was tied to a tree and her clothes were ragged. The woman was tied off from the tree and thrown down into the middle of the clearing near a campfire. Svante left her with four other communitarians while he left with River, Nirvana, and the two that carried the killing.

Two of the communitarians carried poles that appeared to be like torches, while the others were unarmed as their rifles were behind them. The unarmed communitarians continued to kick the woman while the others left. Once they were gone, Diana continued to watch. One of the communitarians, a male, stopped and laughed disgustingly as he unzipped his trousers. Diana could not hear the foul words that were spoken as the others proceeded to hold her down.

"Are you just going to watch while an injustice is committed?" Rei questioned, alerting Diana. "Hurry, go along and save that woman!"

"I- I don't have any training," Diana complained in a whisper. "Isn't the purpose of all this that I be trained by you? I don't know how to properly fight…"

"I will be with you, just go," Rei replied.

Diana sighed and went on, sneaking her approach towards the clearing and hiding in a shrub. She brought her hood over her head and covered her mouth, produced her short sword, and then jumped out. The communitarians looked at her, the man stood up as he was about to violate the woman and looked at her.

"Put your sword away and put your hands forward," Rei instructed. "Do not hold a fist, keep your fingers available and hands ready to grab. Put a foot forward, and another back, but stay on your toes. Be ready to pounce back, grab forward, jump to the side. Keep your eyes on your opponent…"

"Look at what we have here," the communitarian remarked, zipping his trousers. "Another beauty…"

The man reached around for his rifle.

"Strike now," Rei stated. "Run forward and kick him down."

Diana obeyed and ran forward, jumping up and kicking the man down.

"Watch for the man behind you," Rei remarked, forcing Diana to turn around and see the other man attempt to strike her. "Duck down and roll out of the way."

Diana ducked down and did as she was told.

"Now strike!" Rei commanded.

Diana remained low and gave a low kick to knock the other communitarian down.

"And take them down," Rei instructed.

Diana punched the second man she had knocked down while the others ignited their torches and approached Diana. Diana evaded as they attempted to swing at her with the torches, singeing her breastplate as the fire touched her chest.

"At the next strike, evade left and grab the wrist," Rei instructed, causing Diana to do so as told. "Now bring your other arm up and around the joint of the arm, flexing and spinning them to your left to bring them down."

Diana proceeded and dropped the communitarian down. He dropped the torch and it fell onto the floor. Diana took it and hit him in the head before turning to the other as he made his approach.

"Again," Rei insisted.

Diana moved in as he attempted to strike at her and grabbed him by the wrist before taking him down. By then, the others had stood up and readied their fists to fight her. Diana ducked down as they attempted to take another swing at her and she kicked the man down again. She then stood up and ran forward to tackle the other one to the ground, punching him in the face as soon as he fell before turning to the other. Diana picked up a rock that was a part of the campfire and bashed it against the side of the man's face, knocking him out. She then stood up and turned to the others. The torches had burned out, but two of the three that remained had picked them up to use as a club. Diana panted at a careful pace and returned to the bladed stance that Rei had taught her to take at the start of a fight.

The communitarian with the rifle behind him moved to take it into his hands. Diana rushed in to kick him down as he held his hand at the rifle. She then picked it up on the floor and hit him in the head with it. She then quickly ducked as another attempted to strike at her with the torch handle and rolled out of the way. The other went at her, but Diana grabbed the man's wrist as she evaded to the side and pulled him down once more, taking the baton and hitting him in the head with it before deflecting an oncoming blow with the stick and then grabbing the wrist of the other and taking him down. The communitarian went down and Diana hit him in the head, knocking him out.

At the end of the fight, Diana looked around and saw the men scrambling in the dirt, concussed, and slowly spread out to leave her in the clearing. Diana looked for the victim and realized that she had run off during the fight. All that was left were the weapons, the torch handles, and some bloodied rope near a tree. Diana went to fetch the rifle, but as she grabbed it, it faded and dissipated.

"You will not need this, and you will not be trained in these," Rei stated. "Although there is something here that you should recover for your journey onwards."

Diana looked around.

"The torch sticks?" Diana questioned.

"No."

Diana continued to look around, at the fire, and then to the rope. She picked it up and organized it so that she could carry.

"There are many uses rope can possesses, and if none are available, you are best off retrieving some as it becomes available," Rei stated."

Diana brought the rope around her shoulder and then continued to look around.

"Where did that woman go?" Diana questioned. "Should I follow her?"

"It's none of your business," Rei replied. "It's unlikely that a ninja should have to engage in combat like that, and in the future I will instruct you in the proper techniques, but for now we've focused on basics, such as kicking, punching, and evading. Your task now is to continue the hunt for these bandits."

"How? I've lost them for sure since I had to save that woman," Diana replied. "How am I going to find them now?"

"Put your mind to it," Rei simply stated.

Diana sighed and looked around. She could see some boot prints in the soil, but most of the ground around them was grass and didn't leave the same print. She span around the clearing and then focused on some blood that had been left behind, most likely from the killing. She looked at the shrub where blood had stained some leaves. She then looked forward in the right direction for her to continue on her quest.

Act 4, Scene 4

Charlemagne sat in the cargo hold of the G.D.P. V-TOL as it flew over Beijing. He continued to have his beard, but had changed out of his fisherman uniform for a black suit lended to him by Ms. Black. Tristan had also changed out of his uniform and switched into a black suit. The pair of them appeared tired and simply sat together as the vehicle travelled over the city. Charlemagne had a rucksack next to him with all his belongings, and he had his journal in his hand.

Director Black sat across from them with a laptop on her lap, typing out. She sat next to two Guardians. The other two of the squad were at the front, and one of which included Brenton Carse. Director Black slaved away as she typed and talked, wearing a Bluetooth earpiece in her right ear. The V-TOL slowed down and soon came to a halt, and the back door opened for them to exit and step onto the helipad of a skyrise in the Chinese capital. Charlemagne put his journal away and stepped out with Tristan and the director.

A thick haze drifted over Beijing, which made seeing the ground from their height impossible. However, unlike the citizens below, they were perfectly able to see the skies above them, which were clear. The sun was bright and it was late afternoon. The group went to an elevator and entered. Only two Guardians travelled with them, while the other two remained at the V-TOL. Once they reached the ground floor of the building they were in, they stepped out. Charlemagne and Tristan attempted to walk with the director as she continued to talk. From the lobby they had reached, they were able to see the city outdoors. Beijing was similar to Tokyo from what Tristan could tell from where they were.

Director Black finished her phone call and then turned around to Charlemagne and Tristan.

"I've been in contact with the Japanese authorities, and they've been included in the search for your daughter," Director Black stated. "We'll open whatever resource we can to find Diana – I do this not only because you're assisting us, but because I had personally fought and trained with her in Kennte, and couldn't imagine if she were harmed in any sort of way. In addition, we'll widen our search across the island and see if the Yakuza can be of any help – I'm sure they owe us a hand or two for some help we've provided, but in the meantime, I need you to focus on the task at hand."

"What's the mission?" Charlemagne questioned with a sigh. "Why are we in Beijing when we should be in Gansu?"

"Our informant wishes to deliver some important intel on Zimmerman's progress in China. Today, you'll have a meeting with Chinese officials in the Forbidden City at seven o'clock to discuss the current pandemic and what Cabernet Industries will do to assist…"

"We shouldn't be doing anything," Charlemagne muttered. "They've started the bloody mess…"

"You will be courteous, and pleasant, and put on your best diplomat expression – you'll also shave, for heaven's sakes. Afterwards, you'll meet this informant in the palace museum, which will be closed due to the pandemic, and thus provide privacy for you to exchange the information. The information delivered could be vital to our own efforts, and our informant wished to hand these to you and you alone."

"How can we be certain that this individual is not a double agent of some sort?" Charlemagne questioned. "If he knows I'm involved with you over this orb, and he is not trustworthy, then

Zimmerman will have known why I was in Tokyo and been able to organize my assassination at Cabernet Electronics."

"Our agents with counter-intelligence are looking into the possibility of a mole, but I'm confident of our agent – you'll recognize him. I believe the two of you have worked together before," Director Black stated. "You will travel with four of my agents who will provide security – the Guardians will keep an eye on Tristan from the hotel."

"Very well," Charlemagne replied, eyeing a limousine arriving outside of the lobby of the building they were in. "Let's get on with it."

• • •

Later that evening, Charlemagne travelled with several G.D.P. agents through Beijing and to the center of the republic under a police escort put together alongside the G.D.P. Charlemagne looked out of the limousine and listened to the sound of sirens of the police motorcycles. The limousine was in the midst of a large and long motorcade that included other SUVs and sedans. The flash of blue and red could be seen from the front and rear of the car. On his right, Charlemagne could see the Tiananmen gates to the Forbidden City, and on the left he could see Tiananmen Square, which was empty and clear, much as Chang'an Avenue was. Tiananmen Square contained a large rectangular monument in the center with stairs on either side that went up to this elevated monument. From Chang'an Avenue, Charlemagne could see two wide rectangular signposts that were red and contained Chinese Mandarin characters in white that stated something he could not read or understand.

The limousine made a turn and was guided down the side of the plaza, and brought to the front of the Great Hall of the

People. The structure was large and the façade was rectangular with pillars along the front. Behind the pillars were gold-framed doors that went into the foyer of the structure at the top of a wide staircase. Above the pillars were friezes with the emblem of the People's Republic of China in the middle. Above the friezes, an orange roof rimmed around. At the other side of the square was the National Museum of China. The architecture was simple, consisting of a beige brick. The limousine stopped before the red carpet to the government building where agents waited for Charlemagne to open the door and guide him to the building. From the limousine, he was brought up the wide staircase and into the seat of power of the People's Republic of China.

Charlemagne walked up and was met with the Chinese Permanent Representative to the United Nations and the Foreign Minister of the People's Republic of China who greeted Charlemagne before he was brought into the Great Hall of the People for their meeting with the G.D.P. agents at his side.

At the end of the meeting, Charlemagne exited the building and looked out to Tiananmen Square from the top of the steps of the structure. The skies were orange as it was now late evening and the sun was setting. Charlemagne's eyes were focused to Tiananmen, the gate into the Forbidden City where there was a portrait of Chairman Mao Zedong in the center. The base of the gates was a saffron red rectangular box with a central entry point, or tunnel, that went through and above this tunnel was where the portrait hung. At each of the corners of the base were poles with the red flag waving. Above the base was an example of classical Chinese architecture, a two-story structure with hip roofs.

Charlemagne walked from the Great Hall of the People down to the square and across the street to the heavenly gate where there were G.D.P. agents spread out. Charlemagne made eye contact with them and then proceeded through the gate via the central tunnel to reach the other side, which came to another square that looked out to another gate, similar to the one before. At the side in the midst of the plaza were poles with CCTV cameras pointed out at almost every angle. Charlemagne eyes these cameras as he calmly walked along as though on a causal stroll.

G.D.P. agents stood at either side of each gate as Charlemagne continued along, walking past another, and then another larger one to finally reach the central plaza of the Forbidden City which looked to the old palace. Charlemagne walked down the steps from the central tunnel and began to cross the quiet plaza to reach up the steps to the entrance into the palace. He looked at the sides of the many doors and saw the design of traditional Chinese dragons below window screens. He then walked inside, through the open gates and into the throne room where there were many red wooden pillars made of the local sandalwood on approach to the Dragon Throne. The pillars nearest to the throne were covered in gold. Above, on the ceiling, there were further etches of dragons in their serpent-like form. The ceiling was heavily designed and in a grid-like manner. Above the throne was a caisson, or heavily decorated panel with a six-point star made out of two golden squares. The throne stood atop of some steps and had five dragons coiled around the back and hand rests. The screen behind it contained nine dragons. On the carpet of the steps, there were green dragons etched into fabric.

Charlemagne stood before the throne where there was no one seated and simply looked at it and all the dragon motifs that stood around him. He was soon accompanied by a figure that stood two-meters apart from him and looked at the throne.

Charlemagne did not look at this figure, who passively looked at the artefact with him.

"Interesting symbology, the dragon contains," Charlemagne stated. "In European culture, the dragon is a fearsome and evil beast that must be destroyed. He sits on treasure and disrupts the flow of wealth, and in connection with Christian tradition, he is a symbol of Satan or a demon as the final form of the wee serpent that led man astray. It is within all of us to slay a dragon, our inner demons. I stand here, in the heart of a communist nation, when my grandfather used to be an ardent anti-communist who called for the dismantlement and slaying of the Bolshevik dragon in the Soviet Union. What a contrast in culture..." he went on and said. "In China, the Chinese are seen as the descendants of dragons, a shift in what was formally believed where the Emperor was the descendant of a dragon, which comes from the tales of Yangdi and Huangdi, where Yangdi was conceived when his mother telepathically communicated with a dragon, and with the help of Huangdi, the two tribal leaders established what has now become China... but the dragon is not the same as the dragon in our culture, or does it carry the same symbology. The dragon in China is a protector and a mystical, omnipotent creature that brings good luck and fortune. They don't live in the skies, but in the seas, rivers, and lakes..."

Charlemagne finished his sentence and then looked next to him to the informant. He then dropped his expression into one of surprise as he saw who the informant was. Charlemagne frowned and turned to him, walking over to shake his hand.

"I expected someone else," Charlemagne said, shaking the hand of Johnathan Southern, "but this doesn't surprise me any more or less than who I thought would be here. You betrayed me, and now you're betraying Zimmerman."

Johnathan, or 'Johnny' as he was named, did not respond and instead showed Charlemagne the envelope he had in his hands. Not much had changed in Johnathan's appearance aside from his thick brown beard and long hair. He was dressed in a simple coat and cargo pants with boots.

"Zimmerman is having difficulties with locating the Dragon's Den, but he's narrowed the location to several points and is touring the country to cross each off his list," Southern stated in his Yorkshire accent. "Of course, he's having difficulties with the Chinese government, who consider his presence in the country to be illegal and have also taken an interest into the artefact themselves."

"What credibility do you have?" Charlemagne questioned him.

"I'm Zimmerman's primary archeologist – I mentored under you, so that makes me the best apparently," Southern replied, "but your people know that, and they've made me an offer I can't refuse."

"My people? And who do you know to be my people?"

"Interpol," Johnathan simply stated. "Who else?"

"Right…" Charlemagne muttered, moving his hand to receive the documents.

Before Charlemagne could receive the papers, he flinched as a gun was shot, but not at him. Charlemagne looked down to Johnathan's abdomen as blood seeped into his clothing. The envelope fell between them and Johnathan fell over. Charlemagne quickly moved out of the way and produced his handgun from within his suit as he hid behind a pillar. Charlemagne then saw a shadowy figure dash away from the entrance into the throne room, causing him to raise his gun and take shots, but the figure dashed off. He ran outside and looked over, seeing a couple of agents below in the plaza with their guns drawn out and proceeding to open fire at the figure as he attempted to make his escape. Charlemagne took shots until a pair of G.D.P. agents arrived and proceeded to attempt to force him away.

"Wait," Charlemagne protested, "the papers…"

"We'll get them to you later," an agent replied, attempting to force him away. "You need to leave. It's not safe."

Charlemagne caved and allowed the agents to pull him away. He saw many more agents appear as they responded to the assassin. Charlemagne was brought back to Chang'an Avenue where the limousine was pulled up. The agents physically assisted Charlemagne into the limousine and then banged the top for the car to drive off while the others dealt with the mess and took Charlemagne to safety. He looked at his bloodied hands and stood up to sit down on a seat as he was on the floor of the car. Charlemagne was alone in the passenger seat area of the car and let out a sigh. His phone rang. Charlemagne picked it up with his shaking hands.

"H-hello?" Charlemagne questioned.

"Good riddance, you're alright," Director Black responded. "What happened?"

Charlemagne explained that he met with Johnathan Southern and that he attempted to hand him some documents on Zimmerman's progress, but he was then assassinated. Charlemagne said he was unsure who assassinated him, but was sure it was most likely authorized by Zimmerman.

"My agents will take care of this 'assassin,' but in the mean time we need to get you back to the safety of the hotel," Director Black replied. "If Zimmerman has deduced the location of the scepter to nine locations, then we need to act fast…"

"I can deduce the location to one exact point," Charlemagne replied. "All I need is to travel to a certain segment of the Great Wall in Gansu to triangulate the position…"

"Consider it done," Director Black replied. "You'll set off as soon as you arrive to the hotel. I'll see you then."

Director Black hung up on him. Charlemagne dropped his bloodied phone beside him and looked out the window as the car drove through Beijing and returned to the hotel. He slouched back and looked out with a dismal expression, and with tired eyes and body, when the car arrived, he exited to resume the adventure.

Act 4, Scene 5

Diana continued through the Koga Forest, following the trail of blood that was left behind from the sacrificial offering hidden underneath the grey wool blankets. Rei had fallen silent as Diana methodically followed the trail at a calm pace, ensuring she did not miss any stains, while also keeping low and out of sight in the tall grass. With the rope Diana had acquired, she rappelled down a short cliff and continued to reach the outskirts of the commune where she could see the communitarians at work. The commune had no gate, wall or fence surrounding it and was open to the forest around, but there were a lot of communitarians about. Diana analyzed the area as she hid in a bush.

"The art of ninjutsu lies in the ability to remain in the shadows," Rei stated. "You will need to infiltrate the commune and reach the longhouse where they've taken that unfortunate soul to meet his fate, but you'll need to act quickly."

Diana continued to analyze the area.

"How?" Diana questioned.

"I will guide you," Rei replied. "Follow my lead. Quickly, to that shack directly in front of you."

Diana moved out of the bush and kept low as she ran across and hid behind the shack. She then went to the corner and peaked out before taking her head out. There was a woman setting laundry on a clothesline. She reverted back and forth between setting the clothes and turning around to pick them up from a wooden basket. Once the woman had her back turned, Diana dashed across and to the next structure where she hid and went to the corner where there was a man raking leaves.

From where Diana was, she could see the longhouse as she remembered it with the guards at the front carrying their spears. Along the rooftop, there were entry points that Diana eyed from the side where smoke billowed out. Diana made her dash across to the next building as the man turned his back. She then continued across the shack to reach a lodge where there was a man positioned on guard with a spear in hand at an alleyway. Diana tensed back as the man made his approach towards the outskirts of the forest, but paused as he looked out and then turned back around. The lodge next to them was quite long and Diana and the alleyway went straight to the side of the mess hall, while a garden rested ahead.

"You will need to take this man out in order to continue," Rei stated. "When his back is turned, approach him and take him by the neck."

"What?" Diana questioned.

"You need to incapacitate him and move forward," Rei restated. "Push on and I will guide you."

Diana moved forward and went towards the man as he had his back turned.

"Move your right arm around and with your other hand, secure a grip around the neck."

"Won't he yell?" Diana questioned.

"He will struggle, but we can work on techniques that prevent them to alert later on."

Diana moved in and moved her arm around and then supported her arm as she squeezed on the man's neck and choked him. The man, who was taken off-guard, struggled, but panicked and thrashed about. Within a short moment, the man passed out and Diana was about to drop him to the ground. Diana looked at the unconscious man and saw that he breathed.

"You hold them for a few seconds until they pass out to knock them out," Rei remarked. "A little more, and you can kill them."

Diana moved on and reached the ladder at the side of the mess hall and climbed up towards the roof, but diverted to enter a window that went to an attic loft. The mess hall was lit via candle light below, which created a shadow in the open attic across the web of beams. Diana hid behind a bale of hay and then proceeded over the beams, holding her balance. There was a small group of people below that Diana averted, reaching the other side, which was another loft and window to escape out of. Diana looked out the window and saw a metal wire tied between a two-story home and the longhouse over an alleyway between the two structures.

From the window, Diana jumped down, falling to her side before moving around the back of the house to get out of the open. Diana looked out from around the side and could see the field where there were some workers still at work, sowing seeds into the tilled soil. Diana then moved out of the way and crashed into some tools behind her. There were various gardening tools, and among them was a six-foot long pole with no bristle or metal-piece attached. It was simply a pole.

"Take that staff with you," Rei instructed. "It will assist you later. And with it, make your way to the top of the longhouse. You don't have much time left."

Diana looked around the exterior of the two-story home and tried to look for a way to the roof. The house had an exterior set of stairs that went to the second story. Diana went up them and then climbed onto the railing to climb onto the roof. Once atop, she lingered on the side that didn't face the field or rest of the commune, and went to the wire.

"Use the wire to cross to the roof," Rei stated.

"Won't it collapse?" Diana questioned.

"Not if you use it properly," Rei replied. "Take the wire by your hand and then wrap your legs around the other end to pull yourself over. Place your staff on the attachment behind you to store it."

Diana did as Rei explained with the staff and got down to her knees. She grabbed the wire and started to pull herself over to bring her legs out. Once she was out, Diana wrapped her legs around and proceeded to pull herself over. The suspension of her weight caused her back to drop back and for her to hang. Diana looked to the side to ensure that it was clear, and then resumed to pull herself over and reach the rooftop. The staff at her back poked into the side of the building. Diana hung awkwardly as she looked around, struggling to pull herself from the wire to the roof.

Finally, Diana pulled her body up and then extended one arm over to climb up. She then kept low as she went towards the openings in the ceiling, looking down. The longhouse was a circular structure with beams and wires among the ceiling. Diana was able to lower herself onto one of the beams and take a look at what lied below.

The interior of the longhouse consisted of a perimeter platform where the Elders sat atop of mats, cross-legged with a bonfire in the center. The victim of these cultists was placed atop of an altar before the bonfire, and the young boy, two or three years younger than Diana, was stripped of the blanket and all his clothes. He was gagged and tied at the wrists and ankles, bound to the altar.

Diana lowered herself down to a platform that wrapped around the room, looking down below. She saw approximately twelve advisors in the room, including Nirvana and Svante. There were also guards with staffs, but these guards wore masks over their faces and were shirtless, the women bare-chested. Diana looked unceasingly as Svante, who had removed his shirt and was bare-chested with a cleaver began the ceremony. The victim, who was very much conscious, was crying, but immobile. At each column around the second-floor platform, there was an iron wire that was stretched across and connected to a column on the opposite-side. Diana climbed atop of the rail guard and raised herself to grab the wire and pull herself over until she was above Svante.

Upon sight of Svante raising the cleaver, Diana dropped down and landed atop of the sinister man, knocking him out. She then looked out at the other advisors, who looked back at her with astonishment. Diana produced her short sword and looked out to the others, especially the guards who immediately moved to a defensive position.

"Put your sword away and take out your staff," Rei instructed. "You will need it to counter those spears."

Diana complied and put her sword away, pulling out the staff instead, and then pulling the victim over the altar to hide. Once the boy was over, Diana stepped onto the altar and jumped over to engage the guards that moved forward with their spears pointed towards her. The room proceeded to slow down as Diana looked at the four guards who were soon accompanied by another two that had entered the room from outside while the Elders evacuated. Diana closed her eyes.

"You will need to disarm them before they can poke you with their spears," Rei said. "I will guide you through the process."

Diana opened her eyes and then looked forward. The foremost guard pointed his spear towards Diana with intent to strike.

"Bring your staff forward and strike near his wrist from within him," Rei said. "You want to move the spear to the side and force his hand off from its grip."

Diana hit the spear with her staff.

"Now, pull in and hook yourself, and wrap your staff around the pole and twist it clockwise," Rei added.

Diana hooked the staff with the spear and proceeded to pull.

"Lift!" Rei warned as the spear nearly hit Diana in the face.

Diana lifted upwards, pulling up with her backhand and forced the guard to bend over as he continued to hold onto the spear.

"Quickly, press down with your foot and incapacitate him with a simple strike on the head or neck," Rei then went on.

Diana hit down and disarmed the foe. She then hit the man down before looking over to the others who were pointed towards her. A guard thrusted his spear towards Diana. Diana blocked the spear and brought it down to the ground.

"The neck is open," Rei pointed out. "Strike fast."

Diana looked to the neck of the guard and brought the staff up to hit him in the neck. She then pushed him back, hitting against his bare chest.

"Behind you!" Rei shouted to Diana.

Diana turned around and intercepted an incoming jab.

"At the pressure point at the side of the thigh," Rei remarked. "Hit it."

Diana swung at the side of the thigh and caused the woman to come down onto a knee. Diana then brought the staff down onto her neck before intercepting another jab. She moved the guard over and disarmed him as she did to the first. Diana then hit him down and jumped out of the way as another attempted to jab at her. She quickly turned around and looked at her foe as they took careful steps towards her. Diana held her staff with caution as she looked at either of them.

A guard moved in for a jab. Diana deflected and brought the staff down, locking it and then pressing down to disarm her foe. She then pushed the foe back to handle the other, deflecting the attempted stab and pushing the foe back. Diana moved to the other and hit them in the thigh. She then hit them in the head before looking to the other. Diana intercepted the spear as it almost stabbed her and brought the spear down like the other. She then pressed down with her boot and kicked the guard down, squatting him with her staff to look at the others.

An unarmed guard attempted to strike at Diana. Diana pushed him back with her staff and then hit him in the thigh. She then brought him down and kicked him in the head to ensure he stayed down. Another two guards stood up and faced Diana. Diana rushed forward before one could grab a spear. She knocked him back and then hit him in the head before turning to the other. Diana hit him in the back and knocked him over. The unarmed guard immediately moved to run away instead as he recovered.

Diana looked around the room and saw that she had managed to handle the guards to submission and defeat. She continued to hold her staff and returned behind the altar where Svante was. The victim had disappeared. Diana looked away from Svante and around the room, and then noticed that the hostiles she had taken on had disappeared, and when she looked down to Svante again, he was gone. Diana then looked over to the door out of the longhouse where a bright light filtered in from outside.

"You've fought well," Rei stated. "There is much for you to learn, but you appear capable and willing to fight. There was not a moment of hesitation within you…. Leave this space… I will wait for you at the dojo."

Diana didn't respond and instead walked out of the longhouse. She stepped out and found herself in the forest, similar to the forest she had fallen asleep in Japan as she was no longer in the coniferous forest of her memories. Diana moved forward and through some bushes. She continued to hold the staff in her hand, but the rope she had collected had disappeared. Diana walked a short distance until she saw a structure in the midst of the forest, atop of a hill.

After a short hike, Diana reached the steps towards the dojo and entered through the gates. The courtyard was quiet. Diana walked forward and met with a figure at the front of the training center. The woman was dressed in a similar uniform as Diana, but was a young Japanese woman, perhaps in her late twenties or early thirties with black hair. She was armed with a longsword, or katana, and a short sword. She was also equipped with a staff behind her, but her staff was not made of wood, but of metal.

"Welcome," Rei greeted. "Are you ready to train with me?"

"Yes, ma'am," Diana replied. "I am ready."

"Good, because we have much to learn in what will feel like weeks to you," Rei said, pacing before Diana. "What you have with you is known as a bō staff, and as you saw in the longhouse, it proved useful against enemies with similar staffs or spears. In the weeks to come, you will not only complete your basic training in ninjutsu and jujitsu, but also bōjutsu and sōjutsu, the art of the bō and the spear. By the time you finish, you will have a better understanding of each craft and be able to venture without my assistance. Do you understand?"

"Yes," Diana replied.

"Come inside," Rei invited, "your training begins now."

Act 5, Scene 1

Diana pointed her bō staff like a rifle towards her opponents on the floor of the dojo. She was faced with four ninjas in a similar uniform to herself. The ninjas moved in, and Diana deflected their attacks with ease, attempting to disarm them, but taking priority in avoiding to be hit. Diana hit a ninja in the thigh and caused all of them to yield. She then jumped back as another attempted to strike at her, sweeping her bō to hit her in the thigh before focusing on the other two as the third was down. Diana continued to spar with these ninjas, disarming one and causing her to yield, and then hitting another before facing the last.

The two paced in a circle as they faced each other. Diana pointed her staff outwards again. Her foe went forward, and Diana deflected her staff with hers until she was able to land a strike in the chest, pushing her back and then quickly disarming her before forcing her to the ground. Diana pointed the staff directly at her foe, and then froze as she heard the voice of her master, causing the ninja on the floor to jump forward and posture herself. The two stood straight and looked forward as Rei stepped into the room.

"Good," Rei remarked. "Very good."

Rei stepped towards Diana and looked at her.

"You've learned lots in the last several weeks, but you have learned all that you can at this dojo and must now go out and prove yourself," Rei stated to her. "The classroom is nothing compared to the battlefield and the experiences the real world has to offer, so you will instead set off tonight on a journey to fashion your longsword in the heart of the Aku Mountain, but the path to this cave will be difficult... Once you have your fashioned sword, we will be meet again to further your training..."

"When do I leave?" Diana questioned.

"When you are ready," Rei stated. "I will follow you, but will not provide assistance..."

"Thank you, sensei," Diana replied, bowing.

Rei left the room and Diana fell at ease. She looked to her side and noticed that the ninjas she was fighting with had vanished. Diana then looked to the ground and left the room.

• • •

The next morning, Diana awoke and had breakfast before leaving the dojo with only her bō staff, a canister of water, and her short sword. She also brought with her small items, such as throwing stars and smoke pellets. Diana then looked ahead, to the Koga Forest she supposedly ventured through at the start of her journey, but to see a large chain of mountains in the horizon ahead that loomed over. Diana let out a sigh and proceeded to start her hike.

The initial journey was simple. Diana hiked for several miles and then rested to build a fire, cook whatever food she managed to scavenge whilst walking, and fill her canteen. Afterwards, she continued for approximately six hours until she stopped again, but this time to rest. She was unable to reach the mountain within the day, and so she decided to rest at sunset and continue in the next morning.

After another dreamless sleep, Diana awoke refreshed and continued the hike, but this time, traversing the slightly mountainous and rugged landscape of the base of the mountain. Rei was silent with her as she simply hiked, and it began to snow lightly the higher she was to the point where there was snow at her feet and it became too difficult to navigate the terrain due to the slope and snow. Diana proceeded to hike along the sides of the mountain, going upwards only when the terrain was acceptable to do so. On the second day, Diana stopped at a point where she was able to see the breadth of the forest in her mind as she ate the snake she had captured, and then continued on.

Once Diana was fed, she continued through the snowy forest of the mountain until she could hear the sound of some motors in the distance. Diana looked around. She then saw a blur of motion not too far ahead, forcing her to quickly hide. Diana climbed the nearest tree and hid among the snowy branches. She then looked down as the snowmobiles stopped not too far ahead. Diana watched from above as a small squad of men in white camouflage uniforms hopped off the snowmobiles and went to the tracks in the snow left behind by Diana.

The men proceeded to speak in Russian, which Diana could not understand. They looked around as if they were looking for her, and within her sight, she saw the accursed logo of the huntsman spider on the shoulders of these men. The Huntsman mercenaries proceeded to speak to each other. Their arms were behind their backs. Diana watched them for another second before she hopped down and landed on one of them.

Diana quickly produced her bō staff and swatted the other mercenary in the thigh as she took them by surprise. The mercenary attempted to reach for his pistol, and Diana swatted at that hand and then brought them down to knock them out. The other two ahead reached for their rifles, and Diana moved in to quickly engage them to prevent them from arming themselves. She knocked one back and then hit the other in his hand to cause him to drop his pistol. Diana then struck him in the neck side-by-side before hitting the thigh and then knocking him out.

The Huntsman mercenary that had fallen over rolled to his side as Diana attempted to lunge at him. He then stood up and raised his hands to engage in close quarter combat with her.

Diana pointed her staff towards him. She then moved in and attempted to hit him in the thigh, but the mercenary grabbed the staff and pulled Diana towards him. He then went forward and attempted to grab her, but Diana ducked and slid underneath him, letting go of the staff and hitting him in the thigh with a punch to force him down onto one knee. The mercenary span around and Diana jumped back.

Diana kept her right foot forward and raised her hands. The mercenary went in with a kick to the side, but Diana deflected. The mercenary then went for a kick higher up, but Diana deflected. At the third kick, Diana deflected sideways and grabbed the mercenary's thigh, and then brough a hand around his back and to his abdomen, while simultaneously kicking his other leg off balance to bring him down into the snow. She then held the leg used to kick at her as he fell to the ground and stood over him, bringing a fist down to punch him. The mercenary blocked the punch, but Diana grabbed his arm and twisted his arm out of the shoulder socket, causing him to scream out in pain.

Afterwards, Diana stepped back and looked to where the others were, but had disappeared alongside the snowmobiles. Diana turned around to the mercenary she had just wounded, but he was gone too. She looked down to her staff in the snow and saw that it had been snapped in half. She picked each piece and then tossed them into the snow. Diana looked around to refocus on the path ahead of her, and then she continued to hike up the side of the mountain, through the forest where the trees began to spread out as she continued on her quest for the cave to construct her katana.

Act 5, Scene 2

"My agents were unable to recover the body of Mr. Southern at the Forbidden City, or the documents, and we've failed to track the assassin," Director Black briefed the team. "I can only hope that you are more successful in Gansu than we have here."

"We'll keep you updated," Charlemagne replied, looking to a TV screen across the cargo hold of the V-TOL.

"Goodluck," Director Black responded before the screen went black.

Charlemagne and Tristan rode aboard the V-TOL as it flew over China to reach the segment of the Great Wall of China that Charlemagne needed to be at in Western China. They travelled with a squad of Guardians. Charlemagne looked at a map of China drawn in his journal with coordinates in the right corner. Each of them were dressed out of their suits, and in casual clothes for the outdoors. Tristan wore a black leather coat and cargo pants, while Charlemagne wore a casual beige suit with hiking shoes and a light blue dress shirt.

The V-TOL made its descent in the temperate rainforest of the Chinese wilderness and came down. Once the aircraft was set, the back door opened and the pair of them could exit. Charlemagne carried with him a long bag and faced before him a section of the Great Wall of China, in its authentic state as they were in the midst of a forest in the Gansu region. The stone wall was approximately two-feet tall and the top crumbling as it stretched left and right. Tristan looked at the section as he exited the V-TOL.

"That's the Great Wall?" Tristan questioned.

"It's a part of it," Charlemagne remarked. "Outside of Hebei and Shanxi, the wall has suffered the test of time, and segments like this exist where the CPC have yet to adjust, or simply see no reason to restore, but no matter. These bricks leave us a trail, and we can follow them to where the wall picks up again. We need to find the pass so I can make my measurements…"

Charlemagne carried the long bag he had across his back and proceeded to walk towards the wall, looking both left and right, and seeing the wall pick up in its size to the left. Tristan followed.

"Mr. Merrick," a Guardian stated, walking over to him.

Tristan turned around. The Guardian held a briefcase and opened it for him.

"A present from Ms. Black," the Guardian said.

Tristan looked at the long bow inside the case and saw that it was made of a type of carbon fiber and titanium. He picked it up and examined it.

"We have some ammo for you in the V-TOL," the Guardian explained.

"Yeah," Tristan replied, looking at the bow. "Thanks."

Tristan left with the Guardian and returned to the ship while Charlemagne took out a sort of old-fashioned cellphone, which was in fact a portable GPS. He looked at his coordinates and compared them to the ones in his notebook.

"We're a little off," Charlemagne grunted, "but I suppose we can take a little hike…"

Tristan returned with the bow behind him and a bag of arrows at his side. Charlemagne looked at him.

"We'll need to hike a bit to the west to reach the pass," Charlemagne said. "I need to set some points, one from each of the watch towers at the old gates."

"Sure," Tristan replied.

Charlemagne looked to the Guardians.

"We're going to have to hike a little," Charlemagne said. "We won't go far... I don't think we have to worry about Zimmerman around here, so you can just wait here for us."

The Guardians simply stood where they were as Charlemagne and Tristan proceeded to walk off on their own.

"Are you really confident about Zimmerman not having his pawns ambush us?" Tristan questioned as they walked. "Or the Chinese?"

"The Chinese know we're here, and they know not to interfere," Charlemagne replied. "The Chinese are a part of the Committee, so they have a stake in our work."

Charlemagne continued to follow the collapsed segment of wall as they went up a hill. The wall began to grow taller, and soon the two found themselves climbing up stone bricks to find themselves on the battlements. The wall was still thin, and they were not that high up from the ground. Charlemagne led Tristan onwards as they continued to hike along this wall, climbing up steep cases of brick steps and rubble.

Within several minutes, the pair had found themselves at a wider portion of the wall with proper battlements and a watch tower not too far. They continued onwards and passed through the watchtower, continuing atop of the wall and looking out to the area around them. They were in the middle of nowhere and only the tops of trees could be seen alongside mountains in the horizon on one side, and a vast desert beyond some trees on the other side – the outskirt of the Gobi desert.

Charlemagne led Tristan along the Great Wall until they reached a distinct section of the wall at a watchtower, which branched out to the left to a crumbling, thinner wall below and wrapped around to form a sort of fort. From the watchtower, the Great Wall curved out and quickly came to another watchtower, where the wall then curved around again to reach another watchtower and mimic the same design on the other side. At these inner watchtowers, there was a distinct appearance to them from the others as they were taller. Charlemagne and Tristan went around and came to the center of the concave section of the wall where they stood above a portal, or gate, in the wall that entered into the fort. Tristan saw around the inner space of the fort where there were a sort of ruins, overgrown by the forest and most of the structures inside were mere rubble to what they were. In the center of the fortress was a sort of shrine with dragon statue atop the peak of the roof, spread out with an open mouth facing towards the gate. Charlemagne took a set of stairs up the main watchtower to reach the top lookout point. He then followed his GPS and went towards the corner facing the south where he noticed a dragon head pointed out. Charlemagne ran his hand atop of the dragon statue, and then he dropped the long bag behind him and unzipped it to take out a total station, or an electronic device used to survey land and measure distances.

Tristan looked out as Charlemagne set up the total station on its tripod. He then turned it on and began to look through the eyepiece. Charlemagne adjusted the height so that it was approximately on level with the dragon head as much as it could be, requiring him to bend over. Once the device was set up, Charlemagne took out his journal and set it on the ledge of the tower and took out a pen.

"I need you to look in and give me the measurements that'll display," Charlemagne said, opening a fresh page and tapping his pen.

"Sure," Tristan replied, stepping over and leaning over to look in. "What am I supposed to be aiming at?"

"We're aiming for that statue in the center there," Charlemagne replied. "Williamson's notes say that by calculating the angles from each tower to the protector of the wall, we should be able to precisely triangulate the position of the tomb."

"Okay…" Tristan replied, looking back into the optic piece and aiming for the dragon. "We're… about two-hundred and three meters from the statue…"

"I need the exact coordinates to the fifth decimal at least, please…"

"Sorry," Tristan apologized. "Two-hundred and three meters, point three-zero-zero-five-six."

"Perfect…" Charlemagne said, noting the distance. "Help me move it to the western corner."

Tristan picked up the tripod and moved it to the other corner so that they could measure the distance between the two towers.

"One-hundred and forty-four meters, point zero-zero-zero-five-zero" Tristan said, straightening up as he moved his eye away from the total station. "Charles, if the dragon statue points to the tomb, why can't we just follow the statue?"

Charlemagne looked at him. He stuttered to answer and began to flip through his journal.

"The bishop was specific about triangulation… The distance reveals the location… The bishop is not exact in his words, but there was a long preamble about Pei Xiu and the ancient history of cartography and surveying originated in China… We could follow the dragon for miles and miss this tomb… but with these exact distances, we'll know where to go exactly."

"Right," Tristan replied, helping Charlemagne pack up the total station so they could move it again, "and why couldn't we just simulate all this on a computer? With some satellite images?"

"Satellite images aren't accurate, and if it is to scale, then we must be as precise as possible because one centimeter could possibly mean a kilometer."

The two moved from the watchtower and went back around the curved segment of the wall where the portal was. They both stopped at the center as they felt a vibration at their feet. The two looked at each other. Tristan then looked out and into the forest, but he couldn't see anything.

"How peculiar," Charlemagne noted. "Perhaps we should hurry…"

Charlemagne and Tristan went to the other tower and climbed to the lookout point to position the tripod at the southern corner where there was another dragon statue. He pointed the tripod to the statue in the center and then Tristan leaned over to read the distance.

"Two-hundred and three meters, and point three-zero-zero-nine-six," Tristan read. "About the same as the other."

"Not a perfect margin of error," Charlemagne grunted, "but this appears to be an isosceles triangle."

Charlemagne took out his cellphone and turned on the calculator function so that he could do some quick trigonometry. He wrote down the angle from the towers as sixty-nine point two-two-six. He then calculated the distance between the midline as one-hundred and nine meters. Once he had this distance, Charlemagne took out his laptop from his backpack and started to input the distances on a program that displayed a globe of the world.

"I need one more thing…" Charlemagne said, typing into the computer. "I need the coordinates from this point…."

Charlemagne pointed to the corner of the right triangle where the right angle was.

"I'll go down and fetch it," Tristan said, opening his hand. "I'll be quick."

Charlemagne took out his GPS and handed it to Tristan. Tristan then left and took the stairs down to the bottom of the tower and then out so that he was in the open court of the fortress. Tristan walked forward and stood in the center so that he was facing the middle of the portal and the dragon statue. He then froze the GPS so that it recorded the coordinates, and went back to Charlemagne who took them into his hand and inserted them into the program. Charlemagne set the coordinates as their current location and then drew a straight line down the globe. He then scaled one-hundred and nine meters by ten to receive one kilometer and ninety meters. Charlemagne set a waypoint there, and then he went further and multiplied the former coordinates by another ten to measure approximately ten kilometers and nine-hundred meters.

Tristan watched with uncertainty as Charlemagne fiddled with his computer. He then turned his face out to the forest, looking out and towards the desert plains behind them before going back towards the forest.

"Charles..." Tristan said.

"Not now..." Charlemagne replied, measuring one-hundred and nine kilometers from their set location. "I'm almost done."

A flock of birds flew out from ahead and scattered eastwards. Tristan watched with discomfort and then looked back to Charlemagne.

"Can't you do that in the V-TOL?" Tristan questioned. "I don't think we're safe out here."

Charlemagne looked back at him. He then sighed and nodded.

"Very well," Charlemagne remarked. "I have some preliminary coordinates we can check – pack up the theodolite and let's get a move on then."

Act 5, Scene 3

Diana continued upwards towards Aku Mountain as a breeze of snow fell down. She kept her face covered with snowflakes scattered across her veil. The parts of Diana's skin that were visible from the slot for her eyes were as white as the snow around her. Diana trekked along the side of the mountain where there were no trees, but only a gentle slope towards a ridge that would lead to the peak of Aku Mountain.

At the side of the mountain, Diana could see several snowmobiles parked at the outskirts of a cave entrance with two mercenaries posted on guard duty. The blizzard worsened as Diana attempted to focus, but with the quicker speed of the winds, Diana too moved quickly and began to rush along the left to approach the mercenaries. She moved so that she was in their peripheral vision, invisible to their eyes as she moved with the storm. Diana paused as she was less than fifty feet from them. She stayed down and got a better view of the mercenaries before sprinting forward and tackling one on the ground.

The other mercenary turned and looked over with surprise. Diana kept down and quickly lunged upwards to spring upon him, bringing him onto the ground and dislocating his shoulder. Once this mercenary had been swiftly dealt with, Diana jumped over to the other, keeping him down and taking him out. Diana quickly disarmed any weapons from them as they cried out in pain, and then she looked into the dark cave that lay ahead. She checked the mercenaries for flashlights and managed to find one on each of them, but as she turned them on, she saw that they would not light. Diana banged the butt of the flashlight and then discarded it into the snow.

Diana let out a sigh as she looked back into the cave and saw the pure darkness that awaited her. She then moved forward and stepped inside with careful steps. Diana took out her short sword and held it out. She shuffled each step, making sure one foot was forward and within a couple of yards inside, she turned around and looked at her only source of light behind her before continuing inwards until it was but a spectacle behind her. Diana paused again and took a deep breath. She closed her eyes and felt around her. After a moment, Diana continued.

There a total silence around Diana as she walked with careful steps through the darkness. The silence was soon interrupted by a whisper. The whisper turned to chatter alongside a gentle roar. Diana opened her eyes and she looked forward to what was an orange glow ahead of her. Diana continued to move carefully, but approached the light like a moth and got closer and closer. The chatter was near, and it was in Russian between these mercenaries that were in open space ahead.

Diana reached the top of a ledge that looked down to the open space where there was a sort of mound in the center with a fire roaring from out of it like a low chimney. Fire shot out from small holes at the base of the mound. The area was a sort of forge with molten metal pouring simmering in crucibles. A large Japanese man, who appeared distinct like Shinji, Rei, their uncle, and most of the residents in the town with double eyelids, a thick black beard and long hair tied back, stood on his knees in a beige smock with his hands tied behind his back. A mercenary stood before him with an assault rifle. Diana looked about and saw that there were at least five other mercenaries spread out in the breadth of the cavern with tunnels surrounding the perimeter and branching off left and right, ramping down on the right to reach the ground floor below, and then rising again further ahead to wrap around. There were occasional openings, such as where Diana stood, that allowed one to look down. Diana could see two walking about the tunnel paths, while there were three on the ground floor, including the one before the hostage.

Once Diana had a look around the place, she moved off to the right and approached a mercenary from behind. She moved with quiet steps and came from behind to knock him down and take him out. Once he was unconscious, she moved back around the other side to do the same. Diana could hear the gentle chatter in Russian between the mercenaries as she wrapped around and checked her corner to see the other making his approach. Diana awaited around the corner, and once he was near, she jumped before him and quickly moved her right arm around and brought the mercenary down as she pulled back and flexed her left arm around his neck alongside the right to squeeze at the vein with a tightened grip. Once the mercenary had passed out in the ten seconds it took, Diana dropped him to the ground and continued forward.

A stunned whisper could be heard as Diana passed an opening, ducked down, casting a large shadow against the wall. Unbeknownst to the mercenaries, two of their comrades had already fallen, but three remained. Diana came down the ramp at the end of the passageway and looked out from behind the stone walls. She could see another mercenary on approach, so she waited patiently for him to come around so that she could jump out, headbutt him as she grabbed at his vest and then repeat the same procedure to constrict blood flow and knock the opponent out. Once the mercenary was out, Diana continued into the open space, but behind the large infernal stove that burned in the center. Diana turned the corner as she saw the mercenary take the Japanese man hostage, forcing him to stand up as he pointed the rifle to his head. An annoyed shout echoed as the man spoke in Russian, and he looked around as the other mercenary discovered one of the bodies.

Diana looked out as the two remaining mercenaries argued with each other. The one with the hostage looked around the room with slight paranoia. Diana waited for him to turn his back, and once that was done, she snuck behind him and brought an arm around, tipping the assault rifle so that it shot upwards. Diana quickly bashed the man's head against the furnace and then hit him with the butt of his own rifle before looking up to where she had started, where there was an opening and saw the last remaining mercenary look down towards her with his own rifle. Diana quickly took out some throwing stars and threw them before jumping out of the way.

Shots fired and Diana couldn't see where the stars had hit, but she could anticipate that they landed as the mercenary shouted out in pain. Diana quickly ran up the other side of the passageway and kicked the merc down, knocking him out with another kick and a bash against the head with his assault rifle. With the room clear, Diana collected her throwing stars and then looked over to the man she had freed.

"Thank you," the man said, bowing to her. "My name is Goro Kaji and I am a swordsmith who has crafted from this volcano like his ancestors before him for centuries."

Diana stepped down from the ledge and met with the man. She bowed to him.

"You are a woman," Kaji said. "Are you from the temple?"

"Yes," Diana affirmed. "I have been sent by my master to meet with you so – I have recently completed my basic training with Sensei Oishi Rei and was tasked with asking you to create a katana for me so that I can continue my training with her."

"I see," Kaji replied. "For assisting me with these fiends who have come for my work, I will reward you with a handcrafted sword that I was in the process of making, but you will need to be patient and wait a few more hours for it to complete. Is this acceptable for you?"

"Yes," Diana responded, bowing. "I am most grateful for this gift and will wait as long as it takes as I cannot return to my master without this sword."

"You are free to stay the night with me in my forge," Kaji stated. "You do not need to worry about the smoke inhalation as the structure of this cave sees the smoke rise up and out of the cave – I have spent days in this cave without sunlight as have my ancestors, and they have not faced any complications of their health. There is even a mat for you to lay on and I can offer you some food if you'd like."

"Thank you, but I would prefer to rest – it has been a long day for me."

Kaji nodded. Diana looked to where she had defeated the mercenary that had taken Kaji hostage and saw that he was gone. She looked around and was sure the others had disappeared as was custom in this realm. Kaji continued to tend to the flames of the furnace.

"In this furnace, I am smelting a special type of steel known as *tamahagane* – a pure steel that is used to fashion the blade of your sword," Kaji stated before going to another furnace, different to the large mound. "I have been working on this blade for months now and it is nearly finished. When it is done, it will be yours."

Kaji withdrew the piece of steel that was in the furnace and took it out. He laid the red molten piece on a type of anvil and proceeded to hit it with a hammer.

"What I am creating is more than simply a blade," Kaji remarked. "It is more than just a weapon, but a sword that you must regard as a part of you – of your soul."

"Like the bō as an extension of my limb?" Diana questioned. "Master Rei taught me that the bō is to be treated like an extension of my limb."

Kaji looked to Diana and replied, "More intimate than that. The katana *is* a part of you in spirit more than in body."

Diana observed as the smith flattened the piece of steel out. It had the shape of a katana blade, but it was rough around the edges and blocky.

"I have not slept for days... the work is that hard, and without help, I must be vigilant of the cooking process, but I keep myself occupied," Kaji remarked. "For eight centuries, my family has dwelt on this noble craft. What of yours?"

Diana did not answer.

"I do not have the privilege to know of my ancestors," Diana replied. "I am an orphan and my father himself was an orphan."

"Pity."

With these words, Diana left to the other side of the open space where the mat was and she sat down. She said a quick prayer and then laid down, rapidly falling asleep through her exhaustion.

At the next instant of Diana opening her eyes, she looked forward to see the swordsmith on his knees with his back to the mound. He was performing a sort of ritual before a small shrine. He had the completed blade in his hands, but it was missing a handle. Diana closed her eyes and opened them again to see the smith away from the shrine and behind the mound. The mound had been destroyed and in its place lay a jagged rock, similar in appearance to the meteorite vessel, but slightly smaller. Almost as large as Diana herself. The smith was behind the rock and polishing the blade on a set of stones.

Diana watched as the smith finished her blade. Once he was done, he stood up and stepped over to Diana, presenting it to her.

Diana took it into her hand and then looked back at the smith. She carefully examined the sword, looking at its unique pattern on the blade that was the skin of the metal.

"You will need to polish it for two to three weeks once you return to the academy," Kaji stated. "However, for all its purposes, it is complete."

"Thank you, very much," Diana replied, bowing to the swordsmith.

"Do not forget of the effort that was placed into making this weapon," Kaji remarked. "Go in peace."

"*Hai*," Diana replied, stepping back and gently waving the blade to create a *whick* sound as she cut the air.

Once Diana was finished admiring the sword, she left the cave with a torch and returned outside. She looked to the left, towards Aku Mountain and saw not too far in the distance, a structure she had not seen previously. With her sword at her side, Diana hiked the short distance and reached the outskirts of the dojo for her to return to Master Rei and continue her training.

Act 5, Scene 4

Charlemagne and Tristan sat in the cargo hold of the V-TOL as they flew over the forest south from the Great Wall of China where Charlemagne had completed his triangulation. The aircraft flew at a moderate pace as it hovered in place as opposed to flying off at its max speed. Charlemagne shouted coordinates as he looked at his laptop set on his lap. The V-TOL then continued to move. Charlemagne kept looking at his computer and writing in his journal.

At a sudden notice, a red light began to flash in the aircraft and a console beeped off. The pilot drove the V-TOL violently to the side, causing it to shake and spin until order was restored. Charlemagne had fallen over, and his journal and laptop had crashed into the floor, causing the screen to smash. Tristan managed to hold on as he quickly grabbed a handle above him.

"Oh no…" Charlemagne muttered. "What in the hell was that…?!"

A Guardian assisted Charlemagne onto his feet while another picked up the laptop.

"My scanners had detected that we were being locked on by a surface-to-air missile!" the pilot replied.

The warning system went off again.

"Everybody, brace yourself!" the pilot shouted.

Charlemagne sat down and a safety bar was brought down to secure him as the V-TOL shot off. The aircraft shook as an explosion detonated nearby. The shaking worsened and lights began to flicker. The momentum of the V-TOL broke and Tristan felt in his stomach as they went down. Charlemagne closed his eyes as they made impact with the earth.

Tristan looked forward and removed the safeguard around his chest to stand up. He picked up his longbow and then looked to Charlemagne. A Guardian stood up and went to check on the pilots, while another assisted Charlemagne up.

"Both dead," the Guardian stated. "We'll have to move on foot…"

Another Guardian broke a glass case and forced the rear door to open. The doors came down and the four of them stepped out into the forest to look forward at the clearing of forest where the V-TOL had crashed through. Charlemagne looked to a Guardian as another attempted to contact G.D.P. Command.

"I- I need a weapon," Charlemagne said, putting his journal in his coat pocket. "Give me a rifle in case we come into contact with hostiles."

A Guardian handed Charlemagne a rifle from the V-TOL and some magazines. Charlemagne and Tristan looked towards the forest as they heard a vibration in the distance.

"Come on," the Guardian encouraged. "We need to move away from the crash. Let's go!"

Charlemagne nodded and looked to Tristan.

"Tristan, let's go," Charlemagne said with haste.

Tristan nodded and turned around. He proceeded to follow Charlemagne as they began to run through the forest. Within a few minutes of running through the forest, they reached a ridge and a creek below. Tristan's ears twitched as he heard the barks of dogs not too far behind them.

"Come on, evac site is not much farther," a Guardian encouraged, waving to Tristan to help lower him down.

Charlemagne was already ahead and crossing the waters of the creek. Tristan came down and then crossed the shallow creek to reach the other side where the Guardians assisted Charlemagne up the ledge. Tristan climbed up behind him and they continued their sprint through the forest. Charlemagne and Tristan both heard the rotors of a helicopter above them.

In an instant, Charlemagne turned around and quickly grabbed Tristan to move him behind a tree as the rotary cannon of the helicopter span up and opened fire below. Bullets slashed against the wood of trees around them, but thankfully nobody was hit. The helicopter made its pass and went ahead, allowing them to continue their journey forward. Charlemagne paused as he saw a bit of smoke ahead. His head then jerked slightly to the right as he spotted movement.

"Hostiles!" Charlemagne shouted, going into cover.

The four of them came under fire. A small squad of unknown soldiers could be seen ahead, emerging from the plume of smoke. Charlemagne readied his rifle and turned the corner to provide supporting fire. Tristan froze behind the tree and struggled to ready an arrow.

"Where's this evac site?!" Charlemagne questioned a Guardian. "We can't hold off whoever these fiends are for much long – they'll overpower us soon enough."

"Perhaps you have no idea who we are or what we're capable of, Mr. Cabernet," the Guardian leader replied.

"Oh, I have plenty of an idea," Charlemagne responded, reloading and then returning fire.

Tristan breathed slow, careful breaths and hesitated to turn either way to fire a shot. His eyes then looked forward as he saw a rustle of movement. An East European Shepherd with a greyish-white coat like a wolf then jumped out from a bush and crashed into Tristan, biting into his left forearm. Tristan struggled with the dog as it tore into his flesh.

Charlemagne looked immediately and pointed his rifle at the canine, opening fire at the savage beast and shooting it off Tristan. Charlemagne then looked behind him as more dogs and their masters arrived from behind.

"We're being flanked!" Charlemagne yelled out, moving over to go to Tristan.

Tristan looked at his bloodied arm. Blood dripped down and landed on his shirt. His forearm had various nicks where the teeth of the animal had dug into the deepest layers of his skin and into his muscle. He breathed rapidly and then over to Charlemagne who helped him up. Tristan and Charlemagne fled sideways, Charlemagne assisting Tristan for a brief moment before the two ran on their own. Tristan carried his bow with him.

The two ran off, and as they ran, Tristan heard the rabid barks of another dog behind him. He stopped and looked to see the dog rushing towards him. Without a moment of hesitation, he took his bow and shot an arrow at the dog, hitting it in the skull and causing it to crash into the ground. Tristan didn't stop to look as it fell and instead continued on as he and Charlemagne ran for their lives. He could hear the shouts of a man behind them, perhaps a Guardian, shouting out in pain with the snares of a dog in sync with the yells. The two continued along and went a fair distance from the fight when they stopped, mostly so that either of them could catch a breath.

"How?! How?! How have they found us?!" Charlemagne questioned. "How is this possible?"

Tristan didn't respond and instead quickly examined his wound. Charlemagne noticed and took a look at it.

"Are you alright?"

"I'm…" Tristan didn't finish his sentence.

"I don't have any bandages to wrap up that wound and stop the bleeding," Charlemagne remarked, examining it as held Tristan's forearm carefully. "Can you manage?"

"Y-yeah," Tristan replied, not looking at Charlemagne, but instead at his wound.

Charlemagne looked at Tristan and then behind him.

"Come on, let's venture a little more forward," Charlemagne said. "They're still on our tail."

The two continued through the forest at a moderate pace. They didn't run, nor did they walk, but instead it was a type of jog as they jumped over all sorts of fallen debris that posed itself in their way. Tristan grabbed ahold of a trunk to vault over, but his left forearm gave in and caused him to collapse in pain. Charlemagne stopped and went back to help him up. Tristan pushed him back as he attempted to help himself up.

"I'm fine," Tristan quickly said.

"You're not fine," Charlemagne argued. "You're injured."

"I can make it," Tristan replied. "I'm not used to being like this, but I can do it."

"Honestly, Tristan, where are we even going? We're in the midst of China without any money, or any support whatsoever, and who knows if I'll be able to disinfect that wound and dress it before it can become infected?"

"I'll be fine," Tristan argued with him. "I can't get sick, remember? Come on, let's go."

Charlemagne hesitated to turn with him and continue anymore.

"Charles?"

"There's no hope, Tristan," Charlemagne confessed. "We're attempting to run from an enemy that is going to catch up with us eventually."

"Maybe we can find a village, or something... there'll be something. When Diana and I ran off to Montana, there was something for us in the midst of the forest when we came under attack by the assassin. Sure, it was not the most pleasant of communities, but it was a shelter, and we're going to find something like that – I know it."

Charlemagne looked to Tristan and then at him arm. He blinked and kept his eyes closed for an extra second before taking his rifle and removing the magazine.

"What are you doing?" Tristan questioned.

"I'm sorry, but I have to look out for you before I consider this quest," Charlemagne remarked, unloading the loaded cartridge. "Abandon that bow and throw down those arrows. We're surrendering."

Charlemagne climbed back over the fallen tree and carried his rifle by the top. Tristan simply stood where he was, in slight shock as he held the bow in his right hand like Charlemagne carried his rifle. Charlemagne walked the reverse direction they had been going and when he saw the shake of some bushes ahead, he raised the rifle up alongside his other arm to surrender.

Tristan climbed over the fallen tree and watched as around a dozen of mercenaries came out of the bushes with their rifles pointed forward. He recognized them as Huntsman mercenaries, dressed in a different brand of camouflage, a dark green as opposed to the purple-black or white-grey they had worn before. Charlemagne knelt down, dropped the rifle at his side and placed his hands behind his head as they all pointed their rifle towards him. The left-side of the mercenaries pointed their rifles towards Tristan. Charlemagne noticed and turned his neck.

"Drop the bow," Charlemagne stated. "Please."

Tristan held on to the bow as he looked at the six or so mercenaries that had their rifles pointed to him. He tightened a fist around the handle and looked at them with a glare of hatred.

"Tristan!" Charlemagne scolded.

Tristan dropped the bow. He then removed the pouch of arrows from his side and dropped it too. Once that was done, the mercenaries moved in and arrested them, bringing their hands behind their back as they had done once before.

Act 5, Scene 5

Charlemagne and Tristan were brought out of the forest and towards a dirt road where a small convoy of vehicles were stopped. The convoy was led by a tank similar to the ones that were part of the occupation of Allabrese. Behind the tanks were various armored personnel carriers, and then a luxurious black convertible that stood out from the other cars. Charlemagne and Tristan were pushed forward and fell to their knees

The pair looked forward and Charlemagne looked at a recognizable face of a man that led the mercenaries. He was dressed in the same uniform, but he appeared to be considerably older of the bunch with a white beard and scar at his right eye. He also had short hair.

"Well, if it isn't Mr. Cabernet and his young son," the Huntsman leader said, stepping forward. "You're a hard man to find, you know that?"

The Huntsman leader whistled to a mercenary who ran down the convoy and towards the convertible. The door of the car opened at the back and a group of three men stepped out. Meanwhile, one of the mercenaries passed from behind and handed the commander Charlemagne journal. He spoke in Russian to him.

"*Spaciba*," the commander replied before turning to the men that approached.

The mercenary that handed him the book stepped aside and stood next to the commander. Tristan recognized him from Egypt. He was Kodiak Alexandrov and the man with him, the commander, was therefore none other than Bogdan Alexandrov, the leader of the entirety of the Huntsman Legionnaires.

Tristan looked back at the three men that were approaching them. Charlemagne was shocked to see one of the three men to be Johnathan Southern, who less than two days ago, Charlemagne had seen him be shot at and bleed out. The other in the group was none other than Audric Zimmerman, dressed in a white suit with a pink dress shirt. He wore a white safari hat. Charlemagne eyed a ring at his index finger, it was bound in a silver-like metal, but at the top there was a black jewel similar in darkness to the orbs. The third man of the group was someone Tristan did not recognize, but Charlemagne knew. His name was Franklin Dulles, an American businessman and board director with Zimmerman Corporation and husband to the CEO of the corporation, Cynthia Dulles. Mr. Dulles had medium-length black hair and wore black-rimmed glasses. He also had fair skin and brown eyes. He was dressed in a grey suit and had an average figure.

"Mr. Cabernet," Zimmerman said in a cheerful tone. "I haven't seen you since... I suppose it was in France. How have you been?"

Charlemagne frowned at him, especially as he squatted down before him.

"Do you expect me to say anything nice to you? After you obviously led us to a sort of ambush in France, sent an assassin after myself, kidnapped my daughter and ex-girlfriend, and then later sent an occupation force to takeover my hometown in search of Bauer, sent that same assassin after my children once again, murdered Tristan's mother, and have now kidnapped my daughter again, shot down the aircraft I was travelling in, had my son bitten by one of those foul beasts your pawns have, and now hold us hostage?"

Zimmerman looked at him. His eyes scanned Charlemagne and looked over to Tristan. He stood up.

"He had only this on him," Bogdan said, handing Zimmerman the journal.

"Thank you," Zimmerman responded, taking the book and flipping through it.

Once Zimmerman had finished flipping through the book, he passed it to Southern and looked back to Charlemagne.

"Well, Charles, this is a bit of predicament, isn't it?" Zimmerman said. "Now, I'd like to help you out. I really would, but you see, I'm at a crossroad and we've been having a real hard time locating the scepter of Alexander the Great... How about we make a deal?"

Charlemagne did not respond.

"How about you help me locate the scepter, and... perhaps, I help you return to Canada?"

"Where's Diana?" Charlemagne asked. "Where is she? We know you took her... I want to know where she is and what you've done with her."

Zimmerman looked back at Charlemagne and didn't immediately answer. He instead looked at Charlemagne with intent and then to Tristan. Zimmerman let out a sigh and brought his hands behind his back.

"Well, this is hard for me to express, Charles," Zimmerman said, "but I'm afraid Diana is not with us."

"What?" Charlemagne questioned.

Zimmerman faced the side and looked to them through his peripheral vision.

"She's dead," Zimmerman lied. "I'm sorry."

Charlemagne's dropped a look of shock. He breathed rapidly. Meanwhile, Tristan looked at Zimmerman and sprang forth towards him.

"I'll kill you!" Tristan shouted. "I'll murder you!"

Zimmerman jumped back as two mercenaries tackled Tristan and brought him to the ground. Tristan struggled with them, flailing like a fish with his hands tied behind his back.

Kodiak shouted at his men, pointing at Tristan. Tristan began to headbutt the men.

"Tristan!" Charlemagne shouted.

The mercenaries produced stun batons and began to hit Tristan with them.

"Stop!" Charlemagne protested. "Please, stop!"

Zimmerman said nothing and instead simply watched as the two mercenaries hounded Tristan.

"Make them stop!" Charlemagne yelled at Zimmerman. "Audric, please!"

Audric looked to Charlemagne and then raised a hand to Bogdan.

"*Dostatochno!*" Bogdan shouted in Russian. "*Ostanovite eto, vy zhivotnyye!*"

The mercenaries backed off and Tristan was left on the dirt road in slight paralysis as his body shook. He took staggered breaths.

"Perhaps now you'd like to deal with me," Zimmerman said, turning to Charlemagne. "All I ask is that you assist in locating the Dragon's Den, Charles, so that I can retrieve the final orb. If you do not help me, then I will slaughter Tristan with ease – now, I know that you don't want that happen, that I make do with his worthless life, so don't test my patience."

"Please, don't hurt him," Charlemagne requested in defeat. "Please... not him. I'll help you, just please don't hurt him."

"You're a smart man, Charles," Zimmerman remarked. "I knew you'd see reason, and I know you won't do anything irrational or stupid that might result in Tristan's death. Release him."

Bogdan nodded and ordered some mercenaries to release the ties from Charlemagne's hand. He then tapped Zimmerman on the shoulder with the back of his hand and pointed to Tristan.

"What about him?"

"Throw him into the back of one of the APCs," Zimmerman replied. "Send him to Siberia and keep him in detention until Charlemagne sees through. He's your responsibility until then..."

"Yes, sir," Bogdan replied, turning to Kodiak as Zimmerman, Southern, and Dulles left.

Bogdan spoke to Kodiak in Russian. He then followed the trio while Kodiak shouted to some mercenaries who went and picked Tristan up from the ground. Charlemagne was released from his restraints and pushed forward to go to the convertible. Before he took another step, he watched as the mercenaries picked up Tristan and hauled him towards the front APC where he was dragged inside. Charlemagne was pushed forward again and forced to walk, taking a last look to Tristan before he went to the vehicle and was given his journal to complete the quest.

Act 6, Scene 1

Tristan awoke to the sensation of cold water being splashed upon him as he lay in the center of a cold, damp prison cell. He retained his eyes closed as the water fell and only opened them, squinting at the bright light that came from outside of his dark cell. The room the Huntsman kept him in was small, the walls were made of stone brick, there were no windows, and the floor was dirty and made of a smooth stone. He had only a pair of trousers on, the bandage around his forearm, and the thin blanket that prevented him from developing hypothermia. His orange-blonde hair was dirty and wet. All of his other possessions, including his necklace, had been taken from him.

Several days had passed since the exchange in Gansu, and Tristan had been transported to this prison in the Russian Far East. Two Huntsman Mercenaries shouted at him and then entered his cell to force him up. Tristan immediately reacted as one of them grabbed him by the arm. He grabbed back and attempted to pull the merc over, but the other responded and raised him up, pushing him against the wall. Tristan's arms were tied behind his back and he was then pushed out of his cell and through a narrow corridor to another dark room. This room was slightly larger, square-shaped and with a drain in the middle and a single lightbulb hanging from the ceiling.

Tristan was brought to the center of the room and his hands were untied and brought from behind him to in front of him. They were then tied again. A mercenary brought down a chain from above and the hook at the end of the chain was hooked into the rope that tied Tristan's wrists together. The chain was then raised so Tristan was forced to raise his arms up. He was raised to a point where he was pulled up slightly and dangling from the ceiling with a mere inch between his feet and the ground. Once Tristan was set, it began.

The mercenaries proceeded to lash him. The whips hit him in the torso, but Tristan cringed and held, gritting his teeth. He could only hold on for less than a minute until he let go and yelled out in pain. The lashes kept coming and all Tristan could do was let out by yelling as they continued to whip him, jerking his head up with every hit until even the strength to do that left him. The mercenaries began to stop less than five minutes into the session.

Tristan had urinated himself and tears were flowing from his eyes, running down from his face and onto his torso where it mixed with the blood. His entire body shook as he wept, and yet even in this display of public emotion, he attempted to hold back. A mercenary cracked a whip at him again. Tristan yelled out and his sorrow was made louder. The other whipped him as well. Tristan shouted out.

By now, Tristan was barely conscious as they had whipped him for an extra minute. The mercenaries put the whips away and went to lower him. Tristan instantly fell to his knees and continued to shake. He had stopped crying, kept his head down, and did nothing more than stay on his knees with his hands together before him. His torso was covered in cuts from the whip and the uncut skin was pink. Some of the lashes had cut into his trousers and some had hit him on the arms and shoulder. Tristan's eyes were deeply tired, with bags beneath them and the shadows around his eyes were as dark as ever.

Tristan then suddenly began to move. He attempted to raise himself, but his body shook with weakness. He raised his right leg up and managed to position himself so that he was on one knee. The mercenaries noticed this and took their whips to continue beating him. Tristan fell back down. They went at him for another few minutes, bringing him onto his side. At the end, they looked at him. He looked dazed, but he was conscious. Tristan began to attempt to raise himself with his arms.

"*Kto dumayet, chto on mudak?*" the Huntsman questioned, tossing his whip aside and readying his fists.

The Huntsman came down on him and beat him with his own fists, delivering strike after strike to his body. Tristan continued to cry out in pain.

"Eh, who do you think you are?" the Huntsman questioned in English, spitting at him. "*Pedik mal'chik!*"

The Huntsman kicked him with those final words and stepped away from Tristan. Tristan laid against the wall, defeated. His body only vibrated. Tristan's eyes had closed.

"*Tri dnya ... i on vse yeshche derzhit...*" the other Huntsman remarked.

Tristan half opened his eyes. He breathed slowly, but gasped breaths.

"I..." Tristan said in a cracked, broken voice, "... am a wolf..."

A tear fell down Tristan's eye. The Huntsman went towards him and placed a wet towel onto his face. Before Tristan could react, a splash of cold water came with it. Tristan jolted from where he was as he choked. Another splash came from another bucket of water. The Huntsman then went over, removed the towel, and picked him up. They dragged him back to his cell and threw him inside, and there he stayed on the ground for the rest of the day. The Huntsman removed the ties at his wrist before leaving. Once they were gone, Tristan stayed put for close to an hour as he wept, but no more tears fell from his eyes, or at least it didn't seem visible since his face was wet.

Tristan crawled towards the corner of the room where there was a tap. He turned the tap with his shaking hands and water poured out for him to drink. Once he had a small drink, Tristan laid on his back and passed out.

• • •

Tristan opened his eyes at the sound of a hatch at the bottom of the door opening, and a tray being tossed in. He looked over and saw his dinner. Tristan sat up and went over to the tray. He looked at the unappetizing food that was there. A wooden bowl of a murky brownish substance. Tristan simply looked at the meal.

In less than an hour, the doors opened again. Tristan was sat at the back of his cell with his back against it. He squinted again as the door opened and two Huntsman stood before him.

"The Subcommander would like to see you," the Huntsman said. "On your feet... and cover yourself."

The mercenary threw a white tunic to Tristan. It no dirtier than the trousers he was wearing, but he put it on to cover his torso and back. Afterwards, Tristan stood up and with weak legs, he stepped forward. Tristan stepped out of his cell and the mercenaries handcuffed him before they walked with him, not right, but left down the other side of the corridor. The mercenaries took him out of the detention block and along another short corridor to reach a set of doors with bright light pouring from the cracks. The mercenary went to open the door while the other held Tristan by his arm.

Tristan could hear the downpour of rain from outside. The door opened and Tristan looked out to where it was bright out, but the clouds were dark grey and it was raining intensely. The mercenaries led him outside and out of the prison to a small yard in the center. The ground around them was muddy. Tristan looked over to a group of mercenaries that were stood together in the yard.

Kodiak Alexandrov looked to Tristan from the crowd. He was in his uniform, but unarmed. In fact, only a few mercenaries in the crowd of dozens were armed, except those that were along the walls of the prison looking down at them. He wore the standard black-purple uniform as did the others, but his came with the short single shoulder cape that came down to his elbow and distinguished himself from the others. Tristan looked at Kodiak, and Kodiak appeared young to him – perhaps a couple of years older than Tristan, twenty-years old or more. Kodiak looked at Tristan with intent as the mercenaries removed his handcuffs and freed his hands.

"I've heard from my men that you have been troublesome," Kodiak said, stepping forward and towards Tristan, "… that you've been resisting…"

Tristan simply looked towards Kodiak with a blank face. He was mute and expressionless.

"I admire your determination, perhaps even your stubbornness, but I cannot have you having my men look like fools…" Kodiak stated. "I will offer you a deal, Merrick. If you can defeat me in a simple fight, then you can leave and return to your country – the Huntsman will turn a blind eye."

Tristan did not respond. He continued to remain emotionless and mute.

"And if I win, well, nothing… You're mine until Zimmerman sees fit to either release you, or execute you. Whether he'll decide the former or the latter… that's beside the point…" Kodiak went on and said, taking off his cape and handing it to the mercenary next to him.

Tristan looked at Kodiak. Kodiak became annoyed at Tristan's lack of response.

"Speak! I demand you to talk to me!" Kodiak shouted. "Don't lead me to believe that my men have beaten your senses out of you... I know that you can speak, so speak!"

Kodiak continued to look annoyed at Tristan. The Huntsman mercs behind Tristan spoke in Russian to each other while the rest of the crowd murmured. A mercenary stepped towards Tristan from behind and kicked him forward. Tristan fell into the mud and on his side. The other mercenaries laughed.

"So, this is how you'd rather encounter me, huh? No honor? No dignity?" Kodiak questioned, stepping towards Tristan and splashing some mud into him with his boot. "You're nothing more than a worthless dog... so stay in the mud where the bad dogs belong...!"

Tristan closed his eyes and remained in the same position he had landed in as Kodiak continued to slap mud into his face. Once Kodiak grew tired of that, he stepped towards Tristan and grabbed him.

"Here, eat the mud too, why not? Perhaps you're not a dog, not even a son of a bitch, but a pig...!"

Tristan flinched and his body slightly jerked at those words. Kodiak buried his face into the mud. Tristan mildly resisted as he couldn't breathe. Kodiak soon pulled him up and kicked him onto his back.

"What a worthless shell of a man... Eh, they've taken it from you, haven't they? And it's only been three days... What kind of a man were you before then? Surely not a grand one if it's been this easy..."

Kodiak kicked him in the side. Tristan took it with only a minor grunt.

"You are less than a man... a *podzemnyy chelovek!*" Kodiak shouted, kicking him. "You deserve to cave into the fate that awaits you… to die a lowly death, like that whore girlfriend of yours!"

Tristan's focus shifted. He grabbed Kodiak's ankle with his hand and pushed him back. Tristan then stood up and looked down at Kodiak as he sat up. Tristan looked at him with intent, staring into his blue eyes, and in less than a moment, Tristan lunged at him and went berserk, shouting and attempting to land a strike at him, but Kodiak caught the punch as he quickly stood up and flipped Tristan into the mud on his left.

The crowd gasped. Tristan flipped and came back on his feet. The two boys raised their fists at each other. Tristan went forward and attempted to strike at Kodiak. Kodiak quickly tackled him and brought him onto the ground, bringing himself atop of Tristan and restraining Tristan's right arm with his legs while Kodiak punched him in the head savagely. Tristan thrashed his own legs up, but it was no use as Kodiak's body weight was atop of his torso. Tristan attempted to free his right arm, but Kodiak's grip was tight and it was difficult to concentrate with each consecutive blow to his head.

And soon, Tristan caved. He quit attempting to break out and simply collapsed backwards at the final blow as he was defeated. Kodiak released his viperous grip on Tristan's right arm with his thighs and stood up. Tristan was still conscious, but barely. Kodiak panted and looked down at Tristan. He then turned around and left, speaking some quick Russian. Tristan felt warm blood on his face.

The two mercenaries that brought Tristan out returned and each took an arm to drag him back to his cell with the help of some others. The mercenaries pulled him into the dark room and laid him down. Once he was set, they exited the room and closed the door behind him. Tristan laid in the room, in defeat, in the darkness and looked up to the ceiling with his arms stretched out from where the mercenaries had left him.

Act 6, Scene 2

Tristan awoke with cold water splashing against him and the mercenaries shouting at him in Russian. The Huntsman entered and brought Tristan onto his stomach as he closed his eyes. They handcuffed him and then brought him onto his feet. Afterwards, they took him out of his cell and out of the prison. Tristan was loaded onto the back of a truck and thrown inside. The shutter was then brought down and the engine started. Tristan looked around the hollowed metallic room he was in and felt the truck drive off. He panted as he looked around with fear.

After close to twenty minutes, the truck stopped and the shutter opened with three mercenaries looking in and at him. Two of them hopped up and into the truck to take Tristan by the arms and pull him out. They attempted to get him to stand as they reached the rear and to the ground. The mercenaries soon grew impatient with him and he was dragged over and pulled into the mud. A Huntsman officer who wore a similar cape to Kodiak shouted at them and yelled at them. The soldiers quickly picked Tristan up and the officer waved for them to get moving.

Tristan looked down as they dragged him off. They took him inside and brought him down a corridor with chiseled stone brick floors. There was a sense of heating in this facility unlike the prison and Tristan saw a radiator as he passed down the corridor. The soldier that was not helping to carry Tristan opened a door ahead of them and the soldiers brought Tristan into a locker room with tiled floors. The soldiers brought Tristan into a large shower room and brought him down on his knees in the middle of the room. The comrades spoke in Russian to each other as they worked together to remove the handcuffs, strip Tristan of his dirty tunic, and then shave his head. Tristan could hear themselves mutter to each other distastefully, especially as they then shaved Tristan of the mild stubble on his face with an old-fashioned razor blade.

Once Tristan was clean-shaven, they took off the rest of his clothes and put on gas masks as they sprayed him with a sort of gaseous chemical all across his body. Once the delousing was complete, the mercenaries proceeded to hose him down with a mild power wash, and then the showers were turned on and hot water fell down onto Tristan from above where he was left for close to five minutes with a bar of soap. Tristan picked up the soap and attempted to wash himself as best as he could. His thighs, torso, arms and back were covered in scabs from the lashings and bruises from the beatings over the course of however many days it had been. His cheeks were also sore and bruised from the punches Kodiak had given him. At the end of the shower, Tristan was led out and given a towel to dry himself. Tristan made a minor effort to dry himself. One of three mercenaries that had left returned with a set of clothes for Tristan. He set them down behind him on the bench. Tristan barely moved.

The Huntsman soldiers grew impatient with him and quickened the process, drying him off and then pulling down a clean white t-shirt over his body. A soldier gave Tristan the compressed boxers for him to wear and spoke in Russian to him in a manner that he attempted to insist that Tristan at least put these on by himself. Tristan complied. After the boxers were on, the soldier handed him a set of trousers. The trousers were similar to the ones worn by the mercenaries and had the black-purple camouflage pattern on them. Tristan put them on and then he put on the thick woolen socks that came with them. Tristan was then given a pair of boots. He put them on and tied the laces. They were heavy combat boots. A soldier helped Tristan tuck his shirt in upon setting him on his feet, and once that was done, they took him out, bringing him to a medical bay where Tristan was sat down on a bed.

In the office, a medical officer examined Tristan and checked his vital signs. He checked his oxygen levels, his blood pressure and his heart rate, and afterwards he had Tristan lie down. The doctor unwrapped the bandages of his arm and checked the wound from the dog bite. He then redressed the bandages before returning to his desk to write some notes and do other stuff. The doctor soon then turned around again. At the sight of a needle, Tristan instantly resisted and attempted to sit up. The mercenaries in the room with the doctor instantly moved in to hold him down. The injection was delivered and Tristan's vision began to fade as he lost consciousness.

$$\bullet \ \bullet \ \bullet$$

When Tristan awoke from the injection, he found himself in a dim room. He was no longer in the company of Huntsman mercenaries, but two people in lab coats with clipboards.

"*Kak vy dumayete, etot mal'chik sposoben terpet?*" a female scientist questioned.

"*On byl goloden i izbit v techeniye dvukh nedel' i vyzhil. Ya uveren, chto on sposoben terpet',*" a male scientist replied.

Tristan looked around and saw that he was on a platform that was a part of a machine. The platform he was on was one of five others that surrounded the center of the room where the scientists were. All of these platforms were connected to each other and part of a machine. Tristan attempted to move, but his limbs were restrained so that he couldn't move, but only thrash about. In addition, there was an oximeter clip on his finger, nodes over his torso, and two nodes on his face at his temples as well as a metallic band around his skull and over his forehead. A monitor next to him displayed his heart rhythm in real-time. Tristan attempted to look behind him and saw a tinted translucent window with the silhouettes of figures looking down upon him.

The figures behind the glass spoke to the scientists via a microphone that echoed into the room. The male figure spoke in Russian and the scientists left. Tristan looked around with more caution as the room grew even more dim and had a slight orange-red glow. His heart-rate increased as the male figure started a countdown. Tristan waited in anxiety and at the end of the count, he shouted out in pain. Tristan's body jerked and he moved his torso up and down as the pain continued on and on. The sensation occurred for almost a minute, but felt as though it had occurred for five or ten. At the end of it, Tristan panted and cried, but with no tears.

"What is your name?" the male figure questioned in English, but in a Russian accent.

"T-Tristan Merrick – Tristan Luke Merrick."

"What are you doing here, Tristan?"

"I- I don't know," Tristan replied, "please, let me go."

Tristan felt the painful sensation once more. He pulled his head back, raised his pelvis and shouted at the top of his lungs. The pain then stopped.

"What are you doing here, Tristan?" the male figure questioned.

"I… I'm here because my… my guardian brought me here, to China, and… we were captured by the Huntsman…"

Tristan stopped speaking as the pain returned.

"Make it stop!" Tristan shouted as his body twitched and jerked.

"Wrong answer," the male figure stated. "You were not captured by the Huntsman, but you were liberated. The

Huntsman liberated you… You have always been with the Huntsman."

"W-what?" Tristan questioned. "What is this?"

The pain returned. This time, it went on for longer. Tristan's face grew red and tears began to form as he wept again. The pain then stopped.

"You have always been with the Huntsman, don't you remember?" the male figure replied. "You were taken from us by the ones that called themselves your parents, and once more by the one you know as Charlemagne de la Cabernet. Isn't that right?"

"No," Tristan denied.

The pain returned and then subsided.

"It is right, Tristan. You are one of us," the male figure stated. "You are home. Charlemagne kidnapped you, and because of him, you are here, but because of us, you are home."

"No…" Tristan denied.

The pain returned again and then subsided.

"You are home, Tristan."

"No…" Tristan denied again.

The same result occurred, but with a greater intensity.

"Stop!" Tristan begged. "Please, just stop!"

"Where are you, Tristan?"

"I don't know!"

The pain came again. And it kept coming as Tristan vehemently denied and refused to answer the question to the liking of the male figure. They went on for an unknown amount of time until he finally broke. Tristan cried out like an infant as he begged for the pain to end.

"Where are you, Tristan?"

Tristan hesitated to answer as he panted.

"Where are you?" the male figure questioned in the fiercer tone.

"I-I'm home…" Tristan answered. "I'm home – please, just stop. No more…"

Tristan looked around the room to see that his vision was fading. He struggled to keep his head up and crashed it back. No more questions came. The lights in the room returned to their usual setting and the scientists returned into the room. Tristan heard an older scientist speak.

"*Dumayu, na segodnya khvatit… Zavtra myi prodolzhim. Uspokoit' yego i ostvesti yego v svoyu homantu do zavtrashnego utra…*"

The scientists except for the lead walked over to Tristan. Tristan could barely see their faces. He didn't resist as they injected him with a needle. He instead succumbed to the concoction that was injected into him and passed out.

• • •

Tristan woke up and found himself in a different kind of room to the one that he had been kept in for the past several days. For a start, he was on a mattress, but the mattress was on a metal frame. The room he was inside was almost entirely white from the ceiling tiles, the painted brick walls, and the floor tiles. Even the window was white as it was a translucent window. Tristan attempted to raise himself, but he couldn't. His arms and legs were restrained to the bed. All he could do was simply lie down and look to the ceiling. His eyes were tired and he appeared groggy. In front of him was the exit, which was a white metal door with an eyehole for peaking in, but not out. There were no handles to open the door from the inside, but it was not cold and he wore clean clothes. He had a shirt on his back. Tristan looked to the ceiling and was lightly panting.

"H-hello?!" Tristan shouted.

Tristan waited for close to a minute, but no response came.

"Hello?" Tristan yelled again.

Tristan began to cry wet tears and rested his head against the mattress, continuing to look up to the ceiling with his arms stretched out as the mercenaries had left him.

Act 6, Scene 3

Diana opened the sliding door into the kitchen of the dojo. She entered and stood at attention, facing forward as Rei sat on her knees before the stove pit and poked at the fire.

"You called for me, teacher?" Diana questioned.

"Yes," Rei replied, continuing to poke the fire.

Rei stood up and turned to face Diana.

"Your training is almost complete," Rei remarked. "You have made considerable progress in the weeks that have passed, but the time has come for you to set forth on your final trial."

"What is my objective in this trial?" Diana questioned. "Where am I going to? Who am I meeting?"

"I'm afraid, only you can know this," Rei replied. "Through me, you have become skilled in the art of the ninja, mastered the abilities of the bō, the spear, and the katana, but now it is time for you to leave and face your final trial. From henceforth, you have graduated from my academy and can now go into the world to face your fears head on instead of cowering from them. In the forest, you faced your fear of those cultists that terrorized you and had you attempt to kill the one you love. In the mountain, you faced your fear of the Huntsman who have attacked you and the ones you love. In the future, there will be many more fears for you to handle, and it has been my coaching that has attempted to have you overcome these fears within you so that you may be able to handle the fears that exist without."

"When do I leave?"

"You leave when you believe you are prepared to leave. Do you feel that you are ready?"

Diana hesitated to answer.

"Yes," Diana said. "I am ready."

"Good," Rei replied. "You are well-versed and have been prepared to handle the forces outside… Go, and face what awaits you, for if you are truly ready, then you will be ready to go on and assist your guardian with his quest against Audric Zimmerman."

"Yes, teacher," Diana replied, bowing.

With these final words, Diana left and went to her quarters to retrieve her items. She already had her katana in its holster, but she needed to collect a few items, including her water canister, short sword, and bō staff. Once she was equipped, Diana went to the exit of the dojo where she was greeted by apparitions of ninjas holding their swords before them and standing sentinel.

Diana walked to the exit of the dojo and stepped out, into the cold of the mountain. She turned around and looked to Rei who was behind her. She then turned forward and went off, proceeding down the slope of the mountain to begin her journey. Diana walked to the bottom of the slope, a short hike, and reached a crag where the ground was made almost entirely of volcanic stone. There was a deep fog that prevented Diana from seeing more than several meters in front of her, but she continued her descent from the mountain, journeying blind through the midst of the fog until she noticed the ground at her feet turn into a sand. Diana walked carefully, and soon enough, she was out of the fog and taking steps into a desert.

The desert stretched for miles and consisted entirely of sand with dunes in the distance and the setting sun shining down upon her. Diana looked out and saw that the sand in the desert was of a rugged kind, not fine like that of Egypt and not red like that of Australia, but of a goldenrod variant with bits of flora, including cacti scattered across the landscape. Although the landscape mimicked the desert such as that around Kennte in the British

Columbia Interior, it also resembled Egypt to some extents by the dunes and the terrible heat. The heat that fell upon this land was intense and Diana noticed it as she moved her hand up to cover her eyes from the beaming sun.

Without hesitation, Diana continued on her journey as she proceeded to hike on. A wind could be felt through the desert and it picked up sand that irritated Diana's eyes. Diana continued on despite this minor obstacle and braved through. Within an hour, the wind picked up and began to create a minor sandstorm that made it difficult for Diana to see before her. She covered her eyes at instances where the wind was worse, and as she turned to look forward again, she noticed a change in the landscape. The dunes ahead had been replaced and Diana found herself at the edge of a canyon. The dust storm soon settled and Diana was able to view ahead to her right, a peculiarity. Diana knelt down and observed by some cacti.

Diana saw a sort of spacecraft that had crashed in the canyon with wreckage about, and around the wreckage, she saw Men in Black – not in their individualistic appearance as she had seen them in Tokyo, but in their uniform appearance of unnatural literal white skin, deep red lips, and lack of hair – if anything their appearance to her now was unholier and more unnatural as they also appeared to be taller and lankier in their suits. Diana twitched as she saw one of them finish speaking to its colleague and a tongue slither out of its mouth as though the man were a snake. Regardless to their appearance, these men were armed. Diana was close to two-hundred meters from the wreckage and simply observed.

The sun began to set, which allowed Diana the flexibility of darkness and coldness of the night to maneuver herself. To begin, she moved in the shadows of the canyon walls as she hopped down and began to set her path towards the wreckage.

Diana stopped behind a piece of wreckage and continued to observe the agents at work. She saw some of them looking about, examining pieces of the wreck, while others carried artefacts and returned them to the V-TOL parked nearby. Diana awaited in the shadows for the sun to continue to lower itself so that they were placed in the natural darkness of the night, which allowed her to move in and position herself to ambush one of the agents. Diana produced her short sword and held it behind her as she moved about. She stayed behind a crate and looked at the agent ahead. She then moved in when it was clear and approached the tall figure, jumping up and grabbing the neck to slice the throat. The man hissed at Diana's contact and a green blood oozed out, stinging at Diana's arm as it made contact with it. Diana kept the agent down and its mouth covered as she delivered another blow to it with her blade. She then moved forward, around the outside of the craft as she approached another agent. Diana stopped behind a piece of the outside armor that was stuck in the ground and looked over to where two agents were reconvening together.

The two agents chatted between each other for more than a minute. Diana took notice of several other agents around the area, such as inside the ship through the exposed armor and near the V-TOL as it returned from delivering an artefact. Once the two separated and one of the agents made its approach in the direction of Diana, she waited for him to pass before going around to delivering another strike with her short sword to bring him down. Once the agent was down, Diana moved to the outer perimeter of the spacecraft.

Diana looked inside the modern craft and saw that it was spacious inside, but most of the artefacts had been damaged or removed so there was little to observe or even hide behind. Diana moved in and took cover behind the base of a platform.

The agents had set up industrial lamps that lit up the area. Once she had sight of her target in the center of the craft, she moved in and took him out before moving on towards the one by the V-TOL.

By now, darkness had fallen onto the desert and the agents had switched to using flashlights that sat in the breast pocket of their suit jackets. Diana used the darkness to her advantage as she moved in to strike at the agent by the V-TOL, but as she moved forward, the agent turned to by the corner of his eye and saw her through the lack of light. Diana was stunned at the eyes of the creature, which she saw as they looked at her by the corner of its shades – the eyes were reptilian and peered at her. The agent raised its weapon and aimed it towards Diana, shooting a type of plasma weapon at the ground she had stood on while she jumped out of the way. Diana threw her short sword at the creature, but it dodged with its abnormal reflexes. Diana then produced her katana and charged at the creature as it hissed out to alert the others. Diana rolled to the side to dodge another barrage of plasma and then sliced the creature by the neck. She then set of to hide as the others convened at his corpse.

Diana observed from afar as the three remaining agents reached the corpse. They then looked around. Diana cautiously hid behind a piece of the wreckage, especially to avoid exposing herself. She breathed carefully to catch her breath and then began to move towards an agent as it passed her on its own. The others stuck together and went the opposite direction, so Diana went after this one and snuck behind it with her longsword, taking careful and quiet steps. Once she was at an appropriate distance, she took longer steps and then jumped up to slice the head of the creature clean off with the blade.

The creature made a terrible noise as it died. Diana rushed off and jumped towards the shell of the spacecraft, kicking off the beam of the hull and then climbing up onto the roof to move across and over it to the other side so that she could observe the two other. Diana didn't watch them for more than a few seconds before she jumped off and pounced on one of the agents, throwing her shurikens at the other as a distraction so that she could stabbed the creature in the torso and then pull her sword up to go to the other.

Diana looked at the other creature and at the throwing stars that had landed on its torso. The creature yelled out at her. The Men in Black no longer had its pure white face, but instead a greenish-white one with spots on it. The creature spat at Diana a projectile, and Diana dodged out of the way and then charged to slice the head of the creature off. Diana then looked over to the pile of goo that had been shot at her as it tore into the sand and a piece of debris like acid, bubbling. Diana then looked at the second creature on the ground that she had stabbed in the torso. She went towards it and finished it off as it twitched. Once the creature was dead, Diana looked around and assessed the scene to be clear. She cleaned her blade with her sleeve and then put it back. Diana then proceeded to examine the scene and retrieve her throwing stars, and her short sword.

Diana's eyes flicked upwards and into the cargo hold of the V-TOL as Diana saw a small beeping light. She looked carefully and saw that the light was coming from a container inside. Diana walked up the ramp of the V-TOL and inside. She brought her hands atop of the container and looked down. She then dropped a look of disappointment as she looked through the transparent top. Inside was nothing more than various pieces of spacecraft and artefacts that had been taken from the crash site.

"What am I looking for?" Diana questioned in a whisper. "What is it that I have to do?"

Diana let out a sigh. She then turned around and exited the ship, but as she raised her eyes, she was no longer at the crash site. Instead, Diana's eyes saw the extent of the desert again in all its size for her to become lost in as she continued to wander on.

Act 6, Scene 4

Tristan sat in his room where he was restrained at the limbs and looking up to the sky. Several days had passed since he arrived in this room. The door into his cell opened. Tristan flexed his right arm and closed his eyes, but instead, that didn't come. Tristan opened his eyes and looked to the soldier that stood before him instead of the medical officer. The soldier knelt down proceeded to unlock the restraints one-by-one while another watched from the door. Once Tristan was freed, he rubbed his wrists and then looked at the soldier with a blank face of slight surprise. The soldier looked back at him for close to a minute and then to his comrade. Tristan saw them both look at him.

"On your feet," the soldier said to him in English and in a rasp, but gentle voice "you're done here."

Tristan hesitated to act. The soldier noticed and pointed at the ground.

"That's an order," the soldier demanded in a harsher voice. "On your feet, you are done here."

Tristan didn't hesitate to act this time and instead stood up and looked at the mercenary.

"Let's go," the soldier said, getting him to walk out of the room and placing a hand on his shoulder. "You're done here."

Tristan was brought out of the facility and outdoors where he looked up and saw that it was day. The atmosphere was slightly cold, but the skies were blue and the sun shined down. The mercenary ahead of Tristan opened a door and guided him inside. Tristan was led down a corridor where he looked around to see the stone brick walls and stone floor. The buildings of this facility appeared to be refurbished, but they had the appearance of the old fortress that they were. Tristan was led down the corridor and into a change room similar to the one that he had arrived to when he was brought to the facility.

The soldier that was leading them stopped and raised an arm to point Tristan to the showers. Tristan walked in and he was pointed to sit in a chair in the center. He sat down and one of the soldiers proceeded to shave his hair again, which had grown about an inch since his arrival. Once his hair was cut, the soldier stepped out of the way and he was allowed to shower alone. When he was finished, he stepped out and saw that a set of clothes and towels had been left for him on a bench.

Tristan dried himself and then redressed in the same set of clothes, but cleaner than the pair he had been wearing for however many days had passed. Once Tristan was finished, he looked at the pile of dirty clothes and the towel he had used. He picked them up and neatly folded them. Once he was done, he took them out with him in his hands.

The soldiers looked at him as he stepped out, clean and ready.

"W-what do I do with these?" Tristan questioned.

"Hold onto them," the soldier replied. "You'll have to wash them later."

The soldiers then proceeded to walk the opposite direction they had come from.

"Am I returning to my room?" Tristan asked.

The soldier turned around and looked at him with a tired expression.

"That was not your room," the soldier replied. "We are going to your room. Come on."

The soldiers led him down the corridor and then up a set of stairs in a staircase aside. They went up to the third floor and then stepped out to a long corridor with various doors at either side. They walked towards the end and then stepped in to a door on the left. Tristan was allowed to walk in. He looked in and saw a change in scenery to his former bedrooms.

The room had a desk, chair, wooden frame bed in the corner, a wardrobe, and a window with curtains and blinds that looked out to the horizon beyond the fortress. The bed included a mattress and had freshly made sheets. Inside the wardrobe was another uniform and other renditions of the uniform in different colors as well as various other gear below including a gas mask. Next to all this gear was a black trash bag.

"Your personal belongings are there," the soldier stated, pointing to the black bag. "We will show you where you can wash your clothes later, but now it is time to eat."

Tristan looked over to atop of his desk where there was a lunch tray with a green cover over the plate atop of it. He walked over to the tray and raised the cover. Inside was a plate with hash browns, two fried eggs, sausage, some toasted bread and a side of butter. Next to the plate was a glass of black coffee with some sugar and cream. Tristan looked at the food. His right eye twitched, but his stomach grumbled.

"We will give you a moment to eat," the soldier said, closing the door behind him. "When you are finished, you will begin your training…"

Tristan turned to him with slight surprise, but said nothing more than, "Thank you."

The soldier grunted at him with slight distaste and closed the door. Tristan then looked back at the food and then proceeded to look around suspiciously. He then turned to the food and quickly picked up the sausage and proceeded to devour it into his mouth with haste. Tristan ate everything on his plate and licked it when he was finished. He then poured both the cream and sugar into his coffee and drank it all in one swig. He finished his entire meal in less than ten minutes and then sat down in the chair, panting. The soldiers looked at him as he exited the room and looked to them.

"I'm ready," Tristan simply stated in a polite manner.

Tristan was brought downstairs and then to another building that was a part of the fortress compound. He was brought to the basement and then taken to a dark room, which was similar in dimness to the room where he had been tortured, but this room was larger and was a sort of studio with a desk before a window that looked into a black room on the other side. There was also a bluish hue in this room. Next to this desk was a sort of capsule bed, similar to the platform that Tristan had been tortured in, but with a case so that it could be closed and one left inside. This capsule was hooked up to a large computer on the opposite side of the room, which was hooked up to the desktops on the desk via cables that ran along the floor. The setup was entirely messy. A man in a lab coat stood up from the desk and greeted the soldiers in Russian, saluting to them. The man had blonde hair and appeared to be in his early fifties. He was dressed in grey trousers and a dress shirt underneath his lab coat.

"*Eto mal'chik?*" the scientist questioned.

"*Da*," the soldier replied. "On the bed," he ordered Tristan.

"Yes," Tristan responded without hesitation, going towards the bed and entering inside.

"Lie down," the soldier went on.

Tristan lay down inside and kept his arms at his side.

"*On, konechno, poslushen,*" the scientist remarked.

"*Konechno,*" the soldier replied.

"*Konechno, my, lyudi, nichem nye otlichayemsya ot zhivotnykh i mozhyem tak zhye legko obuchat'sya, yesli ne lyegchye.*"

The scientist turned to Tristan and looked at him.

"Vy mozhete nachat' s togo, chto nauchite yego govorit' i ponimat' po-russki," the soldier remarked before leaving.

"Da, mne pridetsya, no snachala on dolzhen nachat' nekotoryye predvaritel'nyye uprazhneniya," the scientist replied, turning to Tristan.

The scientist walked over to him and looked in. The scientist didn't speak English and had Tristan sit up. Tristan sat up. The scientist looked at his skull carefully, assessing the vertebrae before making marks on his spine. Afterwards, the scientist fitted a helmet atop of Tristan's head with probes that touched around the side of his eyes, went into his ears, and touched at four points of his skull, at the occipital, temporal, parietal, and frontal lobe, and at the segment of the spine that the scientist had marked. Once all was set, the scientist had Tristan lie down.

Tristan lay down while the scientist went to his computer. He simply lay on the bed with his hands to his side and the strange crown on his head. Several minutes passed until he felt a sudden stab in his spine. Tristan shouted out in pain and his vision dissipated and he was set in total blackness. The pain soon dissipated and Tristan looked about in the darkness with slight fear. He looked around for several minutes with anticipation until he bent over and grabbed his head. Tristan screamed out as he felt his eyes burn as if they were on fire. All around him, he saw the passing of words shoot by like high-speed trains. In his ears, he could hear the whisper of many different voices.

"Make it stop!" Tristan begged. "Please, make it stop!"

The pain did not end. All Tristan could do was hold his head and shut his eyes. He fell down to his knees and endured it, and in a sudden moment, it stopped on its own. When it was over, Tristan unclenched his hands from his head and opened his eyes. He looked around and saw that he was still in the abyssal darkness, but the hallucination had finished.

"It is over," a man said behind him.

Tristan turned around and looked at the man. It was the scientist. Tristan pointed to him.

"I- I understood that..." Tristan stated. "I'm... I'm talking in Russian."

"Yes," the scientist replied. "You are in a computer simulation that is plugged directly into your central nervous system through the back of your spine. A prototype technology that I had developed and that the Huntsman use to train the next-generation of soldiers they recruit. The pain you had just experienced was not meant to be torturous – it was not to make you submit to an idea, but what I had uploaded was a computer program so that you could understand the Russian language – at least, understand it as much as a computer program can have you understand, by translating what you think in English and having it come out of your tongue in Russian. Similar to any advanced language translation program on the Internet."

"Amazing," Tristan remarked.

"Of course, it is not perfect and there will be some faults – the aim of the next few weeks will be to patch these disparities as well as to train you in the customs and ways of a soldier so that you can serve the Huntsman and your brothers in the battles to come. Am I clear?"

"Yes," Tristan responded.

"Good," the scientist responded.

Tristan looked around him as the atmosphere shifted. He was no longer in a black void, but in a classroom. The scientist stood in the front of the room, but he was no longer the scientist, but instead a generic man in a brown suit with black hair. Tristan was sat in a desk at the front of the classroom.

"Let us begin," the man said, picking up a piece of chalk.

Act 6, Scene 5

Diana set up camp in the desert and caught some sleep. In the morning, she put out the fire she had made and then set to continue through. She ventured across the landscape and reached another row of dunes for her to climb. Diana noticed the wind pick up as she climbed up. The gust had a certain freshness towards it as the air that it brought to her was cool and crisp. She only covered her eyes from the sand as she stopped to enjoy it. Diana continued over the hills as the wind picked up even more. She stopped and covered her entire face as a cloud of sand made its pass, blinding her. She then opened her eyes again and continued uphill to reach the top. Diana looked down from the hill and saw a city in the distance.

The city was at least twenty miles from where she was and she could only see glimpses of the skyscrapers through the fog ahead that surrounded the city. Diana slid downhill and continued across the desert with eagerness to reach the city. However, the sandstorm continued to roll through and when she reached the bottom of the hill, her sight of the city faded, especially with the clouds of dust that attacked her. The skies were no longer blue as they were yesterday, but grey, trapping the humidity and warmth below, but also blocking the sun from gazing down upon her. Diana carried on in the same direction, keeping her sight down due to the wind, but at a brief second of lowered wind, she looked up and could see a patch of greenery in the desert with trees. The city was nowhere to be seen ahead, however.

Diana trekked towards the oasis in the desert and stopped, kneeling down to wash her face in the water. The water in the pool was fresh and crystal clear. Diana took a moment to drink some of the water and looked up with glee as she felt refreshed.

Of course, at the same moment, it proceeded to rain. Diana looked around herself as she noticed a crackle of thunder and shot of lightning from the clouds. She then looked forward as the wind picked up and a cloud of sand tore. Diana covered her face into her arm and then looked ahead at what had appeared in front of her. She looked up and saw the tall skyscrapers stretch left and right as they had suddenly appeared and tore through the desert. Diana looked back into the water, to her reflection, and then looked around her as she was no longer at an oasis, but atop of a skyscraper with the pond now a puddle that had formed from the rain.

The clouds in the sky were dark grey and there was a thin fog that permeated around her. Diana walked to the edge of the skyscraper and tried to look below, but her view of the streets was blocked by the fog. Diana continued to look around at the various buildings around her, most of which were lit by neon lights, but this was not Tokyo. She looked at the signs and saw they were in English. Diana looked around and saw in the distance Cabernet Tower, with its logo beaming down on her. She was in Harlech. Diana walked around the perimeter of the rooftop she was on. The rooftops were messy. A lot of the structures were closely knit together. Diana assessed the area as she determined where she would go, and once she had a path, she jumped down and proceeded along the rows of rooftops. The clouds grew darker within the first several minutes, and then there was a crack of lightning and Diana began to hear sirens.

Diana looked around as she stopped. She then began to hear dogs barking – deep barks like those of the canines of the Harlech Police Department. Another crack of lightning flashed; Diana stood the heavy rain as she looked around in confusion. She began to hear the cries of a baby and that of a crying woman. Diana produced her katana and assumed a defensive stance as she heard a gunshot, but as she looked around, she could see that no shots had been fired. She slowly breathed and looked around, focusing. Diana then twitched to her right as she saw the sudden appearance of commandos in black uniforms with assault rifles. The commandos wore night-vision goggles before their eyes, which made them look as though they had neon green eyes piercing at her. They were similar to the ones from Diana's earlier nightmare, but also the commandos that stormed Cabernet Manor in October. She quickly dodged into cover as they proceeded to fire towards her and she then ran off, jumping down and landing on a balcony below.

From the balcony, Diana ran inside and into an apartment where the furniture was amess and there were no inhabitants in sight. She ran into the corridor and proceeded down to reach a set of stairs that went down. Diana stopped as she went down to levels and saw the shadows of commandos below her. She opted out a window and slid down a metal awning and then jumped to land on another rooftop. Diana then hurried indoors where she paused for a moment and then moved with cautious steps as she heard another noise, the sound of a man begging for his life. Diana proceeded to the end of the corridor and went up a set of stairs to reach the rooftop. She then jumped out and looked across the sprawl of roofs before going forward. To her right was a tall neon sign that flickered and looked outwards. Diana stopped as reached the midst of the rooftop and a trio of three commandos jumped up in a roll and then presented themselves before her. Diana looked at the commandos and saw they were entirely distinct, sporting masks that gave them red artificial eyes and carrying swords that they held like Diana's colleagues at the dojo.

Diana readied her sword and then proceeded to intercept their strikes towards her. She clashed her blade with one of them, strike for strike, and with every strike she made, the noise of the man intensified. Diana stabbed at one of the commandos and then jumped out of the way as another attempted to strike her. She intercepted another strike and felt the commando press down on her with his blade. Diana kicked back and then flipped backwards. She readied herself for another strike as the two remaining ninjas looked at her. They then teamed up, one of them jumping off the other for a suspended strike. Diana blocked the strike and punched the ninja, delivering a finishing blow to the neck before concentrating on the last. Diana looked at the commando with intent as the two took careful steps. The ninja stepped forward and attempted to jab at her. Diana blocked the jab and the two proceeded to exchange swipes until the two blades locked together and sparks flew between them.

A flash of lightning startled Diana as she looked at the face of the ninja and instead saw Tristan. Diana kicked back at the commando and it vanished out of sight. She breathed for a moment and then she turned around as the voice of the man became more localized. She turned around, but before she could walk to the edge of the rooftop, she heard a loud gunshot and saw a murder of crows fly off. Another flash of lightning lit up the sky and the cries of the woman intensified.

Diana looked around as she stood in the rain. She then turned around and looked towards a neighboring rooftop as more commandos, these with assault rifles and green eyes instead of the latter, tumbled out of windows and took cover. Diana ran to the left and jumped off the roof to land on the rooftop where the ninja commandos had appeared from. She then stopped as she saw more of the former commandos appear and close in on her. Diana quickly jumped back and landed on a balcony and disappeared into the apartment as they shot at her.

At the end of the corridor, Diana entered a fire escape that merged with a sort of conservatory or greenhouse. She moved through and came to a narrow open space in the corner of four buildings where there were various shanties built below. The commandos appeared from the opposite-end and fired at her. Diana crossed left and entered another building, running down a corridor and then taking a step to crash into the floor below. Diana caught herself as she landed, and continued down the corridor, stopping as she noticed a warm glow through the cracks in the floorboard. Diana also heard the cries of the woman to be localized. She looked through the cracks, but she could not see much. Diana followed the corridor and stopped as the cries of the woman were replaced with the cries of a little girl. She looked below, seeing what appeared to be a young girl with black-brown hair knelt before the corpse of a woman with light brown hair. The room was lit in its warm glow by fire burning from fireplace.

Diana brought her head back up as she heard the crack of ice and a large splash. She began to pant.

"Tristan?" Diana questioned, looking around.

Diana could not see anything around her. She attempted to look down again, but the light had burned out and it was dark. She refocused on the sound of the downpour. The sound of the toddler crying had dissipated and been replaced with the cries of a young girl. Diana flinched as a commando jumped through the window on the opposite-end of the corridor and pointed his rifle towards her. She instantly reacted and threw some throwing stars at him, hitting him in the head. She moved in as the rifle was pointed up and took her katana, striking at him in the abdomen and then pulled out. Diana then turned behind her as a group of another three commandos arrived and proceeded to shoot at her. Diana jumped out the window and dodged them. She landed on a rooftop below, but before she could run out of harm's way, she stopped.

"Diana!" Tristan shouted from afar as though in fear for her.

Diana looked around. A flash of lightning lit the skies. The cries of the young girl became cries of a young woman. Diana flinched as she felt shots fired towards her miss her only barely. She quickly ran out of the way and down onto a balcony for her enter another apartment. Diana entered the home and came into the corridor. She immediately felt a warm glow in the hallway, emanating from below. Diana walked carefully down the corridor and looked down. The floor below her was on fire. She walked with careful steps as she attempted to reach the end of the corridor where there was an exit sign pointed into a stairwell. Diana reached the end of the corridor and opened the door into the stairwell, but instead of a stairwell, she instead looked in to see another corridor, but this one completely set on fire.

Diana entered the hallway, seeing that the floors were safe to walk on and that there was a door at the other end. She began to hear the voice of a disgruntled man echo as she took her steps. The voices were of several people talking at once, all in annoyed and frustrated tones if they were arguing with each other, but all speaking atop of one another. Diana walked with hesitant steps, stopping only as she began to recognize one of the voices to be Charlemagne. Diana reached the end of the corridor when she looked down through the cracks of the floorboard and saw two figures move, one with blonde hair and the other with reddish-brown hair. They rushed through a doorway and disappeared. Diana opened the door ahead of her, above, and entered another corridor – this one dark and cold. She could still hear the cries of the young woman as well as the rain. Diana looked at the end of the corridor and saw Tristan standing at the other side.

Tristan looked back at her. He had a solemn face and his eyes were dark. She blinked and he was gone. Diana walked down the corridor, but then turned around as the doors burst open and commandos tumbled in. Diana dodged them and entered a stairwell at the end of the corridor. She went up a set of stairs and ran into a commando that jumped through a window in the stairwell. Diana threw her sword like a spear, hitting the commando in the shoulder. She moved in and took her short sword to stab the commando in the abdomen before retrieving her katana and continuing upwards to reach the top of the roof. She looked around and then up to a tall building that was behind her. The building was surrounded by others and was like an ivory tower with these rooftops acting like steps of a staircase.

A group of five ninja commandos jumped upwards onto the rooftop she was at and stood before her at the start of the pathway. Diana immediately went in to engage them, clashing with one of them as they proceeded to spread out and surround her in a circle. Diana kicked the ninja she was currently engaged with back and then produced her bō staff as she noticed the rest of the ninjas gang upon her. She quickly span around with the staff to get them to back off and then jumped out of the way. Diana raised her sword as a ninja attempted to strike at her in the chaos. She blocked the blow and then the next before catching the blade with her gauntlet and stabbing the commando in the abdomen. Another ninja jumped in to stab at her. Diana turned the body of the one she had just defeated and used it to block the blow to the left while another from her right came at her. She blocked the ninja on her right with her sword and kicked him off, sliding the corpse off her grip and then blocking two blows at once as they came to her.

Diana sucker punched the ninja on her right in the head. She then kicked him off and took the increased movement to stab the other in the chest before going ahead to face the other two. The ninja raised its sword up to strike at Diana, but Diana blocked the swipe and three more before turning her attention to the other as he came towards her. Diana clashed her blade with his and then rolled backwards to dodge a swipe from the lateral side, standing back up raising her sword to block another blow. The two swords met with each other. A flash of lightning lit around them and sparks flew from their swords. Diana again hallucinated Tristan's face in the commando ninja, but when his face disappeared, she headbutted the commando and then stabbed him in the abdomen. She then raised her sword to intercept the last ninja, kicking him and causing him to roll to his side, retaining his grip as he looked to Diana, bent over. Diana brought her sword down to the ninja and the ninja blocked her strike. They exchanged several strikes until Diana managed to pull the foe's sword down and then bring it back like an elastic to slice him in the neck and then finish him off with a stab to the suprasternal notch. Diana then pulled her sword back as the ninja disappeared and disintegrated into ashes.

Once Diana was certain she was clear, she put her sword away and proceeded forward and began to climb up the rooftops. She climbed atop of a billboard and carefully walked to the other side like a balance beam. She slid underneath a vent and then shimmied her way over a ledge. Once she was at the final steps, she climbed them with care until she was at the top where she could look out to the city around her, and more importantly, to what was before her. Diana looked at Tristan's corpse at the center of the wide rooftop, before a series of shanties that portrayed a thick shadow behind Tristan. Around him was a pool of blood and in his abdomen was a fresh wound.

Diana ran towards him and assessed him. She checked for a response as she pinched his finger, but none came. She checked his airway, but no air came. He was not breathing. He appeared pale and lifeless. She brought her lips to his and gave him a kiss of life, but before she could beat into his chest the first repetition of an attempted resuscitation, the body disappeared and she plunged her hands into a puddle of water in the middle of the rooftop. The cries of the young woman were most intense. A flash of lightning lit up the dark skies and a wind picked up. Diana looked around and began to hear a maniacal laugh. She looked around for a source of the laughter before she focused on the shadows of the shelters.

From the shadows emerged a figure through the solid shadowy walls, dripping with a black liquid that was like ink as though he emerged from a shadowy realm. The Mysterious Stranger appeared before her in his original form, gas mask over his face, his human eyes staring out, and tall boots that added an extra two inches to his height so that he loomed five inches over her. The Mysterious Stranger stepped out of the shadows and came to face Diana. He carried with him a harpoon that he hastily shot towards her. Diana jumped out of the way and produced her katana. She then looked to the Mysterious Stranger and charged at him with her sword.

The Mysterious Stranger jumped back and out of the way as she swung her sword at him. He dodged each consecutive swipe with agility. Diana jabbed the sword towards him, but he jumped back and then when she attempted to swipe it down upon him, the Mysterious Stranger lunged forward with his arms and grabbed Diana's hands, splitting them apart from the handle of the blade and then bringing his head down to headbutt her. Diana instantly reacted before he could make contact with her by pulling back and kicking off his chest, pushing him back and rolling him over. Diana fell on her side while the Mysterious Stranger caught himself and spun back around to face her. The

Mysterious Stranger grabbed his harpoon from nearby and then charged towards Diana.

Diana stood up and intercepted the harpoon with her bō staff as the Mysterious Stranger attempted to stab her with it. The assassin was significantly stronger than Diana, but she was capable of bringing him over and forcing the harpoon out of his grip. She then elbowed him in the face, but before she could stab him, the Mysterious Stranger grabbed her wrist and threw her aside. Diana attempted to land on her feet, while the assassin picked up his harpoon again and ran towards her with it. She jumped out of the way and then blocked another attempted jab with her staff, hitting the assassin in the face, but he grabbed the staff off her and quickly broke it in half. The   Mysterious Stranger proceeded to grab Diana by the neck as she attempted to execute a low kick. Diana brought her hands to her neck as she was choked and raised from the ground. She looked into the eyes of the assassin. His green bloodshot eyes looked at her. Lightning flashed, and Diana looked through the mask of the assassin to see Tristan's face. Diana's eyes widened. She quickly raised herself and brought her legs atop of the Mysterious Stranger's shoulders. She then kicked off from him, forcing him to let go of her. The assassin rushed to her to deliver a punch. She blocked. He sent a kick. She jumped back and out of the way.

Diana went into deliver her own punches, but the Mysterious Stranger was more or less unfazed by her attempts and delivered a single strike to her face that sent her back and caused her hood to fall back. Blood gushed out from her nose. The Mysterious Stranger closed it to deliver another strike, but Diana caught his fist and used all her strength to push him back. She then hopped back and held her ground as she assumed a defensive stance.

The Mysterious Stranger kicked Diana's katana and caused it to bounce up. He then caught it into his hands and assumed an offensive stance. The assassin attempted to jab at Diana. She rolled out of the way and to her side, quickly standing up and facing her foe as she landed. The assassin then went in with a horizontal slice. Diana blocked the blade with her gauntlet. The assassin then diverged and attempted to hit from the other side, but she blocked with her other gauntlet. The assassin then spun around and jumped up to come down on her, but she blocked the blade as she raised her arms. Diana then jumped out of the way as the assassin spun around again and attempted to slash down on her vertically once, and then spun around again to come down on her with a jump. Diana blocked the oncoming blow with her gauntlet again, pushing back this time, and then preparing as another slice came as he spun again. Diana blocked it. The Mysterious Stranger jumped off of her thigh and prepared to come down on her. Diana caught his hands and immediately headbutted him to back off.

Diana proceeded to strike at him, punch after punch as he was disoriented. The assassin then hit her in the head with his elbow and then spun around to deliver another side strike with the katana. Diana caught the blade in her hands and the two struggled. Lightning struck again and Diana looked back at the face of the assassin as the light shined against him, and again she saw through the mask and saw Tristan's face, beaten up and miserable. Once his face disappeared, Diana then feinted weakness, hit the assassin in the face with her elbow and then kicked him back. The assassin raised the katana to strike down on her, but Diana caught the blade in one hand, punched him in the other, and then pulled the katana away from him and allowed the handle to rush back into his body before she delivered a kick that forced him backwards. Diana then juggled the katana back into her hands and rushed over to deliver the finishing stroke.

The Mysterious Stranger covered his face, but Diana jabbed him in the abdomen, causing him to yell out in pain. Diana then pulled the blade out and brought it around to position at his neck. She had him at her mercy. The assassin looked back at her as she pressed the blade against the fair skin of his neck. She looked at him through his eyes and brought a hand to the mask, pulling the mask off, but as she did so, the assassin vanished in a cloud of black smoke. Diana's foot fell down to the ground of the rooftop. She looked distraught as the assassin disappeared, looking around as if she expected him to return, but he didn't. The Mysterious Stranger was gone.

Diana looked around from atop of the rooftop. She then looked at the mask in her hand. The gas mask that was a fragment of her darkest fear. She looked at her own blue eyes in the reflection of the eyeholes and then threw the mask over the edge. The rain had stopped as had the crying and the thunderstorm. Diana looked up to the sky as a brightness filtered into the city of her nightmares, filling her eyes until all that she saw was whiteness and nothing more.

Act 7, Scene 1

Diana opened her eyes and looked out around her as she was in submerged in an orange liquid within a tube of some sort of dim laboratory. She thrashed about and attempted to emerge out of the liquid, but she could not. Diana gurgled, but she soon realized that she was alive despite her lungs being filled with this fluid. Diana soon calmed down and looked out of the tube. She saw movement outside and recognized one of the many people about as Shinji.

The liquid in the tube soon flushed out and Diana touched down on the ground. She was dressed in swim shorts and had a swimming bra on. There were various nodes attached to her body. Once all the liquid had flushed out, the capsule opened and Diana was able to step out. Shinji looked at her.

"So, you're alive," Shinji said to her.

"*Hai*," Diana replied, looking at her hands. "How do I know if this is real life?"

"It is real," Shinji responded, "and that's a reality you are going to have to accept as the days go on that you're no longer in stasis. Come on," he said. "The daimyo will want to see you…"

Diana walked forward with careful steps. She then stopped and tightened a fist. She proceeded to turn and attempt to strike Shinji, but he dodged and blocked her strike. Diana stopped as she looked at him. He didn't say anything. Diana disengaged and looked ashamed. The two proceeded to walk out of the lab.

"How many days has it been?"

"It's been about six weeks," Shinji answered.

"It feels like it's been almost six months…"

"Yeah…"

Once Diana was bathed and dressed, she put on her uniform and collected her shorts sword. She looked at her things and noticed there was not a katana for her despite having a holster for one. Diana took out her short sword and practiced some of the skills she had, slicing at the air as if she was still in her dreamland.

Once she was ready, she exited and entered a dim hallway. Shinji proceeded to lead her to the throne room where the Grandmaster waited for her. He looked down upon her.

"I had confidence that you would not disappoint me," the daimyo stated to her in Japanese. "You have been through a lot in the last several months, and if you so choose, my dojo is open for you to return so that you may learn more, but you have become adept in your skills…"

The daimyo then looked to Shinji at his right side. Shinji picked up a case and then walked over to present what was inside to her.

"For your skill in completing your training, I present to you a gift, made from the esteemed Goru Clan who have served the Oishi Clan for centuries. Please, take it."

Shinji opened the case and showed Diana a katana sword, freshly made and brand new. She picked it up and examined it. She then returned it to the case and Shinji closed it. Diana took the case into her hands.

"Now that you have completed your training, you are free to return and continue on your personal quest," the daimyo said, "but never forget what you have learned here."

"*Hai*," Diana replied.

"You may leave."

"*Hai*," Diana responded, bowing.

Diana took a step back, but then she stopped.

"If I may," Diana asked in Japanese. "Can I ask you a question?"

"What is it?" the daimyo questioned.

"Rei," Diana said, "is she real, or was she simply a product of my imagination? I was told that there was a clan of female shinobi at a temple not too far from here, but now I realize that this was not true and just a myth, and that in reality I trained under your eyes in some sort of weird hallucination..."

The daimyo looked to her. He developed a solemn face. The old man stood up and then stepped down to face Diana. He then extended a hand for her to walk with him. Shinji watched as the two left the throne room and entered one of the gardens in the midst of the castle. The daimyo walked with Diana for several steps until they stopped before a pond.

"Rei was my sister," the daimyo stated. "The two of us were taught in the art of the ninja from a young age during the American-Japanese War with expectation that we would need to use our skills during the inevitable occupation of this island, our home. After the bombing of Nagasaki and Hiroshima, the empire surrendered and our emperor was humiliated, but our clan continued to fight these oppressors who had brought greed and crime to our island home, and who had been responsible for the deaths of thousands of our own people in the name of their ideals. They had bested us, but we continued to fight, and in the crossfire, my sister was killed during an operation against our occupiers."

Diana was silent.

"This was over seventy years ago..." the daimyo expressed. "Within Rei was nothing more than a determination for Japan to stand as she was, not before the war, but before the modernization that took place... She, like many of us, simply wanted a return to the old ways when Japan was isolated to the rest of the world… The experience you just had in the last few weeks, her presence, was not a hallucination, but her spirit…"

Diana raised an eyebrow.

"The ability to undergo the training you have just completed requires the skill to speak with the dead, and I knew from the moment that you stepped in here, you held that skill, because it is within you that there is a special gift…" the daimyo remarked. "The process of training you required no more than determination, and that determination you had when you expressed your desire to defend your loved ones. All you then needed was time, and I gave that to you."

The daimyo put his hands behind his back.

"Rei was also Shinji's grandmother…" the daimyo remarked. "Before she died, she had given birth to a boy who took the name of his ancestors, Oishi, and that boy was Shinji's father. Shinji is very protective of this village, his family name, and all that it holds. He takes great pride, and one day, when I die, he will be the master of the clan."

"What of your own children?" Diana questioned.

"My children… they are not with us, in this village… one is a doctor in Tokyo, while the other is a businessman with a telecom company in Osaka. They were sent to be educated in the sixties, but when they returned, they shared no desire as they had been indoctrinated by the new Japanese customs. The fate of this village rests only in Shinji… I hope that you share this spirit of his – to hold dear one's family and tradition."

Diana looked to the master with surprise.

"I have no idea who I am, or where I come from," Diana answered. "Honestly, I wish I knew, but I don't."

The daimyo did not respond. He instead turned to Diana and looked to her.

"In time, you may come to know, but for now, you need to set off and search for Zimmerman. Many weeks have passed, and much has changed since you had started your training. Do you know where to go?"

"No, I don't," Diana confessed. "If six weeks have gone by then they could be anywhere – they're probably worried about and where I've gone. I had no idea it'd take this long to finish this training. I thought it would be three days at most."

"I suggest then that you travel to Kyoto and visit the Grand Shrine. If you pray there, then the spirits of our ancestors may guide you for they are ever vigilant and watch over us. They will recognize you and guide you in the right direction. We will provide you transport into Kyoto and provide you with enough so that you can find your way."

"Thank you," Diana replied, bowing. "I am grateful for all that you have passed on to me."

"You owe us nothing," the daimyo replied. "Find Zimmerman, and put an end to that demon."

"*Hai,*" Diana replied, bowing again.

Act 7, Scene 2

Tristan vaulted over a concrete obstacle and moved in with an assault rifle in hand to take point behind the wreckage of an automobile. He was dressed in full-combat gear, including the standard Huntsman helmet with optics raised over his head. He pointed his rifle forward and looked ahead. He was in the ruins of a sort of slum in the midst of an urban center. Ahead of him, between where he was and a structure to the left, and a construction site behind, there was the wreckage of a helicopter. Tristan focused as he kept his eye down the sightlines of his rifle.

In an instant, Tristan adjusted his aim as he spotted the appearance of a hostile. Tristan opened fire and shot towards the hostile. He then adjusted to aim at another before ducking down as the hostiles returned fire. Tristan quickly exchanged cartridges and then proceeded to crawl away from his point of cover and enter a structure behind him. Once he was out of sight, he stood up and ran up a set of stairs to reach the second-floor of the building. Tristan moved to a window and knelt down. He opened fire and shot back at the hostiles as they continued to appear. Tristan's ear then twitched as heard the vibration of footsteps behind him. He quickly turned around and blocked the rifle of an incoming enemy soldier before producing a knife and slashing at the foe's throat. The foe was pushed aside by the soldier behind him. Tristan took the knife and raised it to stab at the foe, but the foe deflected and grabbed his arm by the wrist, knocking it against a wall for him to drop the knife. The hostile then produced his own knife, but instead of grabbing it as it was brought to Tristan's face, he instead punched to the left of his face with his right hand and lowered the knife with his right hand before raising his leg to kick the combatant in the thigh, bringing the hostile down with his left hand by twisting his arm and then pulling at it mercilessly to dislocate it. Tristan then produced a rifle from a holster at his side and shot the hostile in the back of the head as he screamed out.

Once the hostile was neutralized, Tristan picked up his assault rifle as it hung from a sling around his neck and then returned downstairs. He stopped at the doorway and looked out. He saw hostile movement and turned to open fire.

"Friendly reinforcements to your right," a voice projected from within Tristan's earpiece.

"*Ponimaniye*," Tristan replied, reloading his rifle.

Tristan looked to the side as he heard friendly gunfire come from his side.

"Move in to secure the target," the voice projected in Tristan's ear.

"*Da*," Tristan responded, moving in under the covering fire to reach the helicopter wreckage.

Tristan opened the hatch door at the side of the helicopter and then looked inside to some of the corpses that were inside. His eyes then looked to a female civilian in a grey suit that was injured in the crash. She was a young African woman in her twenties with black hair and eyes. Tristan extended a hand to her.

"We have been sent to rescue you," Tristan said in Russian. "Please, come with me."

The woman extended a shaking hand to him. He took it and then picked the woman up in a fireman carry before rushing off under the cover of friendly fire back to the house. A fellow mercenary helped him inside and Tristan sat the woman down so he could pick up his rifle and assist with the returning fire. The woman was in shock and continued to shake.

"*Zvezda*," Tristan reported over the radio. "We have secured the package. We are ready for extraction."

"Understood," the same voice from earlier projected. "Estimated arrival, two minutes."

Tristan reloaded and continued to provide supporting fire. The sound of rotors in the sky above began to fill his ears next to the barrage of bullets.

"I'll cover you," the mercenary next to Tristan said. "Get her out of here."

"Yes," Tristan replied, lowering his rifle and then going to the woman.

Tristan helped raise her over his shoulders again in a fireman carry and then moved out the back door to step into a street. Tristan looked down the street and towards a helicopter that was making its landing in the midst of the war-torn street. He then rushed over as the side doors of the helicopter opened with reinforcements waving for him to come over. Tristan went over and helped the civilian aboard.

"Target secured," the voice projected.

Tristan picked up his rifle and knelt down before the side of the helicopter as his teammates returned. He watched them with his rifle pointed forward as they returned, opening fire as he spotted hostiles attempt to corner them as they attempted to extract. Once they were aboard, Tristan felt a tap on his shoulder. He stood up and attempted to sit down, but as he turned around, the helicopter was gone and he was shot into darkness of an eternal grid. Tristan lowered his rifle and looked around

"Simulation complete," a monotone voice projected in his ear.

"Good," another, natural voice remarked. "End program."

Tristan continued to look around and then raised the visor before his eyes to look around the smaller room he was in. Tristan was not in full-combat gear, but instead in his uniform without the top piece. Instead, he only wore the t-shirt over his torso alongside the black-purple trousers and boots. In addition, he was covered in a mesh of wires, supports along his arms, and a battery pack behind him that connected to the model rifle in his hands. He stood atop of a circular platform that had rail guards around. He was not alone in the room as all of the teammates that were with him stood with him. They were being watched through the glass of a room adjacent to them, which was the same room that Tristan had started his digital training in.

The lights in the dim room lit and the door opened with the Russian scientist stepping out alongside one of the high-ranking officers, the same one that defended Tristan during his arrival. The officer looked at the recruits.

"All recruits are dismissed," the officer stated in a bold voice.

The recruits proceeded to unpack themselves from the exoframe before they proceeded to leave. Tristan was stopped from leaving and taken aside, and he was kept there in silence until the other recruits left. The age of the recruits varied, some of them were young boys in their late teens, while others were older men in their late twenties or early thirties. The officer was an older man, in his forties if not late thirties. Once the recruits were gone, the officer looked to Tristan.

"Good work, today, Merrick," the officer commended. "You have learned lots in the last while, but I'm afraid the classrooms and simulations can only teach you so much."

Tristan stood at attention as the officer spoke to him.

"At ease," the officer requested.

Tristan relaxed himself a bit.

"I have received word from Subcommander Alexandrov requesting for your immediate deployment to Guangxi," the officer stated. "You will be leaving this evening via helicopter with a small squad of reinforcements that will assist with the excavation to the cave deep within the forests there. Am I understood?"

"Yes," Tristan replied without objection.

"Good," the officer replied. "Dismissed."

• • •

Later that night, Tristan left for China with the reinforcement of soldiers, all of whom appeared to be older veterans than the recruits he had been surrounded with recently. Nonetheless, Tristan held his chin up and simply followed orders as they came. From the Far East, they travelled into Manchuria, and from there, they took a train that went south to Guangzhou.

Within midday the next day, Tristan was travelling in a jeep with his team through a humid monsoon forest. They travelled along a highway for the first hour, then a dirt road, and then off-road until they reached a riverbed where a large camp had been established with various tents and parked vehicles about including a tank, armored personnel carriers, Zimmerman's private car, supply trucks, and two forest cutters. Tristan got off the jeep and walked with his team towards a central tent.

Once inside, they moved about to stand and await their briefing as all the soldiers stood around the perimeter of the tent, leaving the center clear where there was a table with a map drawn out. Tristan looked around at the other soldiers as they chatted about. He was the youngest person in the room. Tristan then flinched as he felt the presence of Kodiak next to him. Kodiak looked at him with a frown. Tristan looked back at him fearfully. Kodiak then smiled.

"Relax," Kodiak remarked, patting him on the shoulder. "You are one of us now. You will come to adjust soon enough, I suppose..."

Tristan did not return the smile nor did his expression change from its serious tone. Instead, he shifted his eyes to the entrance of the tent. Kodiak's father, Bogdan, entered with Zimmerman, Dulles, and Southern. Zimmerman was dressed in a similar white suit as the one he had been wearing the last time Tristan saw him. The four of them went to the table in the center and the briefing proceeded. Tristan focused and stood at attention.

Bogdan shouted out to some soldiers at the entrance of the tent. The flaps opened and several soldiers entered, pushing a figure before them who was dressed in a poncho and had mildly thick silver-white beard around his face. Tristan looked at the man as he held a bunch of papers in his hands. Bogdan scolded the men as he took the upper arm of the man and then brought him over to the center of the room.

The man dropped the papers in his hands onto the table and kept his head down.

"Thanks to the help of Mr. Cabernet," Bogdan remarked to the men in Russian. "We have been able to locate the Dragon's Den to be less than fifty miles from our location deep within the depths of the rainforest."

Bogdan awaited for the muttering to cease before he continued.

"The problem, however, is that the Chinese authorities are closing in on our location with intent to find the cavern before us, so we must move out in batches of two, and move out swiftly if we are to arrive at the prize."

Bogdan patted Charlemagne on the back.

"Why don't you explain," Bogdan spoke in English.

Charlemagne continued to look down, shaking before he cleared his throat. Tristan looked at him from the crowd as though he was a bit of confusion. Indeed, Charlemagne appeared different to him with the beard and weakness within him, but that was not it. Charlemagne looked back at him and stared at him for several seconds in slight surprise.

"We don't have all day," Zimmerman sighed. "Hurry up."

"Yes," Charlemagne replied, clearing his throat again. "My previous assumptions were incorrect... while the points in Gansu did provide us with the location of the den, it was not in a straight line as I assumed, but instead, the points at this portal through the Great Wall, which was an important point for passing trade on the Silk Road, is meant to connect in a straight line with the Forbidden Palace in Beijing. The exact distance from these two locations is to scale with the two guard towers..."

Charlemagne drew on the map of China on the table with a black marker. He drew a straight line from Gansu to Beijing.

"And thus, knowing the calculations of the triangle at the portal and adjusting them to scale with the distance from the portal to the Forbidden City, the location of the Tomb of the Dragon Emperor is in this general area, which... with Dr. Southern's own research, is here..."

Charlemagne pulled another map onto the table. This was a more detailed map of the Guangxi region of southern China. Charlemagne pointed to a mark on the map.

"At the... fittingly named, Dragon Mountain..." Charlemagne stated. "Here, I am certain, the tomb of the emperor lies, and it makes sense..."

"Yes, but who wants to hear any more about that," Zimmerman sighed, looking to Bogdan. "What's the plan?"

"As I've said, we'll move in two teams from two separate points," Bogdan continued in English. "One team will attempt to intercept the advancing Chinese forces and delay their arrival to us, while the other will move under the cover of the other and reach the tomb to collect the treasure... if it is even there."

"It'll be there," Zimmerman remarked, looking at Charlemagne and then to Tristan. "Charlemagne is never wrong, is he?"

Tristan flinched.

"Very well," Bogdan replied, ignoring Zimmerman.

Charlemagne proceeded to tidy the papers on the table. Zimmerman looked at him.

"Get him back to his tent," Zimmerman remarked.

"Yes, sir," a soldier replied, moving in to grab Charlemagne with the help of some others.

Once Charlemagne was gone, Dulles and Southern left, while Zimmerman remained for the rest of the briefing. Tristan looked to Charlemagne as he was pulled away. Charlemagne looked back at him and Tristan could only return another confusing glance at him, almost as if he did not recognize him.

Act 7, Scene 3

Diana knelt down in the Grand Shrine in Kyoto as the sun began to set. She looked forward towards the ornaments of the shrine within the pagoda temple. She was knelt in a simple square room with wooden floors and white walls. The beam of the setting sun came in through the open doors from the garden and Diana felt it against her back.

"Lord," Diana expressed. "I have been sent to this foreign land and thrown into the arms of the Oishi Clan to learn these unforgettable skills to defend that which I love. However, I am now lost and in need of guidance to find them... I need to find them... I've travelled to what is considered to be holiest shrine in all of Japan, and while it is not a shrine dedicated specifically to you, Lord, it is a sacred ground nonetheless."

Diana bowed her head and closed her eyes.

"Help me find them, Lord. Help me find Tristan and Charlemagne. I need to find them before it is too late... before something happens to either of them. I have the power within me to assist them, a power that I've learned to hone and concentrate in the skills that I have been taught... I need to find them."

Diana's hands began to tremble.

"When I was a little girl, I never imagined my life would take such a turn as it has now. I thought – I told myself – I promised myself, that I would be single and poor for the rest of my life. And yet, I have met the handsomest man I had ever laid eyes on, somehow he fell in love with me and I fell in love with him, and I now I only envision my future with him and our children. And at the same time, I also came into the home of one of the wealthiest mans in the world, and although we've clashed, he is my spiritual father... where my father lacked..."

Diana shook her head, looked up and brought her hands together.

"Lord, please inspire me to locate them. For this, I pray... Our Father, who art in Heaven, hallowed by thy name. Thy Kingdom come, thy will be done on Earth as it is in Heaven. Give us this day our daily bread and forgive us for our trespasses, as we forgive those that trespass against us..."

Diana stopped at these words and looked to the side.

"My father... he abandoned me and my mother for his own selfish desires... but at least he still supported us to an extent. Some children never get to meet their fathers... but I always thought that as the nicer alternative... that's why I was happiest when he was dead. He abused me. He abused my mother. I don't understand... but I can't keep running from him, even though he's dead.

For whatever reason, I envisioned Tristan to be the Mysterious Stranger, but I know that is impossible to be true, so why did I envision him as the assassin? Why did I see him? Am I scared of Tristan? I'm scared of him leaving me... the idea's driven anxiety through me ever since the possibility came into my mind when he returned from England. I saw him in those visions with Finn too."

Diana lowered her hands and made a fist.

"Am I really so pathetic that I'm jealous of Tristan's only friend? Have I been secretly pleased that Tristan has no friends but me? What kind of woman am I to do that to my man? If Tristan and I hadn't been living together, him without friends, would our relationship have even been possible?"

Diana released her fists.

"I'm always in constant need of him. I'm dependent on him. Only in the past year have I realized this need because he's been avoiding me. It drives me nuts. Am I scared of fighting with him? Of having an argument about our relationship and the direction it's inevitably headed where we'll be apart? Am I scared of him? Of what he might become? Of what his going on in his mind? Enough."

Diana looked forward again and bowed her head.

"I cannot be dependent on him… but there is no shame of being dependent on him. I am a woman. It is the vice within me where I must be dependent on him, with no liberty to choose to accept it, but instead, I simply have to accept it. No more. I have to find him. I have to have this conversation with him…"

Diana's ears poked up as she heard a footstep behind her. She got onto one knee and pivoted around to look. She then dropped a look of surprise as she saw who stood at the entrance into the pagoda. Director Black looked at Diana with a hand on her hip. Diana stood up and looked at her.

"Hello, Diana," Director Black stated. "It's been a while."

"What are you doing here? How did you find me?" Diana questioned.

"We've been looking for you," Director Black replied, scanning Diana's uniform with her eyes, "but for whatever reason, it's as though you disappeared off the face of the planet for the last six weeks until now when we managed to find you here in Kyoto."

"Can you bring me to Tristan and Charlemagne?"

"I've been requested by your guardian to return you to his security detail in Harlech," Director Black replied, stepping forward and entering the pagoda.

"Where are they?"

Director Black hesitated to answer.

"I'm afraid they've been captured," Director Black replied. "Shortly after you disappeared, they went into China where they were detained by the Chinese authorities. I was able to get them out, but they were then ambushed and their aircraft shot down. There were no survivors from the ambush, but we have reason to believe that they might not have killed Charlemagne who may be assisting them now – whether of his own free will or not, we are not sure. And insofar as to whether Tristan is alive, we are not sure."

"Deploy me," Diana instantly requested. "Please. I've had training – weeks of training for this exact purpose. I'm capable of fighting and defending myself. I can help."

Diana produced her sword and brought the top of the blade to the floor to show the director. She then went on to explain the process by which she had been asleep for weeks, training within a hidden village who had kidnapped her because of her suspected relation to Zimmerman.

"Please, don't take me to the Protection Squad," Diana pleaded. "Take me to China so I can rescue them."

Director Black sighed and then replied, "Because of our failure to secure Charlemagne, the Chinese government has become frustrated with the Global Defense Project and its efforts to stop Zimmerman within their country. They've since deployed their own task force led by one of their generals, and our intel states they're in the process of closing in on Zimmerman as we speak," she explained. "Coincidentally, I am defiant and have put together a small team to deploy to Guangxi and while rescuing your guardian and Tristan is not a priority, it is a secondary objective. You are free to join us, but we must leave this instance as they are hours from reaching the location of the orb."

Act 7, Scene 4

Tristan travelled with his team aboard the same jeep they had travelled from Guangzhou in. The convoy had returned to a dirt road that went through the forest. At the lead of the convoy was the forest cutter, while behind the pack was the T-90 tank. Tristan's team were right in front of the tank as they ventured along the bumpy road of the hinterland. There was a mild rain that fell upon them and it was also humid and hot. Tristan had rolled up his sleeves to cope with the heat, which was vastly different from the weather in Siberia.

Kodiak rode in the front of the jeep, and before them was Zimmerman's private car. Charlemagne rode in the back of the car. Southern was in the front passenger seat, while a soldier drove the car. Dulles was in the back of the car, opposite from Charlemagne. Zimmerman was nowhere to be seen because he had been moved to be protected by Bogdan in a random APC. Due to the nature of the terrain, the convoy moved slowly as they continued forward. Approximately fifty miles from them, north, was the second decoy convoy. Kodiak drank from a canteen as Tristan simply held his rifle at his side by the barrel pointed up.

Suddenly, the T-90 behind them detonated. Tristan turned and looked, but before he could look at the fireball that emerged, a secondary strike hit forward.

"Ambush!" several voices shouted.

The jeep halted and Tristan picked up his rifle. He could hear gunfire ahead emerging from the dense woods. The strikes from above continued to rain down on them from every direction. Tristan quickly got off the jeep and looked to Kodiak.

"Secure the VIPs!" Kodiak shouted, rushing towards the car to assist Dulles.

Tristan went and turned to Charlemagne. Charlemagne looked at Tristan, but Tristan didn't stop to look back at him again as he instead grabbed him by the wrist and pulled him out of the car, forcing him to crouch down.

"Forget that old fool," Kodiak remarked to Tristan. "Secure Dr. Southern."

"Yes," Tristan confirmed, moving over to secure the doctor.

Tristan went and looked into the front of the private car and saw that he had been shot dead from the gunfire.

"Dr. Southern is dead," Tristan reported.

"Then grab the old fool and follow me!" Kodiak replied.

Tristan went back to Charlemagne, grabbed him, and the two moved around the rear of the vehicle and off the dirt road to run into the forest for cover. Tristan stopped behind the tree, securing Charlemagne below him and looked out as the fire continued to come down. The private car had detonated from a shell that fell onto it, and although Tristan examined the trees for hostile combatants, he could not see anyone, but the barrage of bullets that came from within.

"All units, retreat to the southside," Kodiak communicated to the team via radio. "*Zvezda*, this is *Konstantin-Nul-Adin*, we are under heavy fire from the north. We need immediate air support at my coordinates to clear hostiles combatants!"

"Understood," command replied.

"*Konstantin-Nul-Adin*," Bogdan spoke over the radio, "what is the status of target *Semyon* and *Dimitri*?"

Kodiak grunted and replied, "Semyon is down. *Dimitri* and *Chelovek* are secured."

"Understood," Bogdan replied.

Tristan was still unable to see the enemy as they shot at them from the forest. In addition, mortar fire continued to rain down around them.

"What are your directions?" a soldier questioned Kodiak.

"Fallback!" Kodiak decided. "Move into the forest, and await air support."

Kodiak then turned to Tristan.

"Keep an eye on him!" Kodiak ordered Tristan.

"*Konechno*," Tristan responded, picking Charlemagne up and pushing him forward. "*Khodit!*"

Tristan proceeded to move out with Charlemagne in front of him. They moved into the forest and escaped the ambush behind. The survivors of the attack moved with them and they ran off, spread out with mortar fire continuing until they were a sure distance.

"*Konstantin-Nul-Adin*," Bogdan spoke. "This is *Boris-Nul-Nul*, I am sending you coordinates not too far from your location. We will meet there."

"Understood," Kodiak responded over the radio.

Tristan had grown apart from Kodiak as they continued to rush through the forest. He vaulted over a fallen tree and then went down a hill, following a soldier ahead of him. Tristan then jumped back as an explosion detonated not too far ahead of them, grabbing Charlemagne and keeping him under cover, especially as the shrapnel fell, including the assault rifle of the soldier. Tristan slowly stood up once it was over, while Charlemagne went for the rifle and picked it up.

Charlemagne stood up and looked to Tristan.

"Now is our chance," Charlemagne said to him in a hushed voice. "We can escape and rush to the tomb before Zimmerman – come on."

Tristan looked at him and then pointed his rifle at him.

"Tristan?" Charlemagne questioned, dropping a look of surprise.

"Drop the weapon!" Tristan ordered.

"Tristan, what are you taking about?"

Kodiak stopped behind Tristan approximately a few meters away and looked. He went over and placed a hand on Tristan's shoulder.

"What is going on?"

"The prisoner attempted to arm himself," Tristan replied in Russian. "He won't put the weapon down."

Kodiak looked to Charlemagne.

"You better do as he says," Kodiak stated, looking back to Charlemagne. "Now that we know the location of this tomb, we have little excuse to keep you alive."

Charlemagne frowned and lowered the rifle. Tristan then went in and pushed him to keep moving forward. Kodiak and Dulles stayed near Tristan and Charlemagne as they continued through the forest and eventually reached the ruins of what appeared to be some sort of concrete warehouse or factory with attached office spaces. In total, three other mercenaries had survived the ambush. Charlemagne and Dulles were taken upstairs where the rest of the survivors regrouped in a shared office.

"*Sokol-Nul-Adin*, this is *Konstantin-Nul-Odin*. What is your status?" Kodiak questioned.

"We are on our way, but delayed. Please stand-by."

"*Chyort*," Kodiak replied, shaking his head.

Tristan's ears twitched as he heard footsteps from above. He looked up and Kodiak responded.

"We're not alone," Kodiak stated in a hushed tone. "We're moving out and proceeding north."

Kodiak went to the exit and stacked up. Tristan took Charlemagne and Dulles and kept them in front of him as a mercenary stacked up behind Kodiak. Tristan gave a thumbs up to the merc ahead of him as he received a tap on the shoulder from behind. The merc then patted Kodiak. Kodiak turned around.

"We'll exit the way we came," Kodiak remarked. "I'm on point."

Kodiak then exited out. The merc behind him followed with the two VIPs. Tristan followed afterwards as they entered the corridor and kept their rifles raised as they proceeded forward. They came to a four-point intersection and stopped to take cover behind a wall. Tristan took cover behind the opposite-side and looked out as smoke began to develop.

"Open fire!" Kodiak shouted.

Special Forces dressed in black jumped down from an opening in the ceiling and shots were exchanged. Kodiak moved in. Tristan turned to check on Charlemagne behind him. He then took him in and kept him down in the room behind them. Charlemagne looked at Tristan as he hesitated to return fire, but said nothing.

"Push forward!" Kodiak yelled, moving in again.

Tristan stood up and forced Charlemagne up. He followed the rest of the team as they continued down the hallway once it was clear. At the end of the corridor, they came to a balcony that surrounded the entirety of an open factory or warehouse space. The ceiling above had collapsed. The team spread out in this area as they came into contact with hostiles on the opposite-side. Tristan kept Charlemagne down with one hand and began to return fire, but missed his shots. His hands were trembling. Charlemagne took notice. Tristan continued to fire and then stopped to reload.

"I'm wounded!" a mercenary shouted from the left-side.

Tristan kept his head down. He then looked up and then kept his head down again as bullets passed him. Tristan looked to his right and breathed slowly.

"Leave him!" Kodiak remarked. "We need to leave!"

Kodiak began to shuffle to the side to reach while another mercenary threw a grenade over. The grenade went off and the others opened fire to clean out the rest of the hostiles before proceeding down to reach the stairwell to come to the ground floor. Kodiak looked across and saw a damaged shutter that was slightly open to the south.

"We'll exit from there!" Kodiak yelled, pointing. "Come on!"

Kodiak took point and led Tristan, Charlemagne, and the two other mercenaries to take cover behind some rubble. Hostiles rappelled into the room and opened fire. A shot pierced Dulles through the skull and caused him to fall over. Tristan instantly took cover and kept Charlemagne's head down as he shot some sporadic shots.

"There's no time to lose!" Kodiak remarked. "Get the old fool out of here!"

Charlemagne ran on his own and crawled under the shutter.

"You two," Kodiak remarked. "Get out and make sure he doesn't flee!"

The two mercenaries evacuated, leaving Kodiak with Tristan. Tristan took some shots, but missed contact with the hostiles. Kodiak cleaned up the two on the roof before turning to Tristan as he stood.

"Let's leave!"

Tristan stood up, but immediately flinched as a troop swung from above and kicked Kodiak onto his side. Tristan pointed his rifle at him, but the hostile raised his rifle up by the barrel and disarmed him. Kodiak looked at Tristan as he was engaged and took out a knife. Tristan was knocked to the ground while Kodiak engaged the hostile. Tristan watched from the ground and attempted to recuperate as his hands searched for his pistol holster at his thigh.

Once Tristan had found his pistol, he produced his own knife and stood up, charging the foe as he had Kodiak on the ground with a pistol aimed and boot on Kodiak's chest. The hostile pointed the pistol at Tristan as he charged him. Tristan grabbed the wrist of the hostile with the same hand he held his knife, and with his pistol he knocked the foe back. He managed to disarm the hostile as he dropped the weapon and proceeded to kick him down before pointing his own pistol back at him as he stepped away.

Tristan looked at the Chinese soldier and into his black eyes that looked at him through the balaclava he wore. He had his hands slightly raised in front of him and appeared stunned. Tristan continued to aim the pistol at the hostile, but did not shoot. Kodiak recuperated and stood up. He then picked up the pistol on the ground and looked at Tristan.

"What are you waiting for?" Kodiak questioned in English. "Shoot him."

Tristan continued to hesitate, and by then, he developed a frustrated appearance as he simply would not take the life of another man. Tristan's hands shook.

"Shoot him!" Kodiak yelled.

Tristan froze. Kodiak scoffed and walked over to stand behind the man. He pointed his own pistol down at his head and shot him in the head. Kodiak then looked at Tristan, annoyed, and waved for him to hurry off. Tristan put his pistol away and picked up his rifle. He then turned to leave as Kodiak pushed him down to crawl under the shutter.

• • •

The team of four continued with Charlemagne through the monsoon forest until they met up with Bogdan who was with Zimmerman and six other mercenaries.

"Is this all?" Bogdan questioned his son.

"We experienced heavy casualties and were ambushed at original waypoint," Kodiak replied. "Unfortunately, I was unable to safeguard either Mr. Dulles or Dr. Southern..."

"It doesn't matter," Zimmerman replied, holding a pistol in his hand.

Kodiak looked at him with surprise. Bogdan was unmoved.

"We have enough men – let's move on foot," Zimmerman stated. "We'll have whatever is left of your other battalion meet us at the exact location once we reach it – if any survive."

Bogdan accepted Zimmerman's proposal. A Mi-25 Hind-D helicopter soon arrived at their location and provided them with air support as they began to proceed east towards the Dragon's Den as per Zimmerman's demands. Tristan continued to obey his orders to watch Charlemagne as they hiked, and Charlemagne kept an eye on Tristan as they continued through the forest.

Act 8, Scene 1

By the time the sun was setting, Charlemagne and Tristan arrived at the mouth of the sculpture of a Chinese dragon dug into the side of a tall rocky cliff. From the mouth, atop of a short hill, mist poured out, creating a haze around the entrance. The two of them stood at the top of a hill that looked towards the entrance into the Dragon's Den. Once they had caught a glance, they walked with the rest of the troops as they went downhill, crossed a stream, and then proceeded up the side of the hill to reach the entrance into the tomb.

Bogdan stopped at the mouth of the tomb. The Hind-D had left them to refuel, but he had the eight troops that remained take point at the entrance. Tristan readied himself at a mound as he prepared to defend the entrance. Bogdan whistled to him.

"Merrick, you are with us," Bogdan stated.

Zimmerman looked at Tristan as he stood up and went over to them. Once the rest of the troops proceeded to entrench themselves under Kodiak's watch, Tristan went with Bogdan, Charlemagne, and Zimmerman into the mouth of the dragon. They proceeded to travel along a short tunnel that led them to a foyer with pillars at the side. Before they proceeded any further, Zimmerman turned and looked to Charlemagne.

"What now?" Zimmerman questioned him, holding his pistol in his hand.

Charlemagne opened his journal and flipped through the pages.

"I told you," Charlemagne replied. "Only those that are strong enough to overcome the evil within… will be able to enter the Tomb of the Dragon Emperor."

"Well, then it is settled," Zimmerman replied. "Send Tristan."

"What?" Charlemagne questioned. "Please, I implore you. We had a deal, and for whatever reason, you've turned my son into… a sociopathic monster who can't even recognize me. You said that no harm would come to him…"

"Actually, I said that we wouldn't kill him," Zimmerman replied, "and the way I see it, if he goes in and dies, or if he doesn't, then that's still blood off my hands."

"Please…" Charlemagne begged.

• • •

Diana rode in the second V-TOL that belonged to the Global Defense Project alongside four Guardians, including Brenton Carse and Leroy Mendez.

"ETA one minute…" the pilot remarked from the front.

"UAV is detecting at least eight hostiles at the entrance of the tomb…" a Guardian reported. "We'll land nearby and engage from the opposite hill."

"Copy that," Mendez reported. "Diana, are you sure you want to join?"

"I'm confident," Diana replied. "I need to get in before anything happens to Charlemagne or Tristan."

"What plan do you have in mind then?" Carse questioned.

"I won't impede," Diana remarked. "Proceed as you were, but I'm going to sneak behind them and proceed on."

"Roger that," Mendez replied.

The V-TOL made its landing in the monsoon forest. The Guardians rushed out and began to move towards the Dragon's Den while Diana covered her face and then went off to the right-side, away from the rest of the Guardians. She ran through the woods and began to hear the exchange of gunfire as the Guardians came into contact with the Huntsman mercenaries.

From the V-TOL, Diana moved swiftly and came to the bottom of the hill. She kept low as she crossed the stream and then began to climb the river on the other side.

Diana moved uphill and proceeded to climb the trees and used them to move as she found it easier. She moved behind the Huntsman and reached the side of the sculpture. She continued up and moved so that she was atop of the head. She then dropped down and fell atop of the snout. Diana looked down and saw the mercenaries as they shot back from their trenches, but she then turned around as she heard echoes from within. Diana looked at the eyehole of the Dragon and saw that there was space for her to climb inside. She proceeded.

• • •

"Send me, please," Charlemagne argued, walking to Zimmerman and dropping to his knees. "I can confront whatever evil lies ahead... He... he's just a boy..."

Zimmerman motioned Bogdan to move Tristan in.

"Alright, time for you to go," Bogdan said, moving to Tristan and pushing him forward. "All you need to do is go forward and report back whatever you find. Understood?"

"Understood," Tristan stated in a neutral tone.

Tristan looked ahead at the dark tunnel before him. He turned on the light of his rifle and began to walk over.

"No, stop! Tristan! Stop!" Charlemagne begged.

"Bogdan," Zimmerman remarked.

Bogdan moved over and picked Zimmerman up.

"Get up, you worthless, *nyem*!" Bogdan remarked, picking Charlemagne up and pushing him back.

"Stop!" Diana shouted from atop of a platform above.

Diana had drawn her sword and looked down upon them. Charlemagne looked up.

"Diana…" Charlemagne reacted, eyes watering. "Y-you're alive!"

Bogdan raised his rifle and pointed it to her. Zimmerman walked next to him and placed a hand on Bogdan's shoulder, which caused him to lower his arms as he patted it and whispered to him.

"How nice of you to join us, Diana," Zimmerman remarked in a cool tone. "Why don't you come down from there and let's talk."

Diana jumped down and looked towards them. Tristan turned around and looked over to Diana. He stood at the entrance of the tunnel with focused eyes on the shadowy figure. His ears twitched as he heard Diana's name. His face picked up and his eyes were focused. Diana pointed her sword towards Zimmerman. Charlemagne stood up and stood behind her.

"You're done, Zimmerman," Diana stated. "Your numbers have been thinned and the troops you have outside won't last long as the Global Defense Project take them down."

"Very impressive, Diana, but you forget one thing," Zimmerman replied, whistling and waving over to Tristan for him to come over.

Tristan walked over and Zimmerman stood back. He then raised his pistol and pointed it at the back of Tristan's head. Tristan accepted the gun at the back of his head as though it were an order.

"Now, I'm glad you've arrived to join us, because I wasn't all that confident about Tristan's abilities, but you… I am confident of," Zimmerman stated. "You'll be able to enter and defeat what's inside – I know that, and you'll do it, or I'll blow his brains out. Understand me?"

Zimmerman grabbed Tristan by around the neck and pulled him aside, keeping the gun pointed at his head.

"Be calm, Tristan…" Diana said to him.

"Don't bother," Bogdan remarked. "He probably doesn't even recognize you… He's been brainwashed to believe the Huntsman are his brethren, and the likes of you and Charlemagne are his enemies."

"That's right," Zimmerman replied, "so without any further delay, go on and face what lies ahead, Diana. We'll be waiting here – once you've found the orb, don't touch it – simply return, and I'll release your lover back to you."

Diana looked at Zimmerman with frustrated eyes. She then put her sword away and sighed.

"Fine," Diana replied. "I'll do it."

"No," Charlemagne protested. "Diana…"

Diana hushed him. Charlemagne went to her and gave her his journal.

"Let her take this," Charlemagne said to the others. "So it can guide her…" he added before looking at her. "Be careful… within you will have to fight a terrible evil. I have been skeptical as to what 'evil' this refers to, but my best hypothesis is that it is some sort of psychological test, so take easy steps because who knows what poison lurks within to cause such a manifestation."

Diana nodded.

"Are you done?" Zimmerman questioned.

Diana turned around and put the journal in a pocket. She then proceeded forward, walking past Bogdan, Dulles, and Zimmerman. Everyone in the room watched her as she proceeded into the dark tunnel with only her swords and a few tools at her disposal. Diana walked forward and proceeded through a cavernous corridor where there was a thick haze around. She continued to walk with careful steps through the darkness when she began to hear the giggles of a little girl. Diana looked around in a cautious stance, hand at her sword handle, prepared to draw. She circled around, but then looked forward as she saw bit of bright light that she had not seen behind her. Diana walked towards the light and soon found herself in a dim room where before her was a large black dragon.

The dragon looked down at her with its effeminate blue eyes huffed fire from its snout. The scales of the beast were a deep black, and it had beautiful black wings with horns from the top of its head. At the side of this the center of the room were staircases that went around to a circular platform directly behind the dragon. At this platform, there was a sort of chandelier or group of mirrors above that looked down to a shrine at the back. Diana saw various lanterns hung around, which provided enough light to see around.

Diana froze as the dragon let out a mighty roar towards her. She immediately ran to her right as the dragon inhaled and then breathed fire behind her. With each step the large dragon, approximately the size of an average dinosaur, ten feet tall and at least thirty feet long, including the tail, which the creature whipped towards Diana in an attempt to lash her. Diana jumped out of the way and then continued to run up the stairs. She came to the central platform and jumped down to land atop of the dragon, stabbing her katana through the tough scales and piercing through. The dragon shouted out in pain as it was stabbed.

The dragon attempted to get Diana off, but she continued to stab into the back of the dragon until finally she was forced off. The dragon then attempted to stomp her, but she rolled out of the way and then ran off as the dragon inhaled and breathed out a flamethrower of fire towards her. Once the full extent of the dragon's breath had been exhaled, Diana rushed towards the hand of the dragon and proceeded to stab at it. Diana fell off the hand as the dragon raised its arm

Diana then rolled aside and stood up as it attempted to stomp at her again. The dragon moved its hand onto the staircase as Diana attempted to climb back up to attack its back. She then jumped out of the way as it attempted to bite at her. The creature then attempted to stomp on her again, which prompted Diana to roll out of the way again before running to the other side. The dragon slowly made its way fully around, but by the time Diana was at the top again, the dragon had just managed to get around to dig its claws into the stairs on its right. Diana hopped down and stabbed her sword into the back of the dragon. She then held onto a horn that protruded out from the outline of its spine, and then climbed up to the top of the head to attempt to dig down into its skull. The dragon flapped its wings and proceeded to fly up. Diana noticed it was closing in on the ceiling, so she jumped down and returned to the creature's back, stabbing her sword into the vertebrae, which caused the creature to become paralyzed as it bashed its head into the ceiling.

The dragon lay on the ground as Diana took her sword and went back up to stab it into the head of the dragon. The dragon was still conscious and started to shake its head, which eventually caused Diana to fall off and land on the ground below. The impact caused Diana to lose grip of her sword. The dragon inhaled and then breathed out towards Diana, forcing her to run to the side. The beast then dropped its hand down before her to cut off her escape, which resulted in Diana vaulting over as the dragon singed its own hand. Diana then looked over to where her sword was as the dragon attempted to stomp her again.

Diana rolled out of the way and proceeded to return to the opposite direction to retrieve her sword. She stopped at the base of the staircase as the dragon blocked her path again and proceeded to breathe out fire at her again. Diana produced some throwing stars and threw them at the dragon as she made her sprint back to the other side. The shuriken interrupted the burst of flames, which allowed Diana to redirect herself to go to the hand of the dragon and bring her sword into the arm. The dragon shouted out as Diana attempted to cut through the arm in an attempt to cut the hand off.

The dragon easily flung Diana off, but she held on to her sword with a tight grip as she hit the wall and fell forward. The creature roared at her and then flew forward slightly to punch the wall. Diana jumped out of the way and then ran towards the beast, under its arm and proceeded to run up the set of stairs to attack it from behind again. The dragon inhaled and attempted to burn her with another throw of its flames, but she jumped down and stabbed into its lower back, holding on as it moved its tail about to shake her off. Diana held on, especially as the creature hit its tail into the surrounding wall. The dragon began to almost climb up the wall of the cave, standing on its hind legs as if to have gravity pull her down.

With her other hand, Diana took her short sword and stabbed into the flesh of the beast. The beast cried out in pain. Diana then took her long sword out and proceeded to climb on the back of the creature as though it were a wall of ice. Diana stopped as she was halfway up. The beast was paralyzed in place.

"You can do it," Diana whispered to herself. "Just don't look down!"

Diana retrieved her short sword and continued to climb up. She pulled her katana out as she got closer to the neck of the beast and proceeded to move towards the side so that she could stab it where the jugular would be for a human. Blood gushed out as she withdrew the sword and held on by the short sword.

The beast howled and punched the wall with its fists before bashing it with its head.

The dragon came down onto both its legs and eventually Diana fell and landed as it proceeded to trample around the room, whipping its tail at random. Diana covered herself and then quickly grabbed her sword as she saw the belly of the beast. The beast roared at Diana. Diana ran towards it. The beast raised a fist to stomp down on her, but as it came down, Diana slid out of the way and pierced her sword up into the belly. She then stood up and slid the sword along, crouching as she ran until she was at the end. Diana then slid out of the way, rolled onto her side, and ran up the set of stairs. The dragon yelled out in misery as Diana saw blood spill out from beneath it. Diana then continued up the stairs as the dragon inhaled and let out another volley of flames from its mouth.

Diana took cover behind a fountain at the top, but the flames had disappeared by then. She stood up and looked down and saw the dragon approaching towards her, standing on its hind legs as it looked at Diana, howling in pain. Diana looked back at the dragon, the two looked at each other through their shared eyes. The dragon then rolled onto its side and collapsed into death.

The dragon was dead. Diana panted as she looked down at the dead dragon. She then looked at her katana in her hand. When Diana looked back at the dragon, she opened her eyes and looked above her. She was no longer in the shrine, but in the tunnel again. Diana stood up and looked forward. Before her was the entrance into the cave, but it was dimmer as there were no lanterns, but still a shred of light. There was no dragon about, but still a set of stairs at either side that connected to a central platform above where there was a shrine and a fountain.

Diana walked up the set of stairs with a hand at her katana, and as she reached the top, she looked at the fountain that was in the center. The fountain did not shoot out water like a typical fountain, but was a crystal blue basin where there was a clear bluish liquid. Diana looked up and saw a large stalactite that hung down. A drop of the liquid came from the formation and dropped into the basin, which appeared to be full, but despite the additional drop, the liquid did not overflow. Around the basin were various intricate treasures, and behind the basin was a shrine with the sarcophagus of the dragon emperor surrounded by various items. Diana's eyes then looked at what was above the sarcophagus on a ledge of the shrine.

The Scepter of Alexander the Great laid on the ledge with a golden frame and head of an eagle. In the mouth of the eagle was a bright orb as white as natural light. Diana looked around the rest of the treasures and then brought a hand to her neck to give a light cough. She then looked down and back towards the cave exit. Diana took out Charlemagne's journal and began to flip through the pages.

"There must be something here, anything…"

Diana spent a bit of time looking through the journal, kneeling down as she did. She then found a page about the mythical dragon tears in the basin and their power to cure any ailment and heal any wound. She continued to flip through.

"Come on…"

Diana stopped as she saw a picture of the Mysterious Stranger, drawn towards the back of the journal. She looked back at him and at his face, the gasmask, he wore. Diana paused for a moment and then stood up.

"I understand," Diana remarked, walking over to the treasures.

Diana picked up a chalice from the treasures and brought it over to the basin. She dipped the cup in and took out approximately half of the liquid that was within to fill half of the cup. Diana looked at the liquid and then took a drink. She then set the chalice down and took a deep breath. Diana then walked down the set of stairs and went into the tunnel to return to the others.

Act 8, Scene 2

Diana returned to the foyer of the tomb where Zimmerman was waiting. He raised his gun and pointed it to Tristan's head as he saw her. Charlemagne stood up from where he was sat and looked at Diana with surprise. Bogdan held his arms crossed.

"So, you're alive," Zimmerman remarked. "I knew you'd be able to defeat what was within…"

"In order to cross through, you'll need to wear gasmasks," Diana stated. "There's a noxious gas emitting through the tunnels that causes one to hallucinate…"

"Hm…" Zimmerman responded, stroking his chin. "Thank you, Diana."

"Of course," Charlemagne remarked, clapping. "How else?"

"Do you have masks?" Zimmerman questioned Bogdan.

"I have one for each of us," Bogdan replied.

"You can have the scepter – it's waiting inside," Diana remarked, holding a fist, "but release Tristan and Charlemagne, and let us go…"

Zimmerman looked to Bogdan. Bogdan looked at Diana.

"I'm afraid, that simply isn't possible," Bogdan responded. "I told you – Tristan's mind has been wiped and he is no longer the boy you remember him to be."

"You told me we had a deal!" Diana yelled at Zimmerman.

"We had a deal, but the truth of the matter is that Tristan wouldn't want to return with you," Zimmerman responded. "He belongs to the Huntsman – don't they deserve something for all the trouble you've put them through?"

"I'll kill you!" Diana replied, producing her sword.

"Bogdan, take care of her," Zimmerman remarked, pointing his gun at Diana, "but don't kill her. Restrain her."

"Yes, sir," Bogdan replied. "*Vyi slyishali yevo! Zaderzhat' yeye!*"

Diana charged at Zimmerman with her sword. Tristan moved and intercepted her, grabbing her by her arm so that the two were in a struggle. Diana looked at Tristan in slight shock. He looked at her with indifference. Tristan easily overpowered her and brought her to the ground. Diana looked up at her boyfriend in defeat.

Tristan raised a foot and pressed down on her armored chest. He then produced his pistol and aimed it at her.

"What is he doing?" Zimmerman questioned.

"Don't just point it," Bogdan remarked. "Shoot her!"

Tristan hesitated to take a shot again.

"Stop," Zimmerman protested. "I didn't say kill her, I said restrain her!"

"Do you really want to keep her alive?" Bogdan questioned. "Let me have some retribution for the men I have lost!"

Charlemagne watched in horror as Tristan continued to aim the pistol, but he also looked confidently at Tristan.

"I won't say it again!" Bogdan remarked to Tristan. "Shoot her!"

Tristan's hands shook. Diana looked up at him.

"Tristan…" Diana whispered.

Tristan's eyes widened.

"Insubordinate fool!" Bogdan cursed, producing his own pistol and aiming it at Diana. "I'll show you how it is done!"

"Stop!" Zimmerman protested again, aiming his pistol at Bogdan.

Shots were fired. Tristan looked down in horror as he saw a bullet had penetrated through Diana's chest plate and blood began to seep out. Charlemagne looked at Bogdan who had been shot in the head and fell over dead. Tristan quickly brought his pistol over to Zimmerman, but Zimmerman raised a hand over to Tristan and he was forced to drop the pistol as he brought his hands to his head and yelled out in pain. A deep purple glow came from Zimmerman's eyes.

"I've had enough," Zimmerman remarked. "All of this nonsense… I've had enough of it! Worthless old man… I should have sent you to die in Allabrese! You stupid Russians can't get anything done right except to stall my enemies! I've had enough of relying on humans only to receive nothing! Any smart Russian would know better than to work with someone like me – the same type of people who plunged Russia into famine for their own selfish purposes. What an idiot! I was going to dispose of him eventually once I had the scepter, but now is a good time too – now that I'm on the cusp of attaining ultimate power."

Tristan fell to his knees and then onto his side as Zimmerman relaxed his hand, his eyes returned to their natural green, and then he pointed his pistol at Charlemagne.

"You, with me!" Zimmerman shouted.

"W-why?!" Charlemagne questioned.

"Because, in case Diana's laid a trap ahead, I need someone to act as bait – now grab a gasmask and let's move!" Zimmerman yelled.

Charlemagne did not argue and went to grab a mask from Bogdan's corpse. He grabbed one while Zimmerman took the other. Charlemagne looked over to Tristan and Diana as he put on the mask. Tristan attempted to crawl towards Charlemagne, but the two adults left into the tunnel as he failed to move another inch. Instead, Tristan sat up and looked over to Diana.

"Diana…" Tristan remarked, kneeling before her and looking at her wound. "Please, don't die… don't die on me…"

Tristan began to produce some first aid from a pouch on his belt, but it seldom helped to stop the bleeding. He applied pressure and proceeded to cry as his efforts did nothing.

Charlemagne travelled with Zimmerman down the cave. Zimmerman lit the way with a flashlight, while Charlemagne led the way with careful steps. Charlemagne turned to the side as they walked.

"How is it that you possess psionic powers?" Charlemagne questioned. "In my mind, you were nothing more than a spoiled, nouveau riche brat obsessed with artefacts, but all this… You're insane."

"You of all people know how one comes to possess psionic powers, Charles," Zimmerman responded. "It takes a great suffering through life to become awakened – not a good person. I have my intentions in mind for what I seek to do, and when I retrieve that scepter, there'll be nobody to stop me anymore, including you."

The pair reached the end of the cave and entered the tomb. Zimmerman forced Charlemagne up the stairs, and when they reached the top, Zimmerman instantly gravitated to the scepter while Charlemagne looked at the fountain. He watched as a drop of liquid fell down from above into the half-filled basin, but it effectively did not increase in volume. Meanwhile, Zimmerman picked up the scepter and then brought his hand to the orb inside, tearing it out.

"Finally…" Zimmerman remarked. "After all these years, I finally have both orbs in my possession."

Charlemagne looked over to Zimmerman as he held the orb in the same hand that he had the ring with the other stones. He looked slightly concerned as Zimmerman held orb the way he did, especially as it began to glow brighter and vibrate.

"What?" Zimmerman questioned. "What's going on?"

Charlemagne held on to the cavern wall as the cave began to shake. Dust fell down from above and some of the artefacts fell over. Charlemagne then looked back over to Zimmerman who continued to hold the orb in his hand.

"W-what is going on?" Zimmerman questioned, dropping to his knees. "No – get out of my head! Get out of my head!"

Charlemagne looked around as he heard whispers of a quiet voice that spoke a language he did not understand. An aura began to develop around Zimmerman. The aura widened and in a split second, Zimmerman disappeared. The celestial orb crashed onto the ground as he vanished, and the earthquake stopped and all returned to calm. Charlemagne stepped forward and picked up the orb. He then looked up as heard whispers again, but they soon disappeared. Charlemagne put the artefact into his pocket in a handkerchief, and then looked over to the fountain.

Liquid continued to drop down from above. Charlemagne picked up a chalice and filled it with the remainder of what was left. He then brought the chalice to his lips, but stopped. He moved the chalice away.

"If I take this, then there will be little hope for Diana…" Charlemagne stated. "If I don't drink this, then the cancer will surely kill me."

Charlemagne sighed.

"A life for a life."

Charlemagne put his gasmask on and then proceeded down the steps, away from the shrine and back through the tunnel to return to Diana. Tristan continued to apply pressure to the wound as Charlemagne returned with the cup. He knelt down on the opposite side from Tristan, removed his mask, and then brought the cup to Diana's lips to help her drink the liquid. Diana drank, and within a few seconds, the bleeding stopped as the wound healed on its own.

"It's a miracle…" Tristan remarked, looking to Charlemagne. "She's going to live."

Charlemagne looked back at Tristan as Tristan looked at his girlfriend with tearful eyes. Diana opened her eyes and looked back at them. She raised a hand and placed it on Tristan's cheek. He took the hand with his hand and continued to look at her with happiness. Charlemagne then looked over to the opposite tunnel as Guardians entered the room. They looked before them, and as Charlemagne saw them, he understood they were here to return them home for this gruesome adventure had reached its end.

Epilogue

Diana entered the garage of Cabernet Manor from the ground entrance and went over to Zephyr's pen to greet him with a smile. She then walked into the stall next to her horse to pick up a pitchfork, but frowned as she noticed there was no hay. Diana sighed, walked over with the pitchfork and looked upstairs to where there was more hay stored. She then looked over to the ladder and then back up to the attic from below. Diana threw the pitchfork up and then jumped up, grabbing the ledge and pulling herself up to go over and fetch some hay. She pushed a bale down and then side-rolled down before jumping as she felt someone behind her. Diana turned around and engaged whoever was behind her.

Tristan grabbed Diana's arm and attempted to bring her down to the ground as he pulled on it, but the two instead came into a stalemate and instantly froze as they saw each other. Tristan disengaged and the two stepped away from each other.

"Sorry..." Tristan remarked, picking up the newspaper and two tinted brown bottles on the floor. "I, uh... just came down to throw this in the recycling."

"No, I'm sorry..." Diana replied, blushing. "I'm still learning to control my reflexes."

The couple looked at each other embarrassingly and then Tristan stepped aside to move around her. Diana turned around and looked at him.

"Tristan," Diana said, forcing him to stop and look at her.

"Yes?" Tristan questioned.

"Is everything okay with you?" Diana asked.

"Huh?"

"I mean, we've been through a lot in the last couple of weeks, and we haven't seen each other in that time. You already told me about what happened with you, and Charles, and then what you went through in Russia, and I told you of my experience, but aside from that. Are you okay?"

Tristan looked at her and then gave a soft smile.

"I'm okay," Tristan responded with a reassuring smile. "Honestly."

"Okay," Diana replied, nodding to him.

Tristan walked off and went outside to place his recyclables while Diana resumed to feed her horse. Once she was done, she went upstairs and looked at the stairs. Instead of taking the stairs, Diana jumped and pulled herself up to vault over the railings of the stairs, but then jumped again as she met with Charlemagne before her.

"Sorry," Diana apologized.

"I was looking for you," Charlemagne remarked. "Come with me."

Charlemagne led Diana downstairs and to his study. Diana closed the door behind her and then stood before Charlemagne's desk as he walked behind it. Charlemagne looked at her and she looked at him. Charlemagne appeared to be healthier, had shaved his beard aside from his moustache, but Diana had noticed that he had started to wear leather gloves at his hands. Currently, he was dressed in his grey plaid suit. Charlemagne picked up a folder on his desk.

Diana looked at the unmarked folder. Charlemagne presented it to her.

"You told me about your journey with the hidden village and expressed to me your regret in not knowing where it is you come from, or who your ancestors were, and I must admit that this pain was the same pain that I felt last year with my own heritage. I'm sorry to admit this fact, but I have been sitting on this information for quite some time, but in fairness, in that time I was validating its authenticity…"

Diana opened the folder and looked at the front page which read, 'The Secret Child of King Edward VIII and Wallis Simpson.' In the corner was a heading that read, 'PG File,' and there was also a stamp in the margin that read, 'Classified.' Diana proceeded to read through these papers, some additional papers behind, and then at a family tree at the back, which showed the royal family from Queen Victoria to most of her current descendants. Once Diana was finished, she closed the folder and looked at Charlemagne.

"Wait, does this mean that we're…?"

"Yes," Charlemagne confirmed. "We're cousins."

"And you just sat on this fact?"

"Like I said, I thought the initial idea to be farfetched and mere propaganda from the syndicate, but the truth of the matter is that it is true. I verified it myself, and even conducted this little test a while back…"

Charlemagne took a piece of paper from another folder on his desk and pushed it forward. Diana picked it up and read through what was a DNA report that confirmed genetic similarities between Charlemagne and Diana.

"The truth is that we're both descendants of Queen Victoria."

Diana put the paper in the folder and then sat both of them on the desk. She carried a stunned look on her face.

"Are you alright?" Charlemagne questioned.

Diana stepped around Charlemagne's desk and looked up at him. Suddenly, she opened her arms and hugged him.

"You're my blood-relative," Diana remarked. "Of course, everything is alright."

Charlemagne extended a hand around and patted Diana on the back as they hugged.

"After all this time…" Diana said with relief.

"Yes," Charlemagne admitted, "but Diana, don't be fooled to think that because we know we are blood-relatives now, that it does not mean that we weren't family before or if weren't blood-relatives, could not have been family. I reveal this truth to you now merely to show you where you come from."

"Of course."

Diana opened her eyes and looked down at an envelope on Charlemagne's desk that was addressed to him from 'Vienna and Everest Cabernet,' she then parted from Charlemagne and looked at him.

"Wait, this means that not just you, but all your relatives are my relatives," Diana stated. "Allodia, Derby… and Salmar and Finn."

"Yes," Charlemagne remarked to her. "We're family. I hope you can find the peace you were looking for with this information, especially in regard to your father who had a tougher upbringing than you."

Diana looked at Charlemagne and nodded. She then hugged him again.

"I have a family," Diana said with a smile as a tear fell from her eye in happiness. "I have a family."

"Finally, be strong in the Lord and in the strength of his might put on the whole armor of God so that you may be able to stand against the schemes of the devil."

– Ephesians 6:10

www.ingramcontent.com/pod-product-compliance
Lightning Source LLC
Chambersburg PA
CBHW051420170626
46809CB00006B/2243